Snug Harbor Series

Book I

I0667749

The Launching

F. L H. HUDKINS

ISBN: 069223344X
ISBN-13: 978-0692233443

DEDICATION

This book is dedicated to recruiters of the Air Force, Army, Coast Guard, Marine Corps and Navy who fill the most stressful billet in the United States Military outside of actual combat.

CONTENTS

ACKNOWLEDGMENT

Wilson O. Hudkins for encouragement in publishing this book and for providing a new computer and manual on self-publishing.

Agueda Tonie Teague for providing help in final preparation of this book.

Bill Leaseburg, *The Starving Artist*, who illustrated the cover of this book from nothing more than a rough idea from the author.

Other Books in Snug Harbor Series:

Book II - *The Cruise*
Book III - *Fiddler's Green*

CHAPTER ONE

REVEILLE

I awoke when the first rays of the rising sun pierced the heavy timber that crowned Berkeley's Knob, thinking of ancestors, ghosts, witches and such, probably because I had gone to sleep re-reading entries in journals scribbled by a long line of grandparents.

The faded, crumbling diaries and day books I'd discovered in a chest in our family library at about the age of ten led me to suspect the Old Timers' thoughts mainly concerned when the next band of Indians would cut down on them from the top of the ridge. Gunpowder residue around loopholes in the log walls of the foyer, the only remaining visible parts of the original log cabin, reinforced that idea in my young mind.

Teenaged re-readings of the old documents made me wonder at the motives of the early settlers who had taken the effort to quill pen happenings by the light of candles or a fat pine knot. Their chronicles of terrible hard work, buying and selling, dance and frolic, church meetings and revival, courting and marriage, birth, sickness, natural death and killings made it apparent they had things, other than Indians, on their minds   The Journals also suggested my two hundred plus year old house had a long history of haunts lurking about the premises. I had not seen anything in, or near, the old house, nor had I heard anything that I could chalk up to an unknown source. I would have preferred to believe the tales were no more than pure stern wash, but the fact remained that no-nonsense folks had seen apparitions prowling about. Journal entries by generations of my ancestors recorded the occurrence of death tokens, sightings of strange beings and lights of unknown origin passing above the mountains.

My great-whichever-grandmother woke one night to see a man dressed in buckskin standing at the foot of her bed. That lady, who feared nothing, except her Lord, rose from her bed and asked his intentions. He peered at her for a moment, then disappeared. She received word the next day that her brother had been killed by a runaway horse. She saw the apparitions once again -- striding away as if he had just stepped from the wide front porch. She received word the following week that her youngest son had been killed during a Civil War skirmish on Rich Mountain. She wrote that she knew, somehow, the ghost was that of the original Henry Clay Berkeley circa Seventeen Hundred--Early.

According to family legend, Margaret Louise, the gravely ill, aged wife of Henry Clay Berkeley, told her husband and a daughter that she had had a visit from the "cutest little men." Her husband and daughter disregarded her strange remark, thinking she was delirious. My great-whichever uncle stood death watch over his mother that night during which time he saw stubby, bearded, little men standing in her room -- one holding a vase. The fellow with the vase threw it to the floor where it shattered. The little men walked from the room, turned toward the kitchen and disappeared. His mother passed to her reward within the hour.

My uncle later told that story to his running mates in a local tavern, probably when he was stern over tea kettle on stump juice. An Irish woodsman asked if his mother had any connection with Ireland. My uncle told him his mother, the matriarch of the Berkeley Clan, had been the sole Paddy among a long line of Limey ancestors.

2

Proud of his family history, and likely broadside to the waves on stump juice, my uncle expounded at length how his mother, age sixteen, sailed from Ireland as an indentured servant. She met Henry Clay Berkeley, age nineteen, on the dock in Norfolk, Virginia and liked the cut of his jib so much that she married him on the spot without the benefit of clergy. They formalized their vows behind tobacco bales by holding hands and jumping over a stick held by another couple. Their vows having been duly exchanged, they turned sterns to the sea and headed toward the Blue Ridge Mountains at Flank-Speed Legs because she had contracted seven years of her life to the Tidewater planter who paid her passage to America. That they had only the clothes on their backs, a small cooking pot, a rifle and a few other small items didn't slow their speed run to the distant blue mountains.

Their trek led them to a mountain valley deep into the wilderness of Western Virginia, the first white folks to arrive in that particular area. They located a riffle-swift river as a ready source of water, then chose the highest slope above the river as their cabin site. From this couple, during their era, came land holdings and what turned from a rude hut into a six-room log cabin. Two centuries plus later, their cabin had evolved into an odd shaped, fourteen room house with walls and flooring ranging in age from those of their first permanent cabin to the early nineteen-thirties, a time when the Berkeley name was fast becoming thin upon the ground. Berkeley unions were not prone to birthing males.

Their marriage, or whatever they called it, was a success, for it lasted eighty-one years before Margaret Louise died. Henry Clay died the following morning, the day of his wife's wake. The record of their doings, first penned using berry juice on thin sheets of scraped deerskin and later scribed with store-bought ink in rough textured tablets, showed they had lived in harmony when not fighting Indians, fierce animals or the elements. The old journals hinted they enjoyed frolic once neighbors arrived on the scene and they believed in the Lord's decree to be fruitful and multiply. They were obviously quite good at holding multiplying drills, considering they had thirteen children, six daughters and two sons who lived and five children who died in infancy, a baker's dozen spread over twenty-three years.

The Irishman argued, after hearing my uncle's tale, that the appearance of Leprechauns was not unknown at the death of Irish persons of distinguished ancestry. He insisted that, despite Margaret Louise Tinney having shipped as an indentured servant, her ancestors were folks of renown among the Celts, otherwise, the Leprechauns would not have appeared.

I thought it interesting that my uncle had rambled at length about the maternal side of his family, but mentioned nothing of the other side. The first Berkeley of our clan to arrive in America supposedly descended from England's blue-blooded Berkeley family, but on the wrong side of the blanket. Nothing was recorded in the journals about his mother, not even her name. Neither was anything recorded as to who raised him or who paid for his education, which he obviously had as indicated by his excellent ability to write the King's English in his journals.

Henry Clay claimed to have cumshawed a blooded horse from his natural father, then rode at flank speed to Bristol where he sold the horse to a used horse dealer, or some such. The horse dealer must have liked the cut of his jib too, for he shipped him as supercargo with a consignment of horses destined for the Colony of Virginia.

He was waiting on the dock for someone to show up to take custody of the horses when he met Margaret Louise Tinney. He chatted her up, being the sweet-talking devil that he must have been, telling her he intended to head for the mountains once he was shut of the horses. It developed, early in their conversation, that she was indentured to the very same planter who owned the horses and was less than happy at the prospect. The details of what they discussed were not recorded, but one apparently launched onto the other like a lamprey eel and off they went behind the tobacco bales. If he had not known, somehow, that the forest underbrush

4

was too thick for the passage of large animals, a couple of the planter's horses would have likely ended in Western Virginia too!

A staccato of clicking noises on the wide chestnut boards of the hall floor jerked me from my musings of family history. Attack was imminent and inevitable.

The Reconnaissance Squad pouncing on my back didn't hurt, but activation of his Psychological Warfare Element, which entailed screeching and yowling like a set of stripped gears, like to destroyed my eardrums. That diversion, coupled with excellent planning and coordination, enabled the Heavy Weapons Platoon to link up and mount attack just behind the Recon Squad. That sixty-plus pound, four point landing on my back did hurt!

I initiated immediate counterattack, but was overpowered from the onset by fat, hairy bodies nipping and scratching as they tangled me in bed clothing. When I was secured to their satisfaction, they tortured me with growls, yowls, snarls, hisses and slobbers.

The course of battle shifted when the Heavy Weapons Platoon forgot the battle plan and went off-plumb. He grabbed bed clothing in his mouth and lunged toward the door. His lunge unwrapped the bed clothing and jerked me three-quarters off the bed. The Recon Squad, lurking on top of the bed clothing, fared worse. He catapulted eight feet across the room and landed on the back of a white, wing-back chair where he clawed frantically before doing a slow, rump-first slide to the floor. He checked himself for injury, snarled and took a swat at his inept partner who had bollixed the attack.

The attacking force, now split into two fronts, surrendered. They reformed into columns abreast, the padded to the side of my bed. I levered myself from the shambles of the bed, leaned down and petted their excited bodies. "Other sailors have such normal pets: alligators, cobras, Tasmanian devils, parrots, whatever. Not me, Buccaneer! I'm burdened with an overweight, oversexed bulldog -- the hero of every gyp within a four-mile radius. Then,

5

to give any ulcer that might be lurking about a chance for growth, I gotta tolerate an intellectual cat who worries about the Middle East situation, bugs and the horror of shedding hair.

"You fellows trying to put me into a canvas jacket with wraparound sleeves, or what? This morning's attack brings us one giant step closer to disaster of the first magnitude. Missus Jenkins will surely see fit to supply me with one or more nasty notes complaining about scratch marks in the hall wax and my bed looking like the aftermath of an orgy. That'll make over one hundred nasty notes and six hysterical telephone calls in less than two years. We're speaking here of conduct unbecoming!

"No? How about the pay raise I forked over when Jarhead treed the driver of the milk tanker on the grape arbor, or the second raise when he ripped Missus Jenkins washing off the line and rolled it in the mud? We won't even mention the big pay raise when Missus Crites cussed her out after Jarhead whipped up on her Great Dane.

"Don't look so smug, Blue Suit! Your stuff is ragged too. Remember when Missus Jenkins found your collection of hair balls behind the desk in the library? Poor woman thought it was a monster mouse and like to had heart lockup! Or when you fell off the mantle and knocked over the coal bucket and great-whichever-grandpa's muzzle-loader? She like to beat the four-minute mile en route the Post farm screaming about haints heaving coal and firearms at her. She gimp-legged around and wheezed like a horse with heaves for a week and a half!

"We're talking excruciating pain if she leaves us. Shipmates, you'll be semi-orphans with no one to prepare your chow, turn on the TV, brush your hair, wipe slobbers, put you out to potty, or keep Jarhead out of the brig. I'll have to take up compartment and head cleaning. I didn't enjoy that routine when I was a seaman and I doubt technology has since improved the scope of the billet. Mates, you drive our housekeeper over the hill and I double-damn guarantee you'll be better off living with the founder of the *Society to Abolish Pets and House Plants*!"

Blue Suit initiated his sawmill noise and licked at my toes with his wood rasp. He didn't look worried, but then he rarely did until he watched the news. Then, worry came upon him.

"You, Jarhead -- Marine Corps reject! Let us now speak of recent bad conduct. I'm not certain if Lady Lou is your latest exploit, but Mister Hancock pounced upon me in Moe's slop chute last evening. We had a one-sided conversation. He told me, along with yelling, screaming and gnashing of teeth, that if his blue tick gyp throws puppies with wide, ugly faces and short bowlegs, he's going to sue. He was so upset I offered to buy him a beer. Jarhead, where he told me to put that beer shouldn't happen to a bulldog -- even you!

"No way can you snivel out, Velcro Lips. You are the only regulation Limey in seventeen counties and I don't believe Lady Lou round heeled it in a British Doggie Club Med. If he sues, you are going to hire out as a security guard until you pay off the paternity rap.

"Oh stop looking so secure. You slithered out of that problem with Nutter's Irish setter only because all six puppies look like red platypuses with weird, pointy ears. That is the sole reason the blame shifted to Pollard's little Chihuahua dog. I do not believe Carlos the Crazy acted alone, even if he stood on a stump. I suspect you two took turnabout holding one another up!"

Jarhead couldn't very well wag the tail he didn't have, but got his point across nicely by resonating his wide stern like a backstay in a typhoon. He thus maintained his innocence. Folks were always putting scandal upon his name.

Both animals padded after me into the bathroom where I expounded at length concerning their consistent failure to cease and desist pouncing on me at first light.

Jarhead exhibited his rubbery, slobbering grin.

Blue Suit looked smug and put more juice to his sawmill, but he meowed and hauled tail when I turned on the shower. It reminded him of the need to worry about hail, rainstorm and pestilence.

"I was pondering, before you two grabbed me, as to what suitable punishment I could lay on the public affairs moron who arranged the fail-ex interview with that college newspaper, highbrow skin magazine, or whatever sort of rag it is. I considered giving Chief Journalist Curtis P. Longly a bulldog and pussycat, but I can't. The Navy forbids cruel and inhumane punishments."

I inspected my uniform for Irish pennants and other items that tend to detract from the appearance expected by the Navy. Jarhead watched, but didn't comment, so I decided my service dress blues met the standard set forth for the normal, red-blooded, government-employed mercenary. I don't consider mercenary all that bad of a title. I expected to be called far worse before the interview ended.

Blue suit slunk back into the bedroom and whipped a couple of laps across the toe of my shoe, which dulled the shine I'd just buffed. He looked greatly worried. Either he'd been staring at the blank TV screen and suspected a foreign power had lit off The Big One, or he grasp the potential for me knee-capping myself during the interview. I figured it was probably the latter and he had serious doubts as to my ability to support our little family by hawking wind-up toys on the street.

There were old Royal Navy punishments, such as flogging around the fleet, worse than doing an interview with a college newspaper, but not much else. I had a totally negative attitude about the whole thing. I had, more than once and in the same sort of establishment, been called baby killer, murderer, rapist, village burner, and other choice names. Yet, regardless of the lifestyle and political outlook of those who had orally abused me, I had to give the flower children considerable credit.

The flower power folks -- dirty, wearing rags, decked out in

8

beads and flowers -- sold the world the party line that they were a mellow and peace-loving group. Navy PA types couldn't market females in a male prison if the medium of exchange were cockroaches, let alone an idea.

My chances of surviving the interview without infuriating at least one academician equaled the survival chances of a koala bear wintering in a West Virginia sassafras thicket. There was absolutely no doubt in my military mind of what was going to happen. The editor, who had likely soaked her brain cells with mind-expanding chemicals until truly convinced folks wanted to stop beating each other over the head with dried kitty cats, jawbones of asses and other useful weaponry, was going to ruin my day. Either I'd get angry and lift safety valves at her, or she'd get angry and lift safeties on me. Regardless of who lit off their boiler, a cloud of steam belching from somebody's stack was in the Plan of the Day and would occur when:

She broke out the media's *Standard List of Classified Subjects to Which the Military Cannot Legally Respond*, hit me with a few questions from that document, then bad-mouthed me when I wouldn't answer her questions.

She blamed me because many third-world leaders did not subscribe to the Swords to Pruning Hooks Theory and accepted dried kitty cats and other weaponry as viable tools for exercising foreign diplomacy.

She implied military people are dumber than nine-pound rocks and couldn't possibly earn a living another way, except as a rent-a-cop, a strip joint bouncer or entry level burger chef.

I executed my right to play Simon Says and told her what to do with herself.

Given a choice between the interview and marooning, I'd have taken marooning. I had, however, raised my right hand to finalize the shipping over ceremony when I last reenlisted in Uncle Sam's Canoe Club. I was, therefore, legally bound to participate in the interview even though an understudy to a lunatic had contrived the evolution.

After cautioning Jarhead on the perils of running amok and Blue Suit on aiding Jarhead in executing an escape and evasion effort, I set forth with sword and buckler to do battle with a modern day Philistine. I feared the worst when I looked back at the farmhouse and noticed Blue Suit posted himself to lookout duty on a window ledge. That usually meant Jarhead was engaged in plotting a run ashore. It was only a matter of time before my neighbors tarred and feathered me, followed by all three of us being awarded a free ride out of town on a fence rail

CHAPTER TWO

SHANGHAIED

I let the little GSA Ford Pinto coast down the narrow switchback road that made a five-minute crow's flight to the town of Big Otter a tense twenty-minute drive in good weather and a driver's nightmare during winter months. It was easy to believe the mountaineer legend that pioneers charted roads in the path of a black snake drunk on stump juice.

Three small boys and a tiny girl searching for arrowheads in a newly disked field caught my eye as I rounded a steep curve. That suggested an Indian uprising in the making.

It was the kind of day that made me realize growing up isn't what it's cracked up to be. I wanted to be a kid again and conduct totally unauthorized, non-parental sanctioned removal of my shoes and splash barefooted through the silver rivulets of runoff trickling through the new grass in the hillside pastures. I wanted to touch and smell -- and maybe even taste the white and pink and yellow blossoms and squirrel ear sized leaves. I wanted to run wild in the soft spring air and make an absolute fool of myself.

11

Thoughts of a barefooted spring and all it promised disappeared when church spires peeking above the deep valley's morning fog announced the small town of Big Otter on the near bank of the Hemlock River. My morale turned keel up and descended to that of a fellow functioning as training aid for drawing and quartering evolutions. The dreaded interview was well-nigh upon me.

The closer I came to the shabby, money-shy college the more I dreaded the interview. I once admired colleges and the people who frequented them. I then believed colleges generated minds capable of independent thought, promoted freethinking and exchange of ideas and encouraged students to dream grand dreams. I no longer believed that. Almost everyone associated with higher learning seemed to have lashed themselves firmly to the same ideas and identical politics. Those who failed to clone were quickly ostracized. Independent thought appeared neither encouraged nor desired.

I had personally experienced this during a Modern History class in San Diego while striving part-time for a degree in history. We were discussing the Monroe Doctrine when the professor stated it was a horrible concept and we had no right to have treated 'Cubar' so mean because of a few little missiles.

Every clone in the room started foaming at the mouth about what the United States had done to poor Fidel. They agreed, after some overt prodding from the professor, that they would rush to Cuba to help Fidel harvest the cane crop. The fact that they would not recognize a stalk of sugar cane if they tripped over one did not enter their highly educated minds.

I took their ranting until my blood pressure peaked. I then stood up, walked to the front of the class and told them I believed they should help Fidel-baby because their potential as cane cutters far exceeded their potential for anything else except, maybe, manager of a coin car wash. I qualified my statement by saying no matter what function they performed in life, they would bring disaster and ruin upon any organization unfortunate enough to be cursed with them. I hung around a bit to give them their chance, but the professor and students only moaned and fussed and called me names. None of them exhibited any desire to wield a dried kitty cat as a tool of persuasion.

I received notice at my next evening class that my previously perfect grade point average had been 'readjusted' somewhere below freezing level -- Fahrenheit. My name had been moved from the dean's list to another list. I had failed to clone. Rather than become a card-carrying member of the *International Order of Ax Murderers*, I left the campus never to return.

I didn't enjoy the hisses and catcalls I received as I crossed the greening campus, but I maintained course and speed and did not flash the International Signal of Extreme Displeasure. I meandered along, admiring the flora and fauna, mostly the fauna, when I nearly collided with an exceptionally attractive, barefooted fauna carrying a mola-covered book bag and wearing about ten pounds of beads around the neck of her ragged, dirty granny dress.. I excused myself and started to walk away when I noticed her staring at the rows of ribbons on my chest as though she thought them pretty. She shoved her brown eyes through square, steel-rimmed eyeglasses and gave me a look that would have frosted a blacksmith's forge. "You've had a great deal of opportunity, Sergeant."

"I'm not a sergeant, but I might have had a great deal of opportunity, depending on what we're talking about."

"The opportunity to exploit the bodies of economically deprived oriental women, *Sergeant*."

"The Army has sergeants. The Air Force has sergeants. The Marine Corps has sergeants. The Navy does not have sergeants. I am, therefore, not a sergeant. As to the exploiting . . . I don't believe I've ever done any. But I'm willing to learn a new technique, Brown Eyes. Give me your mother's name and telephone number and I will exploit her -- providing she takes showers more often than you!"

What she told me to accomplish was disgusting and physically impossible. I didn't know about economically deprived, but her mother never invested in soap to wash her daughter's filthy mouth. She blessed me like a thirty-year bosun hauling on a fouled anchor as I hauled to starboard and rounded bushes in front of the student union beyond rage range. I was about to mount the wide, brick staircase to go fist and skull with the Philistine newspaper editor when a voice I recognized called my name.

"Good morning, Joan." I greeted the tall, rather skinny blonde. "I forgot you attended this Seat of Higher Learning." I didn't know Joan well although I chatted with her when I was unlucky enough to trip across her steaming in company with my least favorite chief petty officer in the entire United States Navy. Joan certainly wasn't the most interesting of women, but chatting with her beat hell out of listening to Curtis P. Longly motor mouth about his importance to The Recruiting Effort.

"Not for long, Clay. A couple months, then Bingo! Have you seen Curt this morning?"

"Is he supposed to be here?" I hoped he wasn't. If he never again crossed my bow, it would be too soon.

"So he said. One never knows about Curt."

I knew about him. I knew he was a Mark One -- Mod Zero Slimy Creature. But, to give Curtis some credit, he was not Head Slimy Creature in the Naval Recruiting Command.

"Come inside, Clay. Buy me a coffee." she ordered, grabbing me by the hand.

I managed to free my hand after a short tugging contest. I didn't want to hold hands with a woman who held mouth-to-mouth resuscitation drills with Curtis. "Well, I really can't, Joan. I'm supposed to meet the editor of the *Campus Crier*. I've never had the pleasure, but I expect you know her -- Patricia Patterson?"

"Of course I know her! We're on the *Crier* staff. Look, Patty will be delayed. We've time for coffee and a cigarette. You do smoke, don't you?"

"Today, yes. If I can bum off you." I'd pretty much quit smoking in Naval Hospital, San Diego while being put back together from wounds suffered in Vietnam, mainly because smoking was not permitted. I occasionally took it up again when the pressure got heavy.

We had a one-way chat over weak, lukewarm, vending machine coffee with her bragging about Curtis' value to navy recruiting. I thought I'd have to hold a gag and barf drill!

"Clay," Joan said, putting her long fingers on my sleeve. "Would you do me a favor?"

"It's likely." No problem there if it concerned smiting Curtis.

"Great! Look, Patty is one of my oldest friends, but I want you to help me set up a teeny situation -- a trick, sort of."

"A trick -- like in playing a joke?" I didn't know about Patty, but Joan might be willing to turn a few tricks, considering she valued herself low enough to date Curtis.

"Well, yes. Sort of. Look, Patty is a terrible pain. She is the most straight-laced woman on campus. She has terribly old-fashioned moral values, but she's a hypocrite really. By that, I mean she puts up a front because she is secretly frightened to death of men. She does date, but the instant a man gets the tiniest bit off base, she refuses to date him further. Do you understand what I mean?"

I said I thought I did, but there was no doubt in my military mind Joan was discussing an old-maid type who hated all men, except sky pilots, one of those who thump on bibles, criticize

15

everybody and call on the wicked and sinful to see The Light. Patricia Patterson and I would get along well -- about as well as the Greeks and the Turks.

"Clay, in recent days we teased and teased Patty. About you, mainly. Well, about your reputation and the . . . conquests you've made throughout Big Otter County."

"You had some reason, I suppose, other than she's not into playing musical beds?" That question got me a really dirty look!

"It's payback time, you see, for her pestering with her moralizing."

"That's where I come in? Well, I'm not about to get involved in playing a trick --"

"Wait, Clay! I'm *trying* to explain, if you will *let* me."

"I'm listening, but I don't like what I'm hearing,"

"Clay, we really need your help. You cannot fail to get her attention."

"I'm greatly flattered."

"You don't have to be sarcastic, Clay. Listen to me! We've teased about how you are going to affect her libido. She became totally angry and snapped she wasn't about to become sexually excited by a lecherous Neanderthal with the morals of a goat and the brains of a rooster."

"What the hell did you tell her? That I was going to lick my eyebrows, grab her stern, quote dirty stories out of my third grade reader, or what?"

"Don't be foolish! We just told her you are a good-looking man with a lot of charm and that women are eager to accommodate you. We implied she is so inexperienced you would have her bedded if she had courage to date you even one time. We then qualified that by telling her not to worry because she couldn't possibly get a date with you, no matter what she did."

A slender English face with a few scars on my right cheek and forehead and a somewhat crooked mouth where the medical repair job hadn't quite worked didn't add up to 'good looking' by most folks' standards. A head of somewhat wavy brown hair was about it in the good-looking sense. I wasn't a lover either. The women I went after were not difficult. We were after the same thing.

I couldn't help thinking there was a tiger somewhere in the grass. I wasn't at all certain the tiger wanted this Patty person for lunch. With Curtis around, my chances of becoming tiger chow were excellent to outstanding. It was necessary to be paranoid around Curtis.

"Joan, this is not something I'd get involved with. She hasn't done anything to me."

"Don't be a boob, Clay! Just *don't* date her." Joan said, impatiently.

"I beg to inform, Joan, I haven' the slightest idea what you are asking."

"You don't *have* to understand! Just don't date her!"

"Let me explain, Joan. No elaboration. No assistance." I smiled, but was getting a mite hostile. I wondered just how stupid Joan thought I was. Probably nine-pound rock class, if she'd paid attention to Curtis-baby's ideas concerning my dearth of intelligence.

Joan glared for a tick for two before letting out a little sigh, which I recognized as surrender. "We want her to make an ass out of herself. Okay? We want this mainly because Patty obtains positions and honors that rightfully belong to others. She can be *quite* the little bitch, but professors think she is so sweet. They believe she is *so* intelligent and *so* good at everything. Well, there is one thing she is neither intelligent about, nor good at. Men! She has zero concept how modern women relate with men. She is frightened silly of you, but she's stubborn enough to try to prove her point. She bet us each a lipstick she'd get a date with you. If you date her, she'll laugh at us, but you'll be the real loser because you will have a terrible time!"

"I suppose I should thank you for enhancing my reputation, but I won't. Joan, you folks shouldn't have done this. Interviews are rough enough without stirring up the water."

"Don't *worry*! She would never let anything harm her precious paper. You'll help?"

"Not directly. She sounds like the last type of woman I'd date. I doubt she'll even try once she meets me."

"Look, Patty has probably returned by now. You'd better go to the office by yourself, or she'll believe I influenced you."

Joan didn't need to worry. She had not influenced me. I still didn't understand exactly what she intended, but I did understand her operation plan dictated execution of a knifing. Not that a little friendly backstabbing was out of the ordinary in the academic world, but I detected a little friendly hate there too.

"Oh, Clay!" Joan called. "The reason Patty wasn't here when you arrived is because she rushed home to change after she made the bet. You should have seen her! She is *so* frumpy!"

CHAPTER THREE

ENEMY CONTACT

Patricia Patterson appeared quite young, sixteen or seventeen, maybe eighteen, at the far outside. She was wearing a long-sleeved, beige blouse with an ivory colored silk scarf across one shoulder. She didn't look at all frumpy.

She had wavy-curly, sort of rumpled, taffy hair with blond-white strands I suspected were sun streaks. Her eyes were big and gray. Her little nose didn't miss pug status by much. Her lips fit well, but her chin was a bit too strong for her small, oval face. She was slender and tiny, not even five feet tall. From what I could see of her standing behind her jumbled desk, it appeared her basic equipment had been issued in miniature.

While she didn't look at all plain, as Joan led me to believe, she did not strike me as ravishing. I couldn't decide if she was pretty, a tad less than pretty or just basic cute. I'd have bet my GSA Pinto she was a farm girl. She looked the type: bright, clean and healthy -- a perky sort of girl.

She turned slightly pink, so I figured I'd better carry out my part of the ordeal before I embarrassed her further by gawking like I'd never before seen a female. "Miss Patterson, I'm Clay Berkeley

-- here for the interview with your ra . . . er, your newspaper." I expected to be chastised bitterly, for not addressing her as "Miz."

She smiled -- broad front teeth and a slight overbite. I had a weakness for women with a slight overbite. "I guessed that, considering we rarely see that uniform here. Something about the naval uniform provides an air of mystery." (That was when she set her trap.)

"Should I address you as Master Chief or Mister Berkeley?" Her voice was soft and clear, but I detected Mark One - Mod Zero hillbilly in her speech. That made two of us.

"Clay will do fine, Miss Patterson."

"I have been Patty for twenty-two years, Clay. I see no reason to change now."

She was quite a bit older than she appeared, but I was into the initial phase of my lusting years when she entered the world.

She told me I was free to smoke, then seated me in an age-darkened, cane-bottomed chair just off the right, rear corner of her desk. I wanted to smoke, but I had no cigarettes. My chances of bumming were nil. Tobacco had never touched her gleaming teeth.

I hadn't noticed her legs until she crossed them. Even beneath her longer than fashionable skirt, there was no doubt in my mind I'd just caught a flash of the best pair of legs I'd ever seen. They were not large shapely -- not small shapely, but delicately shapely. Her legs would cause the weak, the lame and the halt to dance the hornpipe and sing sea chanteys!

I was having serious doubts about Joan's statements. Patty, although nothing like beautiful, was so unique looking she should have had men lined up in the passageway bearing golden pears, silver bells and other desirable wampum.

"I have this eight by ten inch photograph Curtis provided." She held up my picture. "Is it suitable?"

I told her it was. It was my usual appearance since a host of sawbones fitted my lower face back together. George Washington probably looked that grim when General Braddock told him: *'I say, Washington -- you Colonials are an excitable lot. Indian ambush? Against trained British soldiers? In broad daylight? Really, Washington!'*

"Clay, I have your career biography, also provided by Curtis. May I use it?"

Strange she had twice called Chief Longly 'Curtis' He didn't like to be called Curtis.

"No problem, Patty." Not unless it was produced from the investigation the FBI conducted for my initial top secret clearance. That one probably had a few sticky places regarding liberty incidents early in my career.

"I will ask the questions I formulated, although Curtis said you might be reluctant to answer them. Let me know if I ask something too sensitive and we will go off the record to derive an answer satisfactory to both. OK?"

"Will you promise anything I say off the record stays off the record? I sometimes insert foot in mouth and apply pressure." I trusted the media -- about as much as an outhouse pit full of rabid skunks when I was on the hole.

I liked the way she laughed. It wasn't a polite, phony laugh. It was rich and strong.

"Absolutely! I have no desire to win a Pulitzer Prize for discovering deep, dark secrets of the Navy. I am not pursuing a media career. I intend to teach school after I graduate in June."

"I understand you are thirty-four years old and have served in the Navy for sixteen years. Please explain your naval occupation. I find your range of jobs confusing."

"Sailors have, roughly, two occupations, Patty. A military one, their rank -- and the more or less civilian type job, their rating. Sailors are routinely double-hatted as firefighters, damage control personnel and a host of other collateral duties.

"My rank is master chief petty officer, the highest enlisted rank in the Navy, other than the one Master Chief of the Navy. Master chiefs manage people in more than one rating and operate across departmental lines. One job I've had in this category is Master Chief of the Command. My duties were to advise an admiral on morale and welfare of enlisted members in his subordinate commands comprising forty-odd ships. When something people related got out of trim, I was responsible for tweaking it until the problem was resolved.

"My rating is radioman.

"Putting the rank and the rating together, master chief radiomen usually function as radio officer when assigned to a ship or as communications officer of a destroyer squadron. When I advanced to master chief about two years ago, I was assigned to Admiral Grayson's cruiser-destroyer group in San Diego as communications assistant. I was responsible for voice, record and data communications aboard the flagship and for planning and coordinating tactical communications among the fourteen ships that made up his battle group. I've not had much shore duty. This is my first as a chief petty officer, except for a two-year overseas tour in Madrid, Spain. I'm now performing an 'out-of-rating' tour as a naval recruiter. I'd better explain how recruiting is organized, or you will have no idea what I am taking about.

"The basic level of recruiting is canvass recruiter. These are petty officers responsible for enlisting four people each month. They are experienced sailors trained in salesmanship and all aspects of Navy recruiting. They are among the top ten percent of all sailors in the Navy.

"Next in the chain-of-command are recruiters-in-charge of recruiting stations. These individuals, called RINC for short, are directly responsible for the production, training and well-being of their recruiters.

"RINC's report to a zone supervisor responsible for multiple stations. There are five zone supervisors in our district. I'm supervisor of Southern Recruiting Zone, responsible for thirty recruiters who man sixteen stations located in West Virginia and Kentucky.

"Zone supervisors report to the chief recruiter, normally a master chief petty officer, a very senior one. Ours has been a master chief since John Paul Jones served out chow as a mess cook. He is the captain's right-hand man.

"Next is commanding officer of the naval recruiting district, called either NRD or District. The CO of NRD Big Otter is a captain responsible for recruiting in parts of Kentucky, Ohio, Virginia and West Virginia.

"Others in NRD do pretty much the same as in any command. There is an executive officer. A civilian administrative officer and her staff. Our supply officer is a senior chief store-keeper with a staff of two. He is nicknamed 'Keys' because a set of linked keys is the rating insignia of storekeepers. Our incumbent public affairs officer is a chief journalist who is recovering from heavy surgery. That's why Curtis Longly is here instead of his regular assignment on the commodore's staff.

"NRD reports to an organization, known as Area. This is commanded by a captain who is known as commodore because captains of several districts report to him.

"Area reports to the Naval Recruiting Command, called CRUITCOM, an admiral responsible for recruiting throughout the United States.

"So, you see, Patty, I'm just a rock packer scratching around in the mud, about third down in the NRD chain-of-command if you don't count the administrative side of the house where the executive officer comes into play. The XO has little to do with production.

"How many master chiefs serve in the Navy, Clay?"

"No idea, really. Congress mandated master chief manning to be less than one percent of the total force when they created the rank in 1958."

"Your BIO states you were a hero in Vietnam. What did you do to earn that honor?"

"I had a PBR, a fast river patrol boat, blown out of the water."

"And?"

"I swam to another boat."

"I do not believe you earned that medal simply for swimming. The Silver Star must be near to the top. What did you really do?"

"I was in charge of three boats maneuvering in a tidal river to support a SEAL team, meaning Sea, Air, Land -- frogmen they used to be called. My boat and another hit a mine and exploded. The citation says I boarded the remaining boat, took the enemy under fire, saved the survivors in the water, then extracted the SEAL team." I was glad she was not looking into the Navy's deep, dark secrets. She didn't let go when she got a bone in her teeth.

"It sounds as though you are not certain."

"I don't remember much of it."

"Because you were badly wounded?"

"I wasn't wounded in the fire fight. I was hit with pieces from the boat or mine."

"I will work up something about your service in Vietnam, your Silver Star and that you were wounded in action."

"You don't need to go into detail about the medal. It doesn't represent what an outsider might think. I'd have received a lesser medal if people hadn't gotten killed. Heavy medals are awarded only for heavy combat. People are usually killed before a firefight is deemed as heavy combat."

"Really? Clay, what do you believe happened in Vietnam to cause the war to end so tragically?"

There it was. Armageddon. Patty had acted so sweet I had left a hole in my armor large enough to drive a Sherman tank through. I knew exactly what was going to happen. She'd ask a few well-disguised questions until she got me to say what she wanted, then she'd open fire with a barrage of boilerplate, pseudo-intellectual, bad-mouthing of the war. When she finished, she'd call me names of an unseemly nature.

Being of sound mind and body, but not very bright, I did exactly what Curtis knew I'd do. I leaped smartly upon my soap-box and let her rip! "I'll tell you exactly what I think, Patty, but it's not to be used in your article. I think the military did one hell of a fine job, but there is a host of people who don't understand what happened in Vietnam.

"There were many reasons why things went bad. For one thing, there were too many Slimy Creatures . . . er, too many in the military trying to get their ticket punched. Combat duty looks very good in promotion records. There were so many officers trying to get 'Combat' in their service jacket the military services rotated officers in and out of the field every six months

25

"That rotation played hob with the command structure. Often, because of combat losses, junior NCO's ended up as the only continuity and sometimes the only leader in small organizations. If you really want to know what went wrong, throw away the heavy books written by high-ranking military and civilian folks. Their books don't tell what really happened out in the boondocks. Read *Soldier* by Lieutenant Colonel Herbert, or books written by officer and enlisted grunts who actually fought the war."

"Clay, do you believe the war was just?"

"Initially, yes. But it went downhill because it got bigger and bigger as each service went after a piece of the action. It ultimately resembled a kennel of coonhounds after one small bitc . . . er, bone! Patty, we didn't go there to fight a war. We started out to train the South Vietnamese how to fight their own war. I sincerely believe our actions were honorable and in keeping with United States' policy to contain the Red Hordes. By the time the war ended, no one knew what they were doing. It got really difficult to determine the enemy."

"Goodness! Is that possible in a war -- not knowing the enemy?"

"Outside of the Viet Cong and the North Vietnamese, we had several choices of who the enemy was: the politicians in Vietnam and the spineless wonders in Washington, the war protesters, the media and even some in high command.

"Politicians in Vietnam didn't give two whoops about anything, except lining their pockets and the pockets of their relatives. They destroyed the moral of the country. Our own politicians were, of course, trying to stay in office, even at the expense of their country. The President's spear carriers were never certain how they wanted to proceed. Mohammed Ali couldn't whip an aged wino using the rules of engagement they formulated, then changed constantly.

"Most protesters were not idealists protesting the war. Many were, as far was the troops were concerned, protesting because of fear for themselves or somebody close to them. Some joined the pack just to raise hell, smoke grass and get their bones jum . . . er, have a good time. A few were the usual sincere nuts who protest everything the USA does. The protesters got a lot of us killed on both sides by giving the enemy encouragement, which kept the war going longer than it otherwise would have.

"A handful of our high-ranking leadership was pis . . . er, poor too. They engaged in self-serving practices -- lied to everyone, including their own troops.

"The world media was terrible! I went from admiring reporters to detesting them. They lied and slanted the truth until God, Himself, will have trouble making up their Charge and Specification Sheet when they go to the Big Newsroom in the Sky. I'm not saying our military didn't have some bad actors there. We did. We've had them in every war.

"That's all I'm going to say. That war has as many opinions as there are people, but I know folks in the field fought as well as troops in any other war. We lost hells of middle grade and junior officers and NCO's and thousands of troops to no good end." I finished my piece, then waited. I wondered if I'd learn any new nasty words.

Patty didn't burst a boiler like I expected. She just gave me a sad smile, then said, "It was a terrible war. I feel so sorry for those who lost their lives and those wounded."

While Patty looked over her notes, I watched like a mouser at a rat hole in case she uncrossed her legs. Her damned skirt was way, way too long for legs that could have modeled nylons or graced the cover of *The Refined Gentleman's Skin Book of Choice*.

"Clay, I understand recruiting is difficult. Can you tell me why?"

"I can try, but I'm getting a mite dry from all this off-the-record motor mouthing. Let's get a cup of coffee or something."

Patty, for whatever reason, turned as nervous as a male guard in a female prison after we returned to her office. I had no idea why. I could think of nothing that had happened in the cafeteria out of the ordinary, except when Patty dropped her spoon and banged her head when she bent beneath the table to retrieve it.

"Patty, everyone has an opinion about recruiting problems. Unfortunately, opinions are exactly like as . . . uh, everyone has one. I'm not an expert. I don't believe recruiting experts exist. Listen, I'm speaking only for the Navy, but all services have it tough. Now that we've shifted to the All Volunteer Force, the Navy can't seem to grasp that we can no longer pick and choose from people trying to avoid being drafted into the Army.

"A good part of the Navy's problem is we don't advertise in ways that appeal to people we want. We're trying to sell foreign travel and education when we should be trying to sell interesting jobs, good technical training and the attraction women have toward sailors."

Patty blushed.

"Uh . . . strike that last part, Patty.

"Recruiting is a joke! Everybody at the seat of government has jumped on the AVF bandwagon and dashes around like a new ensign showing off his single stripe. Defense Department keeps telling congress the AVF is the best thing since se . . . uh, sliced bread, but a few more million dollars are needed to fine tune it.

"The AVF will work, but we've got to stop beating our people to death for not making goal. Recruiters are trying hard, but they are starting to look more like whipped pups than the professionals they are. Thousands of contacts by recruiters might get the numbers Defense wants, but will not get the type of people the services need. Right now, all services are accepting men ill suited

28

for military service just to make a quota set by chair warmers. Recruiting women is not a problem; we are enlisting high caliber females across the board.

"What I think we need to do is advertise by honest, this is no shi . . . uh, no kidding spots on television programs teens and young folks watch. We should use real sailors telling why they joined the Navy, what it did or did not do for them, and what they think of their job. The spots shouldn't be too glossy and the people should be average sailors, not sailors who look and sound like actors. The spots should be true. Negative statements won't hurt. They'll help because a person will think: 'Hey, that's a real sailor talking! He or she says the outfit's got some faults, but they treated him or her pretty well. He or she got most of what they wanted. Maybe I can fit in there.'

"What do we do? We throw big bucks to a civilian advertising agency that sells soap to dream up a sales pitch to sell a life style they understand about as well as a city slicker understands pig farming!"

Patty giggled. Cute giggle, that girl. Nice overbite.

"We do the strangest things to ourselves. The Navy cannot directly enlist a minority male, high school graduate, mental group three-lower. The other services love this guy! He is no mental giant, but he's trainable. For us to take him, we must enlist three thick-headed majorities, before we can enlist one thick-headed minority. This system is called Parity and must be the most ill-conceived idea ever to come out of the ivory tower.

"The idea is complex. Somebody decided there are too many minorities in Combat Arms and too few in offices. In other words, the percentage of blacks in dangerous or low skill jobs outnumbers the percentage of blacks in the civilian population. The combat part is not a problem in the Navy! Everybody aboard ship is 'Combat Arms' because there is no rear echelon for ship's company. Everybody contributes to fighting the ship. A cook's battle station is usually in a gun mount or powder magazine. What

29

we have done, in effect, is social engineer a percentage of a race out of the Navy!"

"Gracious, Clay. Is parity legal?"

"It was tested in court and whatever organization defended the program won. Very peculiar program -- parity.

"I'll get off my podium now and maybe we can continue. I'd just as soon you don't put the parity bit into your article, not that it's a deep dark secret. The black community knows all about it. Some even approve."

"What you are saying is fascinating! I would like to hear more, but I have classes this afternoon." (That was when she covered her trap lightly with leaves.)

"I'm willing to talk Navy whenever you want, Patty." (That's when I jumped up and down on the trap's tongue, squarely with both feet.)

"Are you really?" she questioned, then shifted to a sweet, little girl voice that made the hairs on my arms rise. "Could we discuss this in more detail? Oh -- Friday night at a restaurant, maybe? We will go Dutch!"

I considered, briefly, the fate of Joan and her fellow conspirators. I then cast them over the stern and steamed away. "Sure, if you can put up with my big mouth for an evening. Is nine o'clock okay? The Foxfire on Randolph Street is a nice restaurant."

"The Foxfire is fine, but nine o'clock is a bit late for me. "Would seven o'clock be too early? Do you often eat at Foxfire?"

I didn't think I ought to tell her my supper was usually Fall City beer in a rather low-grade establishment she'd probably never heard of, let alone patronized.

"I don't value my cooking, Patty. I rarely eat at home -- except soup, a sandwich or some such. I usually eat breakfast at the Barf and Cho, . . . uh, in the federal building cafeteria. I get lunch in Pedro the Pepper Pull . . . uh, a Mexican place, or in a café down the street. Since I'm at work until late evening, I usually wander across the street for a few White Castles around six. Shall I meet you at seven, or pick you up somewhere?"

"Oh, I love White Castles. I would rather have them than a steak! Our farm is way out on Jessie's Run. I will meet you at Foxfire."

The GSA Pinto would have been a secure bet. Patty was a farm girl. We took another short coffee break. That time she didn't drop her spoon, but I did notice her giving me some very strange looks. They were duplicates of those she whipped on me after we retrieved her spoon during our first coffee break.

As I was preparing to leave, Patty told me she enjoyed the interview. She giggled, nervously, then said she'd heard I was a difficult person with whom to deal, but had found me pleasant, interesting and easy to interview.

In that frankness seemed to be in the Plan of the Day, I told her I, too, had enjoyed the interview and remarked about how enjoyable it was to talk with somebody so intelligent and pretty. My mealy-mouthed comments caused an interesting blush that started on her tanned cheeks, then spread down her neck and up to her ears. I could not recall ever having seen another female activate her blush system, except for a girl in the seventh grade. What we were doing in her barn didn't get very far. Her brother caught us and we had to fork over our allowance for the next four weeks to keep him from ratting us out.

CHAPTER FOUR

TURNING AND BURNING

I was in no hurry to return to my office after the interview. What with the effort I'd put forth, I figured the Navy owed me Big Time. I, therefore, made the only rational decision and wheeled in behind Moe's Mote, for a couple of brews and chow from his steam line.

Moe's Mote was the epitome of a drinking man's bar. It was a square, dingy room with a L-shaped bar. It boasted stools and chairs fabricated for people who carried the standard issue of arms, legs and sterns. Faded, greenish half-curtains hanging on tarnished brass rods protected occupants of the cigarette scorched, drink stained booths from prying eyes of nosy citizens passing on the street. No one knew whether the bar's name contained an obscure meaning or if Moe was bad at spelling.

Moe, somewhere in his sixties, resembled a starving mud turtle with the demeanor of an unhappy water moccasin. He spared no customer, but reserved his most caustic comments for those he liked. He hunted tips like pigs hunt copperheads, making tightwads look like Mafia dons out for a night on the town. He was, in fact, a generous man who'd feed anybody short on funds, no matter how often they showed up. Rumor had it he was a big supporter of the Salvation Army.

If there had ever been a Missus Moe, nobody knew of her. There were rumors of a long-standing liaison with the woman who owned Big Otter Hotel and Foxfire Restaurant. Considering her lady-like demeanor and fine appearance, I considered those rumors nothing more than scuttlebutt.

Females didn't much frequent Moe's bar. Either they felt uncomfortable in a male oriented slop chute, or they realized men frequented Moe's to drink, shoot the breeze and engage in male bonding. A few military and civilian women savvy enough not to complain about smoke, vulgar language, off-color stories and shop talk did frequent Moe's. Those women were much appreciated and rarely hit on. They provided the only touch of class.

Then there were the barflies . . . a group of aged veterans who lived not far away in decaying houses, in a seedy downtown hotel or in a retirement home a couple of streets distant from Moe's. Some owned considerable property, but chose to live where they had always lived, or where others of their age group lived.

The 'flies were not hard up for cash. They all enjoyed a steady income via interest payments, rents or retirement benefits. This enabled them to devise a pool of continually fed, common cash by which they could all stay flush with ready drinking money. When a check was lost or delayed, the 'flies never sweetened the working kitty with alternate money. They instead resorted to caging drinks and bitching about inefficiency in the postal system

The 'flies were mean-tempered, wise-assed, usually in the bag and always talking. Their conversations were limited, mainly, to women of long ago and the happenings during the Big One, WW Two. The group's natural habitat, the spot they protected from encroachment, was at the far end of the bar nearest the men's head.

I liked the 'flies, though they teased me unmercifully after they discovered I was far younger than most of equal rank. They hung the nickname 'Boot Camp' on me and took extreme pleasure beating me out of beer. That day was no exception in that they stuck me for a round of beer shortly after I went to their end of the bar to say hello. They said it was my turn because they had bought me a brew on Saint Patrick's Day.

I wanted to remain at Moe's the rest of the day, even if I had to buy the 'flies more suds, but that was impossible. I needed to visit my office to see what bad cards had been dealt me while I was off doing my bit for Public Affairs.

I stopped down the passageway from my office, located in the Old Post Office Building, to scuttlebutt with Angie Wallace, the RINC of my largest station. I found the place deserted, except for a tall, bony second class electrician engrossed in the contents of a gray, multi-drawer card file. "The Army across the passageway would have grabbed me had I been an applicant!" I yelled, pleased that my voice startled him. "Where's Angie, Willy?"

"Went to run some police checks on a guy she wants to ship to boot camp tomorrow, Master Chief."

"Maybe you know. How many applicants does her station have on deck today?"

Willy scratched his balding head to warm up his thinking machinery. "We still got a chance of getting five. Give me a tick to see what we got in the pipeline for Direct and DEP."

Rounding up X-number of warm bodies each month did not satisfy CRUITCOM. That was too simple. Some had to be folks who entered boot camp directly after their enlistment -- Directs. Those still in school, or otherwise unable to leave near term, were enlisted into the Delayed Entry Program and scheduled for shipment to boot camp on a mutually agreeable date -- DEPS.

"Willy! You actually used the tracking system without griping."

"I can use it, Master Chief, but I don't see why we have to keep all that paperwork to prove we've been working. It eats up my time and doesn't help keep applicants in any better order than when I carried a wheel book in my hip pocket."

"It was designed by jackals for use by lions, Willy, but it has good points."

"A hooker can have good points too and she can still give you a terrible case of gleep!"

After some stunning, nationwide failures to obtain goal, CRUITCOM, with the wisdom of a mentally challenged, three-toed sloth, blamed the failures on everything, except the Navy goat. CRUITCOM planners failed to identify what really caused the failures: lowered college entrance standards and an open job market. Instead, they decided recruiters were losing accessions because they tracked applicants "outta their hats." They also suspected recruiters of driving aimlessly around the countryside and hanging out in beer joints instead of prospecting for applicants.

An administrative process titled '*The Tracking System*' was then foisted upon recruiters by a hungry civilian agency hired to study and improve the situation. This multifaceted system theoretically enabled a recruiter to track a person from nothing more than a name until that person enlisted in the Navy, became ineligible, or until it was known for certain the individual had no interest in enlisting.

"Angie said you went to the college today, Master Chief. Any problems with peace creeps?"

"None to speak of, Willy. A few hisses and the like. The girl who interviewed me was easy to work with. She's smart. Could have made me look like a real flange head if she'd wanted. She's a really nice kid. She's a different looking sorta girl, but I'd have to call her pretty. She was bad nervous too -- something like the duty adulteress at a stoning drill."

"Irene ain't going to like you messing with her, Master Chief."

"I'm not 'messing with her.' Anyway, Irene doesn't own me. I don't own her. If I wanted that sort of mess, I'd get married, which is the single most stupid thing a man can do! I can't understand why any man on an even keel would want to formation steam. It doesn't make sense to give any woman that kinda control over your life. Find 'em, love 'em and get the hell out of Dodge if they get serious is the only way to go."

"Angie says Irene is mighty put out at your tom catting around. Angie says you're going to have to fill out your own travel claims before long."

"Angie and Irene aren't real fond of each other. Enough of this idle chatter. I must toddle along and squeeze some warm bodies out of our zone. The skipper will be after me with his cat-o-nine-tails if we don't get more folks into the Navy."

A conference call to my stations did little to improve my morale. Their projections showed making goal a possibility, barring disasters, but nothing great in the way of production. I tilted my leather chair against the radiator, draped my feet over the corner of the desk and stared glumly over the town while shifting my brain into something approaching deep thinking.

My recruiters were working hard, twelve to sixteen hours per day, but we were not reaping the fruits of their labor. Most months took almost the entire period to make goal, some months were cliff-hangers and a couple were failures. I'd done everything I could dream up to improve morale and production after I'd taken over Southern Zone from the previous supervisor who was fired for lack of production.

THE LAUNCHING

I'd closed four unproductive stations and transferred the recruiters and their assets to the nearest productive station. I'd relieved one-person stations of production-slowing chores by making them a satellite under the RINC of a multi-person station. The change was successful in that every one-recruiter station, unburdened from myriad administration tasks, began making goal. The bad part of the two-three month snuffle was that I had to fire a RINC who couldn't lead without driving people and fire two recruiters who made no effort to improve their performance.

I was still working on the problem of morale and production when the click of a relay alerted me to an incoming call. I grabbed the phone on the first ring -- no use waiting for my CETA secretary to answer. She wasn't there. She'd made her escape on days I failed to appear by 0805.

"Good afternoon, Master Chief." the skipper greeted. "How is goal looking?"

I provided Captain Markham the possible accession tally I'd just badgered from my RINC's.

"Your zone isn't creating records, but it is head and shoulders above the other four. Today, there was a total of only twenty-nine applicants in the examining center from all five zones! We are not, at this rate, likely to get a warm fuzzy from the commodore!"

"Captain, I don't like to crawl out on the yardarm without a safety belt, but projections indicate goal. I might go a bit over goal."

"Hang in there, Master Chief. I'll ring off now and call your counterpart in Eastern Zone who sent six weak. lame and halt applicants to the examining center this morning. All were rejected for problems that should have shown up during blueprinting by the recruiters."

The skipper was one great guy and one hell of a sailor. He was a mustang who had crawled up the hawse pipe from seaman recruit to captain. Along the way, he had been a CPO. He had commanded a shore establishment and a new destroyer leader. It was a far piece to climb for a backwoods boy from Tennessee. He was a fine naval officer and a great leader. He accepted responsibility for the failures of subordinates and credited successes to juniors.

Our commodore, known as 'Confident Claude,' was a citizen of a different realm, not fit to tote the skipper's ditty bag. He had the warmth of a frozen urinal and the personality of a bent beer keg. He'd take suction on a leper to further his career. Failure was in his vocabulary only when he could lay blame on others.

I made my three o'clock call to the examining center liaison petty officer to see how many accessions we'd gotten in the Navy from the eighteen applicants my zone had one deck for enlistment. I was pleasantly surprised. Fifteen had enlisted. Three wood rats unable to enlist were temporary rejects: one with protein in his urine, one with a light rash, one for a missing police check. I now had one hundred and four of the one hundred and twenty warm bodies I needed to make April goal and I had them on the twenty-second of the month. Not so very bad, Buccaneer!

It had been a long day, so when the clock neared twenty hundred, I locked my safe and   stowed non-sensitive papers in a drawer to prevent the GSA cleaning crew scattering them about when they polished my desk. It was past time for the evening liquid repast at Moe's Mote.

CHAPTER FIVE

SHIPMATES, FAIR AND FOUL

"Making goal?" I queried the cluster of Navy and fellow recruiters from the other services, less ill-starred Air Force types who were not allowed in bars and other establishments of ill repute. That was after everyone had a good laugh over Moe's comment about me looking beat to parade rest because I'd been caught using my post hole digger in another man's ground.

"Not unless I score with that fine looking deputy sheriff I just discovered existed." grinned the red headed, recruiting poster handsome NCO in Charge of the Marine Recruiting Station, a man huge enough to butt heads with a harbor tug and my best running mate.

"It's difficult to communicate with sea going bellhops." I said, loudly. "Cut their heads open and there'd be nothing but a legion of little female body parts beating feet about the deck!"

"Oh, you mean Station goal? Like for the Corps? Not bloody likely, Master Chief! I've got the same chance of making goal in April as Jane Flako has of joining the VFW!"

"You trying to ruin my night, Gunny?" snarled Sergeant Major McCormick, my Army counterpart. "I like Ho Chi Minh better'n Jane Fonda. And he got me shot. Twice!"

"They'd busted her for treason if the government had balls as big as a crab's ass!" Angie Wallace piped up. "I'd have volunteered to command the firing squad. I'd made sure bullets hit the right place. POW! Right in her mouth . . . which ain't her most used organ."

Angie was a little plain, a little short, a little pudgy, a little crude and a consistent ball breaker. She was also twice Area Sixteen Recruiter of the Year, and one of the best young leaders I knew. She was strict. She was fair. She was shrewd. She was knowledgeable. Her only fault was she spoke borderline ghetto. I didn't understand why. She was born and raised in Big Otter that had no ghetto. Her mother's grammar was excellent. I'd never met her father, who she never mentioned.

For all her military excellence, she was not respectful to me. She walked a fine line of near insubordination. I suspected she resented my taking the billet of her previous boss. She made it quite plain he walked some inches above water. She hinted I couldn't' even float!

Her recruiters nicknamed her 'Queen Angie,' but that somehow didn't fit her personality and the nickname evolved to 'King Angie.' That was what she was called, but never to her face. She'd have ripped the lips off the person who addressed her by anything, except her rank or real name.

"Yeah, Angie." Gunny said. "You're right as usual."

"Men gots their brains mixed up with their maul. Say, how comes you got no slut with you, Master Chief?"

"You surrender to that shyster yet, Angie?" I retorted, referring to a final year law student who pleaded to date her on a near daily basis.

"Your mammy teach you not to ax personal questions?"

"She did, Angie, but I'm prying into your love life. Same as you do mine."

"The answer, Master Chief, is no!"

"Gunny and I think you ought to go out with that law dog. He's got potential!"

"Potential?" Angie tapped her palm with a broad, stubby forefinger. "Potential ain't getting it. He's gots to have it right damned now!"

"He's a good-looking guy, Angie." Gunny said. "Show him what female sailors are made of."

"I'd tells you to get screwed, if I wasn't so junior. So, gets seduced. The both of you!"

"I'd like to, Angie, but no one'll take pity and lay some love on me. On second thought, I can do without the love part. Rubbin' and purrin' will do nicely."

"You wants Stuff, you gots to pay attention to something 'sides a beer bottle, Master Chief. The sweaty part be hanging fire. Your main squeeze, otherwise known as 'Travel Claims,' be here for a good hour. Not at the bar . . . in the corner booth, motor mouthing with that blonde bitch and that honky Chief Journalist from Area who act like he admire bed sheets as formal wear. Klan done turned him down for membership 'cause he be such a prick."

I looked. Irene saw me and waved. I waved back. Neither Joan nor Longly even looked at me. I could understand that. I'd cut Joan slap out of a backstabbing and lost her the price of a lipstick. Longly was a Slimy Creature who hated me. I didn't understand Irene's action. I expected her to call me over, but she turned back to Longly and his Punchboard. That, somehow, didn't look like a good sign.

41

"Angie, why do I get the feeling you don't like Irene?"

"Might be 'cause I don't likes her, Master Chief. She be a high-toned bitch with ball bearings in her heels. She be a full-blown slut if'n the field wasn't so crowded."

"You're entitled to your opinion, Angie, but I don't believe she's anything approaching a slut." I said, stiffly.

"Course not!" Angie hooted. "You'd swear The Happy Hooker was virgin if she was to lay Stuff on you and takes care of your travel claims!"

That dagger bled me deep and got a really big laugh from Moe and the troops at the bar.

"Angie, why don't you walk over to the Greyhound Station and play with the winos. No, don't do that . . . They never did anything to me."

"I'd shows you my middle finger, Master Chief, but the Navy wouldn't like that. Better I gets my butt the hell and gone before Irene come over here and I steps in me a pile of gunnery sergeant and master chief. Don't catch the gleep, guys."

"She's one hard-nosed gal!" Gunny observed, after Angie paused to give Irene an evil glare before steaming out the hatch with the forward velocity of an attacking wildcat. "Pity she didn't join the Army. She'd have been another Patton."

"To hell with that!" Sergeant Major McCormick protested. "The Army isn't ready for her. I don't see how you put up with her, Clay. I really don't."

"It's not easy, Mac." I sighed. "But you have to understand she's one hell of a fine petty officer and maybe the best recruiter in CRUITCOM. I could spend all my days contemplating Higher Ideals if I had a few more like her."

"We all know what you mean by 'contemplating,' and it has nothing to do with 'Ideals.'" Gunny snorted. "Hey, you hear anything about your transfer to sea duty?"

"I lost that one. I'm stuck in this Land of Opportunity for the duration."

"Hell of a note when a sailor can't volunteer for sea duty!" Gunny grumbled. "It's time to swallow the anchor."

Gunny Thornton would retire when they zipped him inside a body bag or laid him in a ninety-dollar, gray metal casket, if they could find either large enough to hold his huge carcass.

Gunny was flat big and flat strong. He once, single-handed, laid waste to five Royal Marines outside Mam's Bar in Palma, Spain after the poor unsuspecting fellows were foolish enough to refer to American Marines as 'Fairy Bum Suckers.' It is significant that the smallest Royal present was about six-two and two hundred plus pounds.

Gunny had collected his pay the hard way. He'd earned the Silver Star, the Bronze Star and two Purple hearts during the early days of Vietnam. He wasn't all that unique for a Marine, just a run-of-the-mill, upper grade, career NCO with a chest full of medals and a dozen 'Hey! Me too! I wuz there!' medals and ribbons and a body covered with scars. Hero status aside, he was having difficulty advancing because his career field was overcrowded. He had been one grade senior to me when we first steamed together in the Mediterranean. I now ranked him twice.

"Here comes Irene." Gunny whispered. "You got a travel claim to fill out?"

"You didn't call today." Her fingers wrapped my hand and squeezed, quite a contrast between her warm hand and the cold beer bottle. There was no doubt in my military mind that warm was going to win out before the evening ended.

"Tough day, Irene. I didn't return from the college early enough to call you for lunch."

"You sound grumpy, Clay. Are you still tired from night before last?" Her breath tickled my ear and her scent brought vivid visions of the pleasures of her bed.

"You might not believe it, Irene, but beds are also used to sleep in. I rested last night, so a rematch wouldn't be out of the question."

"Yes it would, Shakespeare, for two reasons. It is my time of the month. And I hear you've found a new playmate at the college."

People who criticize old women for being gossips have never associated with military folks -- world class bone carriers, every last one of them.

Irene and I spent time together, but ownership wasn't involved. We both dated others. This was the first time she'd expressed resentment at my falling from grace. I wondered why.

"Everything today was business, Irene. I told you last week your puke PA buddy arranged an interview at the college. Curtis had some idea an interview would lead to students thinking Navy and maybe even get us free advertisements in their newspaper. It turned out to be a typical PA evolution. The editor graduates in June. Now some poor devil, probably me, will have to plow around the stumps again next year. She didn't say she wouldn't give free ads, but I seriously doubt her budget can handle it. Our college looks 'bout as poor as a sailor two days from payday.."

"I suppose the hand holding beneath the table was part of the program? Get real, Clay! She's young enough to be your daughter!"

"I didn't hold her hand! She dropped her spoon. I bent to pick it up. So did she. We reached the spoon at the same time.

Wasn't no hand holding. She's a bit shy. She'd have screamed if I'd hung onto her hand."

"Did she scream when you looked up her dress, or did she reserve her hysterics for when you peeked inside her blouse at those two little bumps on her chest?"

Irene was getting nasty!

"Her skirt damned near dragged the deck. I didn't look down her blouse either. She had this scarf thing tied around the neck of a blouse buttoned all the way to her Adam's apple. Hell, Irene, I couldn't have looked down her blouse with an inspection mirror. And, to clear the decks, she's twelve years younger than me. Hardly daughter age, Puss!"

"With your morals, I'd be very, very surprised if you don't have children near her age. If you don't have bastards running around it couldn't be from failure to participate, not from what people with whom you were raised say."

I was trying to get my gear locker restowed so I could rebut Irene's accusations when Curtis bounded briskly to the bar and illuminated us with one of his bright, public affairs type smiles. I was reminded of Oil Can Harry.

I locked into his almost purple eyes. He flinched. It was one of my meaner looks, but not my best. "Curtis . . . we were just discussing my college caper. I had a grand old time! I held a one-man panty raid, smote three Hare Krishna's and sexually assaulted a peace creep. Didn't you hear about it? You should have. You were there."

"Please! I've asked you repeatedly not to address me as 'Curtis.' Yes, I was nearby. The commodore thought that prudent in event you decided to lecture on the diplomatic benefits of war and upset the editor who is quite unworldly."

"Diplomacy is what got me into a war. 'The pursuit of war is diplomacy failed,' so far as old Carl von Clausewitz and I are concerned."

"I'm sure you would know. Anyway, it was surprising how well it went, really. You may get to hold both of her hands in the next several months, provided you don't leer at her."

"Curtis, my son, kindly follow me."

Inside the passageway leading to the heads and parking lot, I grabbed Curtis by the shoulder and dug in deep. "Curtis, I don't like somebody dogging my tracks who wears the navy blue uniform and didn't earn it at sea. That means you, Curtis."

"I have four years sea duty." Curtis huffed.

"Contrary to your belief, duty in an aviation patrol squadron is not regulation sea duty. Naval air stations do not get underway. Sea duty, Curtis? Sicily and Iceland with cold beer every night and the occasional warm woman? Sea Duty?"

"What you see here represent many flight hours!" Curtis tapped the gold aircrewman wings above his Good Conduct and National Defense Ribbon, his only ones.

"Maybe yes -- maybe no, as the girls in Barcelona say. Many patrol planes are old and shabby and I can't imagine you doing anything dirty that would damage your nails.

"Anyway, Curtis, if you ever again schedule a function for me, or my people, then dog our tracks, it will be deep, dark kimchi time. If you worked for me, I'd arrange to heave your shore lovin' stern on the skinniest, haze gray tin can in This Man's Navy, one that would roll on wet grass! That might give you appreciation for the Navy and the people in it. Since you don't work for me, Curtis, I'll have to calibrate your head some other way. In sailor talk, which you don't understand, I'll make you beg for stevedore duty on a greasy gator freighter, which in case you don't know, is an amphibious force ship used to transport troops and equipment.

46

Fellow, you keep screwing with me and you'll wish your mother had aborted you!"

Curtis' eyes blazed. I could tell he was keeping his anger under check, so as not to give me an excuse to deck him. "I simply carried out the commodore's orders. He insists a public affairs person remain close during speeches and interviews."

"Confident Claude is a paranoid ass who wouldn't trust John Paul Jones." I said, flatly. "No more discussion, Curtis. Oh, one more thing. Real chief petty officers don't tell stories out of school. You shouldn't oughta told Irene about Patty Patterson. Not so very good, Buccaneer!"

"The look on Patty's face while you two were fumbling beneath the table was so . . . strange that I thought Irene and Joan would find it humorous."

"Irene surely thought it funny, Curtis. About like LBJ thought the news media was funny. For the record, I didn't grab any part of Patty, not even her hand. I accidentally touched her fingertips and we exchanged static electricity. Now get the hell out of my eyes!"

I intended to make it a short night after Irene flounced out the door with Joan and Curtis astern, but it didn't work out that way. The talk got good and so did the beer. Manure piled deep while we fought one war, discussed police actions and visited well-remember ports. I finally rolled home in a cab, received a snarl from Jarhead, moved Blue Suit to the other pillow and hit my pit.

I had the oddest dream. I dreamed I was cuddled with a tiny, wavy-curly haired girl in an orchard on top of a green hill. We were heaving apple blossoms at Curtis who, for whatever reason, was slithering around on his belly in the orchard grass. I also dreamed that an aged woman in a long, gray dress stood beside my bed smiling at me. It is extremely difficult to decipher dreams.

CHAPTER SIX

DAILY ROUTINE

Irene looked up from a stack of paper as I zipped past her desk the next morning to pick up guard mail at District. "Come to say sorry, Love?" She smiled, sweetly.

"Didn't know I'd done anything. Did you?"

She issued an order very unbecoming to a lady, or a woman who was not one.

"I take it we're still angry. See you, Love. Duty beckons."

Her second unladylike statement followed me down the passageway. I didn't think her time of the month was causing her demeanor. Either she lied to me the previous night, or she'd lied the week before. Women don't normally have the curse every twelve days.

"Master Chief!" the skipper called from his office as I heeled left on the quarterdeck. "I understand you found someone to help you complete your college degree. I trust this young lady will provide the level of personal attention your travel claims now receive."

Talk about nosy folks!

Back in my office, I read the mail, crunched a few numbers, wove a few words, called one of my stations that seemed to be falling by the wayside, then decided a cigarette and a cup of hot java would round out the morning. I was about to slide down the passageway to bum a cigarette from a FBI acquaintance, probably the only remaining member of the FBI willing to soil his reputation by smoking, when the telephone did its usual sick, hesitant jingle. I suspected it was the chief recruiter with a warm fuzzy for yesterday's excellent production.

"Commodore here! Your captain tells me you expect to make goal. You're confident of goal?"

I visualized the commodore's stubby, slack-bellied body hunched over his desk while his flaccid, liver-colored lips worked his telephone. I wondered if the stove stoker billet in Operation Deep Freeze was available – anything to keep from hearing his slimy voice.

"No, Sir, I'm not. I'm never confident of goal."

"That is a negative thought, Master Chief! Good salesmen have confidence. I should know. I'm the best salesman in CRUITCOM! I tell the admiral I could enlist more people than any recruiter, including your Petty Officer Angela Wallace. Why do I tell the admiral that? Because I understand success. I am successful because of my superior understanding of people. I work harder than any subordinate and I have enough pride to . . ."

I removed the phone from my ear, hung my feet over the desk's edge and studied the street below. The sycamore trees lining Buckhannon Street were leafing nicely, but they didn't yet hide the lovely Sailor Bait tripping smartly down the street.

"You hear, Master Chief?" he screamed so loudly I heard him from the phone in my lap.

"Uh, I hear you now, Commodore. I lost you for a tick. We have serious problems with the telephone system up here in the mountains. Lots of dead cats on the lines."

"So I keep hearing from your captain. Strange how those cats affect only West Virginia. Hillbillies are rather stupid, but I do think they would be able to find those cats!"

"As I was saying before your phone quit . . . you said you were going to make goal in October, then missed by two accessions."

"We didn't miss goal in October, Commodore. We over shipped by three. What District missed was Seafarer program goal."

"Regardless, you missed goal."

"Program goal is the responsibility of the classifiers, not the recruiters. We do the press gang bit and the classifiers sneaky-snake them into programs where we need them. We made goal in October!"

"Bilge, Master Chief, bilge! If you can't do your job well enough to get the bright ones to the classifiers, there is no way they can put them into the proper programs."

"Commodore, how much brain power does one need to enlist as deck ape, which is what Seafarer is? We are logged in CRUITCOM as exceeding number goal in October."

"You can quote numbers anyway you want, so long as they agree with mine!" He was yelling again. That happened a lot when we talked.

"My projection numbers are as accurate as I can make them by guessing. That's what we are really doing, regardless of what we call it. They are exactly what I expect to get at any given moment."

"I'm increasingly unhappy with your attitude, Master Chief."

"Sorry to hear that, Commodore. I believe you have the option of terminating a person from recruiting duty when you are dissatisfied with their performance."

"Do you question that?"

"No, Commodore, I just think you should exercise that option. You're not happy with me and I'm not happy with yo . . . er, recruiting. I'm outta gas, outta air speed -- and outta ideas, as aviators say."

"Master Chief Berkeley, I told you before, you are going to remain on recruiting until your tour is up, unless you step in a bight and I fire you. Admiral Grayson couldn't get you transferred when you went crying to him. Now, jack your people around and make goal. I don't care if you have to work them twenty-four hours per day, seven days a week. If they won't produce, convene a field board and fire them! You hear?"

I heard. I heard. For the eleventy-eleventh time, I heard.

I thought I was "outta here" when Admiral Grayson, my old boss, called in February from his two-star job in Washington. He inquired if I was interested in the communications assistant billet on the staff of a one-star admiral about to deploy to the Mediterranean in the cruiser *Belknap*. Accept the billet? Cat got climbing gear?

It had looked good; admirals usually get what they want. I was awaiting formal orders when the plan crashed and burned. Some little gray bureaucrat in a little gray room in the chop chain discovered recruiting duty was 'The Navy's Highest Priority,' and that I had almost one and one-half years left on my recruiting tour. Those above the 'crat in the chop chain were then obligated to recommend disapproval, which shot my transfer out of the air.

So there I was, stuck with duty I hated, mainly because the Commodore kept pushing me to do things to recruiters I was not willing to do.

Recruiting duty was terrible shore duty compared even with duty in Adak, Alaska. Recruiters worked eight-to-eight, five days per week and until noon on Saturday. They did this until they made their monthly goal of four accessions, after which they were not required to work on Saturday. The twelve-hour day was illusive. Recruiters with applicants had to get up at zero-dark-thirty to transport them to the examining center by six o'clock in the morning. Nobody dictated my working hours, but I worked the same hours as my recruiters. I subscribed fully to an old Army adage I considered the basic principle of leadership. 'First the mules, then the troops -- and then the officers'

That afternoon with the sun shining, the spring air cool and no crises on the horizon, I decided to call my recruiter in Big Isaac to report I was en route her station.

Petty Officer Barbara Randolph, Big Isaac's sole recruiter, wanted me to play Big Brass from Out of Town and assure an applicant's folks the Navy really did pay new recruits several hundred dollars per month. It seemed the last military member of the York family made it to France in 1918 when the going salary was thirteen Yankee green dollars per month.

On the way to the York farm, Barbara warned me the family was 'Real Hillbillies' and I should prepare myself. The slender, ginger-haired Petty Officer wrinkled her freckled nose and chuckled when I told her that I, too, was a native of Wild, Wonderful West Virginia, although somewhat removed from the jug with the corn cob stopper crowd.

Barbara remarked that she, much like the girl she was about to enlist, couldn't wait to graduate Big Isaac High School and charge out into the unknown world beyond the Appalachians. She said it

52

took tours in Japan and Australia and a tour aboard ship before she realized there was no place quite like West Virginia and started scheming to return.

Her first act, the day she advanced to Data Processor First Class, had been to slap a chit into the Chief of Naval Personnel requesting assignment to recruiting duty. Her fine record made it a certainty she would get what she requested. Her second act was to telephone the chief recruiter of NRD Big Otter to request assignment to the isolated mountain town of Big Isaac. She reinforced her request by stating she was willing to remain in the aged destroyer tender, *Yosemite*, until the Big Isaac station was available.

The CR was reluctant to station her at Big Isaac. Not because she was a single female who would serve over seventy miles from the nearest naval support, but because not one recruiter had succeeded in Big Isaac since the draft ended. The station was changed to part-time status after the previous RINC lost his rudder, started believing he was Daniel Boone and stalked Indians through the mountains instead of recruiting. Luckily, the RINC didn't hurt anybody before he was shipped off to a Naval Hospital. He enjoyed no more success finding Indians than finding people for the Navy.

Barbara didn't stress out. She missed making goal only once and over shipped accessions ten of her fourteen months in Big Isaac. Most of her towns were tiny and located in hollows at the end of narrow, rutted roads. Months of beating recruits out of deep hollows in that desolate country should have been enough for anybody. Barbara loved it!

Mister York had a fine crop of derelict cars and trucks on the hills surrounding his sagging log house. The rusty vehicles seemed to be nurturing dogs. At least a dozen dogs commenced to bay and carry on as Barbara worked her car between piles of rusted farm machinery on what could loosely be described as a driveway.

A mob of children poured out the front door and clustered around like pygmies checking out explorers. The almost white-haired children looked like clones, boys wearing white tee shirts with bib overalls and girls in smock-type print dresses. Their threadbare clothing had suffered washing so many times the original colors had faded away. Some wore shoes. Some didn't. None seemed aware of the cold, late afternoon wind whipping through the forest.

Barbara was a prior visitor to the York estate and learned how to contain the masses. She pulled what must have been five pounds of dime store candy from her car and gave the bag to the largest girl. That cleared the area except for the pack of hounds and assorted mongrels, some cats, two goats, poultry comprising ducks, geese, turkeys and chickens and a fat, black rabbit that topped at least ten pounds. I had difficulty believing the white sow rocking away in the porch swing -- grunting and wheezing in time with the sway of the swing.

Mister and Missus York welcomed us like long-lost members of the clan, or kids they'd misplaced some months ago. They pulled us inside the house and slapped us on a couch whose tattered fabric recorded every happening since about 'Forty-six. The rabbit had visited the couch before us . . . or maybe it was the goat.

Mister York offered us a "pull." When we declined the stump juice, Missus York served sassafras tea laced with mint in cracked, mismatched cups. I suspected Job's Turkey could buy and sell the York family, but they damned sure wasn't hungry, not judging by the remnants of the noon meal on the long, unpainted table that, with the help of two benches and a rusty Burnside stove with a crack in its belly, filled almost half of the room.

I broke out the Navy pay scale and explained it to Mister and Missus York and their daughter before giving them that and other Navy literature. They were astonished at the monthly salary. They acted like there had not been that much money in the house since the Great Depression.

I congratulated the tanned, smiling teenager on her extremely high scores on the ASVAB test and said I hoped she'd do equally well on the physical. Miss. Virginia York certainly looked healthy enough. She was positively overgrown in two places.

Just as we were saying our good-byes, the pig came grunting into the house. She made a couple of passes around the oblong, braided rug on which the children were devouring the candy, stuck her nose in the air and squealed. Missus York yelled, "Shift your butts!" as she swatted a couple of kids alongside their heads with her dishrag. "The pig wants to sit down?"

Over an early evening beer and hot dog, I remarked to Barbara that the best efforts of programs started by Presidents Roosevelt and Kennedy had not done a great deal for dirt poor, hill folks like the York family.

"Why, Master Chief, they're not groundhogging it at all! They own acres and acres of land at the head of Brushy River and Mister York sold acres of coal in recent years. I heard he just signed a contract with Blue Diamond to strip an additional coal field. She lowered her voice to a whisper. "There's talk he sells really good giggle-soup he 'stills himself."

That proved, for the umpteenth time, that first impressions are often flat wrong.

CHAPTER SEVEN

RENDEZVOUS

Around seventeen hundred, Friday afternoon, I decided to grant myself a meritorious early liberty to prepare for my date with Patty. I ambled down the passageway, leaned in the hatch of the recruiting station and told Angie to muster me gone.

"You shacking up with that old Irene Johnson again?" Angie threw up her hands. "What a man'll do to gets his travel claims filled out . . . I swear!"

It was obvious Angie and I didn't have a proper military relationship. I was way, way senior to her, yet she treated me like a bastard stepchild. She said things a first class petty officer should not even think of saying to a master chief. She involved herself in suppressing communism, racism, sexism and most other 'isms known to the world -- and seemed to believe I favored them all. She did not approve of my female friends and took extreme pleasure in picking them apart.

"I don't have a date with Irene. And let's knock off the travel claims garbage! See you tomorrow, Angie. Shove your people off early, if you want."

"Then it be that go-go bunny you saved from getting molested behind Pink Place. She owe you, Master Chief. Be better you rents her out. You gets two-three squeaky-clean hookers for what drinks cost where she work now!"

I hauled down my Flag and retreated from the field.

My home phone rang while I was trying to match one of the few non-uniform neckties I owned with my blue suit. I feared it was Irene

"Henry Clay, your bulldog has been eating my mums again!"

"Again? Missus Post, I don't know how he got out, unless the gas or electric man left the gate open. I'm really sorry."

I tried to keep Jarhead cinched down to no avail. My farm manager built a five foot, woven wire fence for the back yard, but still Jarhead escaped when the mood struck him. He had ample accomplices. Everybody who visited the farm seemed in cahoots and left the backyard gate open. I'd read somewhere about a cat that could open latches, which contributed to my suspicions that Blue Suit aided and abetted Jarhead's frequent AWOL's.

"Oh, Clay, there's no keeping that animal penned. I believe that dog can climb fences! I told Jenny -- that's Missus Caffey, just this morning about Jarhead. I said, 'Jenny, that bulldog is a menace! The way he carries on, you'd never know he's the dog of that nice Berkeley boy.' I said . . ."

I'd known Missus Post since I could remember. She was my nearest neighbor and a good one. When I was a kid, I could always count on jellied bread, a cookie, or a slice of pie or cake when I passed her house on my way up the lane from the school bus stop.

She provided a world of comfort during the period I lived alone on the farm after my parents drown. She treated me more

57

like a grandmother would treat a grief stricken, sixteen-year-old grandson than a neighbor boy of no relation. I had not needed food, clothing or money, but I would have had a difficult time with my mind without her concern and kindness. She was the only woman in the world with any claim to my love.

She was one sweet person, but a closed mouth wasn't one of her virtues. She knew every bit of scandal in adjoining counties and had feeder lines into bordering states. Missus Post *knew* and wasn't afraid to broadcast intelligence she gleaned to God-World.

". . . So, I said to Jenny, 'I spanked that boy once for riding through my chicken flock on his bicycle. Now he's a big man in the Navy. He's in charge of a lot of people.' I said --"

"Look, Missus Post." I broke in when it looked like she was getting wound up for the duration. "I've got to run. I have an appointment. I'll jack up Jarhead. I'll replace the mums too. I'll get you a whole tray."

"Now, Henry Clay, you shouldn't fib to an old lady." she admonished, having switched to a feeble voice. "I vow you've got a date -- not an appointment. You're courting that nice little Patterson girl!"

I'd always known she had a great intelligence network, but never suspected it was that good! Since she knew about my date with Patty, there was no doubt in my military mind she'd spread it across several counties. Not to worry. It wasn't the first time I'd served as conversation piece on the Quilting Circle Network.

"I'll get the mums Saturday, Missus Post. Bye now."

"Wait! I've got enough mums. Get me a yellow rose bush. I'll bake you a spice cake for digging the hole."

Patty was waiting when I arrived at Foxfire Restaurant. She was chatting with Missus Moore, the owner and maybe, although I didn't believe it, Moe's Big Love, like she had known her for her whole life. It later turned out she had.

Missus Moore gave me a long, calculating stare as if she suspected me of some ill deed. I'd gotten along well with the straight-laced Missus Moore since I'd known her, probably because I'd never brought any Angie-designated "sluts" into her establishment. All my guests had been reputable members of the community who were in a position to contribute to recruiting efforts, folks I wanted to cultivate as Centers of Influence.

The only female I'd had in Foxfire was Miss. Claghorn, the aged principal of Roosevelt-Wilson High School, whose eyesight was so poor she had difficulty seeing her food. Everyone in the Big Otter County knew Miss. Claghorn couldn't see to find button holes in her clothing and was pale death on booze, fast cars, fun, sex, chewing gum and tobacco, not necessarily in that order. That had not, however, stopped Missus Moore from looking like she suspected I'd taken the old lady steaming about the town and gotten her so smashed she couldn't eat properly.

Now I had Patty in her restaurant. That likely established in Missus Moore's mind that I was working my way through the eighteen to eighty crowd. At a minimum, Missus Moore probably thought I was trying to rob the cradle. I wasn't trying to rob it -- just borrow from it for a while.

Patty must have gone home to change; her clothing looked far too fresh to have been worn all day. She was wearing a pale blue, full-skirted dress with a waist length jacket affair. She had a white, silk scarf bent, looped, tied, whatever, across one shoulder. Pinned on the scarf was a wee teddy bear. Her earrings were so tiny I couldn't quite make them out, but they looked like diamond kitty cats. I had fallen among the bubble gummers!

I became aware as I followed Patty to our table that the slight swaying of her dress was something to behold. It didn't look like conscious swaying. It looked like pure, natural, female-type swaying. I had serious problems with Joan's story about Patty not having had many more dates than a cloistered nun. Men ought to have been hanging around the Patterson farm chewing rocks!

The Foxfire was neither ritzy, nor expensive. It served good food with a minimum of flourish to local workers, visitors and folks who just wanted a meal without the bother of cooking. Plain, tasty, West Virginia food was what they served. I believe they would have eighty-sixed a person who asked for a veggie sandwich on sourdough and a bottle of frog slime water from France. West Virginia was Cholesterol and Cornbread Country.

I had a slab of aged country ham that had served time in an honest-to-goodness smokehouse, tender soup beans and mashed potatoes with milk gravy. Patty had a small steak with a salad. She said she was watching her figure. So was I, what I could see of it from across the table. I couldn't understand her watching it though. Her figure would have disappeared entirely if she watched it too much. She didn't appear to carry one out-of-place ounce of fat on her entire tiny body. If she did, it didn't show on her superstructure. Her amidships and stern looked far too trim and tidy to carry excess cargo either.

Patty was still in her interview mode. She asked a sea bag full of questions about the Navy and places I'd visited, but I managed to extract a few kernels of intelligence. I discovered she was an only child, had lived on Jessie's Run her entire life and intended to get her teaching certification before the next school year. I'd have gotten more, but she went bad nervous whenever I steered the conversation toward her.

I sorta hoped she'd drop her spoon again, like she had in the college cafeteria during our first coffee break. I, a kindly gentleman, had bent beneath the table to pick it up, only to find her already there and reaching for the same spoon. A strong jolt of static electricity discharged between our fingertips. We both jumped and I said something about the air being abnormally dry for spring.

It was not by design that I got a quick glance at a lacy, black bra, what there was of it, when her blouse gaped open. I didn't know they made training bras that sheer! What she wore out of sight damned sure didn't match her outward dress at all. I could have made a career out of picking up that spoon, except I didn't want her to repeat the bang she received when she jumped and hit the underside of the table with her head. And I sure didn't want a repeat of the strange look she laid on me while rubbing her head with her mouth gapped open. She kept laying those strange looks on me throughout the rest of the interview.

I offered Patty a drink when we finished eating. She ordered a non-alcoholic, greenish-white, frothy thing, probably made by little brown elves in a lush, hidden valley where grown up folks couldn't go. After Patty relaxed a bit and stopped fumbling with her napkin every time I flirted a little. I radiated my best sailor-type smile and deemed it fitting and proper to try a little friendly eye contact -- which didn't work all that smashing.

She turned the color of a regulation flamingo and like to tore her purse apart digging in it. I half-expected her to pull out a derringer and have at me, but she extracted only a blue hanky with tiny, white flowers. She twisted it around in her hands twenty-thirty times, then snapped it back into her purse. She looked about as relaxed as a Roman Catholic at a Holy Roller tent meeting. I calmed her by talking how I had enjoyed duty in Spain. I didn't try any more eye contact, for fear she'd break a leg trying to escape imminent molestation.

"Clay, did you know Curtis is my first cousin?"

"No, I didn't." It was not a point in her favor.

"Well, he is." She sounded like she didn't consider it in her favor either. "He said you have spent almost all of your time in the Navy at sea. You never married?"

"Nope."

"Why, you are thirty-four years old! You must have met a woman suitable for marriage somewhere. Spain, maybe?"

I didn't think that needed an answer.

"I am an Aquarius, Clay. And you are a Scorpio, right?"

"Yeah, Patty. One of the bad actors. A Scorpio."

"Why?"

"I have strong reason to believe my folks had something to do with when I was born."

Patty blushed a light rose. "Not that! Why did you never marry?"

"Because my twenty-two-year-old Aquarius, I never wanted to get married."

"I am not your Aquarius."

"Beg pardon?"

"I am not *your* anything!"

"I never intended to imply you were."

She gave me another strange look and whipped out her hanky to give it another fifty or so twists. Her face turned roughly the shade of a ripe cherry when she accused, "Curtis said you are one of those sailors with girls in every port."

"That's not true. I've only been in the Navy sixteen years. I've not been to every port."

"*Well!*" she exclaimed, looking like I had said something dirty.

I suspected I'd made the wrong rebuttal. "Look, Patty. I've never been married. My animals are enough for me."

"*Your animals*?" she gasped.

"Yeah, the dog eats mums."

"*Eats mums*?" Her voice was a little strangled.

"He's some sort of mum freak. Missus Post, who lives down the road, called tonight and said he'd been at 'em again. I owe her a yellow rose bush."

"A *rose* bush, a *yellow* one?"

"He ate her bed of mums and she wants a yellow rose bush as payment for his sins. I'll get her one Saturday and plant it Sunday. That dog keeps me swimming in deep, dark shi -- er, kimchi."

"What is kimchi?"

"Rotten cabbage."

"Oh,"

"Anyway, just last week and the week before too, he was catting around at a neighbor's farm. Their bitc . . . er, dog was in hea . . . uh, wanted to have puppies. Jarhead intended to scre . . . er, he likes girls."

"Jarhead likes *girls*?" Patty sidled catty corner off her chair and scrutinized the door as if she feared it would suddenly slam shut and lock.

"I don't think I'm telling this right. A friend died and the folks who'd been boarding his dog and cat wanted them gone. After I bombed out trying to find someone to take them, I arranged to have them shipped to my farm where Mister Pollard, my farm manager, took care of them until I transferred here on recruiting duty.

"Jarhead, he's a fat, English bulldog. Marine barracks have bulldogs as their mascot, so I named him Jarhead, a nickname for Marines. I never knew his original name. The cat's either.

"The cat is a smoke gray, long-haired Persian. He weighs about twenty pounds. He's got a big set of bal . . . uh, he's a very masculine looking cat, but inside he's a wimp. He's even afraid of beetles! You might not believe it, but he seems to worry about odd things. I ought not tell you this, but he looks worried after he watches the news on TV. Taking all his characteristics into account, I named him Blue Suit, after the Air Force."

Those comments generated that look again. She probably thought my previous duty station was a locked pink room with soft walls and no sharp edges.

"It was very sweet of you to provide those animals a home." she said, softly. "I believe Blue Suit really does worry. Animals *know* things."

"Someone had to take them. Jeff loved those guys. He really missed them and hated to leave them behind when he went to Vietnam. He even wrote letters to his pets."

"How did he die, Clay?"

"The little fellows in black pajamas coated sharpened, bamboo sticks with human shi. . . . er, waste, left them in the sun for a few days, then stuck them around our camp and mortared the bejesus out of us. Jeff noticed kids coming up a path toward the firefight and ran to shoo them away. He hit a trip wire and fell face down into a whole nest of the things. I've always wondered if the VC ran those kids up that path so some softhearted American would dash down the path to keep them from harm. Jeff died a few days later. He had bugs in his system the doctors never even heard of."

"Oh, Clay," Tears brimmed in her eyes. "That is terrible!"

"We lost many fine, easygoing men like Jefferson O. Armstrong over there, men who would have been a real asset to the world after the war. It makes me so . . . aw, forget it."

"I suppose you hate them, Clay. The VC, I mean."

"I once did, but then we bugged out and I put it away. They lost a lot too. Probably guys just like Jeff. Nice guys always seem to get --"

Patty let out a gasp, stood up, grabbed her purse, excused herself and zipped toward the lady's head like she really needed to go. Missus Moore locked right into that maneuver, threw a couple of eye daggers in my direction, then followed Patty.

I cussed myself for upsetting her.

Patty disappeared for so long that I was beginning to think she had crawled out a window and left me standing an alley watch, a situation that happens when a sailor waits in vain for a "B" girl to show up, as promised. When Patty finally returned, she looked pale and maybe a little ill, so I asked if she wanted to leave.

"No, Clay. I asked Missus Moore to bring another drink. I must tell you something."

Missus Moore showed up right on cue with my beer and an ice tea for Patty. She placed them on the table, gave Patty a little pat on the arm and whipped a big, warm smile in my direction. I had no idea what I'd done to please her, but hoped to do it more often.

When I looked back at Patty, the hanky was catching hell. She'd twisted it into a spiral about the size of a pencil and was in the process of twisting it even smaller.

"Patty, is something the matter?"

"Yes, Clay, something is very much the matter."

"I hope I didn't upset you."

"Oh, Clay, you did nothing wrong. I did something to you. It is horrible too."

"I can't imagine you doing anything horrible, let alone to me, who you barely know."

"I *did*!" she cried. "You are going to become terribly, terribly angry, but I must explain."

The little hanky was almost in shreds and still catching hell. I had no idea what disturbed her so badly, nor did I have a clue what I was going to become angry about. "Patty, I'm not an ogre. If you believe you did something to me and feel you have to get it off your breast . . . er, mind, then lay it on me. I won't get mad."

"Clay, I did not want to go with you tonight."

"You didn't?"

"I did not. Oh, I know your reputation. I realize women are happy to date you and I am not . . . was not . . . Oh darn! They always do, do they not? Go with you, I mean?"

"I don't know what you've heard, exactly, but you heard it from Joan and Company."

Patty grabbed herself across her breasts, or rather, their usual location. "*You know*? About my stupid bet?"

"Yes, Patty. I know. Don't ask how I know. I'm not going to tell you."

"You knew what I was going to do . . . I did . . . I mean, I . . . Oh, damn-in-hell!"

I figured I'd have to leave the table if the swear words got stronger.

She took a long drag on her tea and composed herself somewhat. "Clay, I am so ashamed. I was so stupid!"

"You were tricked into the bet, Patty. I've enjoyed this evening, regardless of how it happened."

"I must explain about the bet. Otherwise, you will think I am a twit and a girl who uses people. I am not -- and I do not.

"I am teased consistently about men. The problem is not that I am afraid of men as my friends maintain. The problem is I have no success with men. Either I have no interest in them, or they insist I engage in . . . practices. Do you understand what I am saying, Clay?"

"I think so, Patty, but you needn't explain anything to me."

"You are not interested in my beliefs?"

That was one strange question to lay on a near stranger

"I'm interested, but discussing them seems to upset you."

"That *stupid* bet upsets me! Clay, I want you to understand. Listen to me. Please." she said, tugging and pulling at the little hanky as if to tear it into pieces. It didn't have far to go.

"I am not a . . . one of those type women. I suspect I have the same feelings as any normal female. I simply do not believe men and women should take relationships lightly. Love must mean something! Otherwise it is merely a physical act. I wonder how people . . .perform when they have no feelings for one another. My friends think my ideas peculiar. Possibly they are, but I am not going to . . . er, just to have a boyfriend. Do you understand?"

"I understand what you are saying, but I don't know why you are telling me. I hope you don't think I'm going to drag you off and attack you."

"I do not think that at all! I . . . Girls teased and teased about you. They told me I could not get a date with you even if I were to . . . I am certainly not going to tell you that!

"I am not beautiful, but I do not believe I am unattractive. Men look at me as though I am attractive. You look at me that way, which makes me feel . . . Oh!"

Tomato growers would kill to reproduce the exact shade on Patty's face.

"Men do not ask for repeat dates, one or two -- rarely three. I once believed it was because I am so small. Now, I am certain it is because I do not . . . encourage those I do not like enough to . . . you know!

"I felt I had to prove something. Maybe to my girlfriends. Maybe to myself. So, somehow, I made that stupid bet. I am so ashamed and so sorry. This should not have happened to you, or to me. Oh, damn-in-hell! Why did this happen *now*?"

The little hanky gave up the ghost and joined the Big Cotton Ball in the Sky. There wasn't enough left to wrap a dead canary.

"Let's start over, Patty. Let's have a real date. OK?"

She flashed her slight overbite at me, then her face crumpled. She jumped up and tore toward the head. Missus Moore smiled at me and again followed Patty.

I was one befuddled sailor; all of my halyards were wrapped around the mast.

Patty returned in ten or fifteen minutes and gave me another of those strange looks, then asked, "Are you certain you want to see me again, Henry Clay Berkeley? Not simply because you feel sorry for me?"

I reached across the table to take her hand, but she pulled it away. "Patty, no one needs to feel sorry for you. You're much too nice, both in the way you look and the way you act. I enjoy being with you. You are a sweet woman and a darned cute one too. I'm proud to be with you tonight -- any night, for that matter. I hope you will go out with me again."

That got a nice glow on her cheeks!

"I . . . I am not certain, after what I did to you. I am confused. I will call you when I decide. I simply cannot promise anything just now."

"You have my office number and I'm in the book."

"May we go now, Clay? I need to think. A lot."

I walked Patty to her car, but saying good night took longer than I'd expected. She kept me hanging around the parking lot for several minutes while she chattered nervously about how pretty spring was, how soft the air felt and how good the blossoms smelled.

I nearly had to leg iron myself to a lamp post to keep my hands off her. I wanted to kiss her in the worst way, but I was afraid she'd scream right there in front of God and everybody. Also, if I'd kissed her, she would have had to buy scads of lipsticks, which I suspected were not cheap. She didn't seem the type who would exercise reason and lie about it.

She stepped toward me, looked up with her big, gray eyes and said, "If you wish, you may . . . Oh, damn-in-hell!" She whirled away, yanked her car door open and leaped inside. Then she was gone and I was having mind shattering thoughts that had never before crossed my mind. No doubt about it, I was rapidly going off pier head!

I cranked up Dad's old Dodge Power Wagon and drive directly to Moe's where I ordered a Jim Beam and water, gulped it down. Moe took my money and looked quizzically at me. "Never seen you drink hard stuff. That college kid's boyfriend catch you with your ax in his notch? Or did you just miss getting run over by one of your tool warmers. Irene, maybe?"

"I'd call you a vulgar name, Moe, if I didn't like you. You anus orifice!"

Gunny Thornton appeared from among the barflies at the distant end of the bar, pulled a stool and crawled on it. Rather, he bent his knees and set on the defenseless little thing. "Girl problems, maybe?"

"You heard what I told Moe. Same applies to you, Leatherneck!"

"Did the sweet, innocent, little college girl stiff the big, bad, horny master chief out of some Stuff. Is that your problem, Son?"

"Does the entire State of West Virginia know where I was tonight?"

"You can bet your Navy lovin' stern Irene knows. She stomped in here three-four times tonight with fire in her eye and the devil in her heart! She ultimately left with some fellow I think she knows very, very well, Amigo. Probably in the Biblical sense. I say that because Irene let out a whoop you could have heard in Harrison County when he walked through the door. He didn't get to the bar before Irene leaped out of her chair like a snake chomped down on her stern, and put about six fathoms of tongue down his throat like she was familiar with the territory. They pawed each over one drink, then left. Don't know who he was. Good-looking man."

"Well, whoever he is, he's welcome to whatever she's good for. I don't know what the hell is wrong with Irene. She lit off and has acted like a rabid rattlesnake since I went to the college for that damned interview. I suspect she's really angry after tonight, what with all the flapper valve mouths around here. I took Patty out only because jealous cats ganged up on her."

"What you did was nice, but you'll never get your travel claims filled that way."

Gunny didn't seem to like the look I laid on him.

We had another drink, then switched to beer. We discussed the usual subjects while getting trashed, then Gunny shifted the subject from liberty in Singapore to Patty. Who, strangely, had been shifting in and out of my thoughts

"As little Alice said, it's Curiouser and Curiouser. Patricia Lane Patterson! **Really**?"

"You are the second -- no, the fourth, person who has made some sly comment about Patty. What is it about her? Is she one of them church going twirls . . . uh, girls who pulls double duty as town jump? She's inflicted -- er, infected with chronic gleep, or something? Tell me what with her high moral passables . . . uh, principles and sweet nook -- er, look that she's been boned . . . uh, cloned from an active duty angel. Tell me everyone, even the National Inquirer, knows her's got . . . er, she's got sainthood. Ain't nobody telled me nothing, not even my steaming bloody . . . uh, buddy. And here I am, about to get zapped by The Big Finger for trying to get into her dance . . . er, pants! Which I taint."

"In reference to whatever the hell it was you just said, I don't know her well, even if she does live down the road from my folk's place and was running mates with my little sister from grade school until Heather joined the Coast Guard. All I know is she's a Mark One -- Mod Zero Straight Arrow, if that title applies to females. Don't screw around. Full Stop! Heather told Mom how Patty turned boys off in high school. How she kept fixing her up, only to have Patty date a guy maybe once, then refuse to date him again. After a while every boy quit trying to date her."

"Makes no sense, Gunny. She's not the Catcher . . . er, Creature from the Black Balloon . . . uh, Lagoon. She's a cute girl. Not beautiful by a long snot . . . er shot, but damned cute. She's built like a little slick . . . er, brick . . . Oh, hell, considering she ain't got one hell of a lot of nothing . . . er, a hell of a lot of anything. She's got one pair of legs, I mean nine pair of legs . . . er, nice pair halfway to her bees . . . er, knees, which is all I seen. Titties ain't no bigger than a shot glass, but . . . son of a bitch! I meaned a tea cup, I meaned . . . er, I don't know what I meanted, but they look fine inside her flouse, at least her bra do."

"You're garbling like a Teletype with a busted clutch! You're making about as much sense as Book, that walkin' talkin' pet rock you have for a recruiter. If it's catching, you keep him away from me! You okay or what?"

"Yeah, Gunny. I'd okay." I wasn't okay. Anybody who can't talk is not okay. It was scary.

"Your modulator is FUBAR! You're catawampus on that hard stuff you drank!

"As I was saying, Patty is a strange girl when it comes to men. Don't ask! I don't know nothing about her going for women. She's just strange -- maybe different is a better word. Mom was talking about Patty a month or so ago. She says Patty has nobody strapped down. Not strapped on, you understand. Strapped down, like a steady fellow she's got on the bitter end of her hawser. Mom said there was a truck-sized hillwilliam that she once thought might turn into Patty's steady fellow, but then Patty deep sixed him.

"I think she's a Tight Fitting. Unless she's getting it on with one of their hired hands of which they got some. It was nice of you to help her out, but she could have bought every lipstick in Big Otter County and never strained her daddy's coin purse. He'd got a lot of eagle dust for a farmer. How'd it really go tonight? As bad as you sound?"

"She wouldn't no . . . er, go with me again if'n I wore the chastity belt."

"Surely you didn't try to get it on with her in one date!"

"Gunny, a regulation rapist wouldn't try to get it on with her on the first date! I teated . . . er, treated her like a sister. She was vice, er, nice, but she shooted . . . er, shot me down so hard I bounced when I hit the deck. No, not really. She just didn't say yes to a second date."

"You ain't the first she shot down, Master Chief. I'm surprised she ever agreed to go out with you -- even the one time."

"Why the bell, er, hell not? I'm not pretty like Curtis. I might not be 'good looking' like that fellow Irene left with, but not ugly. A little rugged, maybe."

"Master Chief, listen to me. She's not your type. She's way too young for you. Look! She's no hot skivvy girl. She's a walking piece of class! She knows what she wants and she's going to hold out until she gets it. Patty wants to wear white before she does it!"

"Does what?"

"Gives her all. Extended her precious gift. Surrenders. Does the dirty deed. Damn it, Man! You ain't going to get her legs spread unless you marry her."

"Marry her? You're a sick man, Gunny, nil . . . er, ill even. I only just bet . . . er, met the girl and my chances of taking her out again equals a redneck backing . . . er, shacking up with an ACLU gal. I'm not interested in her anyway."

"You're not?"

"You don't understand, Gunny. The liberty duds Patty paraded tonight cost more than I make in a month, but that didn't bop . . . er, stop her from pinning a teddy bear on her dress and sticking diamond pussycats in her ears. She's like a little girl. She ain't grown. Gunny, you've known me since we were on that ragged amphibious flagship *USS Mount McKinley*, otherwise known as an AMPIG. Did you ever say . . . uh, see any, and I meaned the slightest indication I wanted to get buried . . . er, married?"

"Can't say I have, 'cept maybe that blue-blooded, English Honey. All I can see is you're bad upset about how your night went. You're garbling bad!

"Think about this, if you can. How many times have you struck out with a woman? You always thought it was funny. Joked about it. You ain't doing that now, Shipmate. She's got you thwart ships in one date!"

"Screw you! That goes for your bat . . . er, cat too!"

"Listen, Shipmate. You keep fooling around with her and she'll get your liberty card. Permanently. Young Stuff is dangerous. WHAM -- you're formation steaming!"

"That's it, Gunny! You're lazy . . . er, crazy. I'm going home and soak my bed . . . er, head for even blowing you. Oh, Lord, I didn't meant that! I meant knowing you. Why don't you find yourself a pretty flyboy and play drop the rope . . . er, soap?"

"I don't approve of that kind of sex, but it'd be safer in the long run than an old seadog like you playing socket set with a regulation Tight Fitting.

CHAPTER EIGHT

LIBERTY CALL

Saturday started well, even though I was hung over as a pig with a silo full of spoiled ensilage. We obtained most of our recruiting goal by week's end and the month looked locked in, baring an unhappy doctor at the examining center. Even my secretary, who rarely worked Saturdays, mustered in. Saturday looked even better when tall, burly, square-headed Eugene "Book" Arnet rolled through the door growling like a ship's horn in a fog bank. "Hey, Master Chief! We'uns a-makin' goal?"

"Looks like it, Book. How's the clientele in Falling Ash?"

"They're so dumb th' Army can't take em! Them thet ain't dumb, they got trouble with the law. Then thet ain't got law after 'em is sick some way. Makin' goal in Kentucky is rougher'n uh cob uh corn." Book grinned his big, dumb, hayseed grin. "Hey, Master Chief, yu want t' sneak off to get uh beer?"

"Got no problem with that, but I've got to stick around for a tick. I'm expecting a conference call from the chief recruiter. Get you a cup of java and bug King Angie. By the way . . . did Ellen Ann issue you your liberty card?"

"I done told her I had t' come up here t' cumshaw me some stuff for my station. Thet's kinda true. I'm a-goin' t' tell my old woman thet yu made me stay up here t' do some awful bad work what I'll figger on later. Hey, Master Chief, yu got t' lie t' women folks." Book said, seriously. "If'n she wuz t' catch me flat on top uh gal and come up and slap me smack-dab on my navy blue ass, I'd lie 'bout it. By hell, I'd stick t' hit too!"

"Hit the hatch, Book! I've got work to do." I ordered, after I stopped laughing and got my sea bag restowed.

Book, so called because he wouldn't recognize one without a navy blue cover, was reputed to have failed Tags and Twinkle in the first grade. He could read fairly well and was a mathematical whiz, but his ability to speak and write the King's English was nearly nonexistent. He was a regulation hillbilly! He had, maybe, six years solid education and twenty-odd years in the Navy Reserve, the first four on active duty and his most recent year as an active duty recruiter. His naval service was checkered with constant falls from grace, but no one could fault his performance as a first class engineman. He had a sea bag full of commendations attesting to his ability to get the most out of both machinery and people. His civilian years were spent working in a local Ford Motors plant as a line foreman.

Book was now one of my favorite people, but I'd originally thought him the dumbest acting, dumbest sounding man I'd had the misfortune to trip over. I ultimately discovered Book was sneaky smart and as shrewd an individual as I'd met. His thought train, however, was flawed.

Book fitted just fine in the poorly producing station I'd assigned him. He acted and sounded just like the natives in that area. He straightened out the three-recruiter station in a jiffy and turned it into a top producer. The Army and Air Force recruiters weren't happy with Book because they'd had recruiting their way for far too long. They ganged up on the Navy in general and Book in particular. They made a terrible bad mistake!

First, Book explained during a speech to several dozen male *Future Farmers of America* that the United States needed every military service. He ended his speech by going to work on the Air Force, which had torn the Navy to shreds during their presentation.

"Yu fellers all done heerd terrible bad things 'bout th' Navy here today. Hit ain't none uh hit true and hit ain't right t' talk no-count 'bout no service. But, I jest got t' warn yu'll. Fellers thet joins the United States Air Force has mostly got little, bitty Stuff. Why, their Stuff ain't almost never bigger'n what uh guinea pig packs!"

The Air Force enlisted exactly one man out of the FFA that year, a considerable difference from previous years when they dominated recruiting in that organization. The Navy recruited eight as opposed to two the year before. The Marines got six. The Army got a bunch

The Army NCO-in-Charge in Fallen Ash was a top recruiter. She was an attractive, long-legged redhead with green eyes. She had *no* problem making contact with male prospects. That, coupled with exceptional competence, enabled her to consistently enlist far more than the required number. Hard scuttlebutt had it she picked lovers from among her applicants.

A couple of weeks after Book blasted the Air Force out of the sky, an older than usual applicant walked into Book's station, saying he was tired of being laid off from his job and wanted to know what the Navy had to offer. Book blueprinted him, found no police record or medical problems and that he had already taken the ASVAB test on which he obtained a high score. Book whipped the six-year enlistment on him. He outlined enlistment in pay grade E-3, two years of technical schools and automatic advancement to petty officer third class upon completion of the initial school. He closed his sales pitch by telling the prospect he'd take him to Big Otter the following morning for processing into the Navy.

The prospect backed and filled before he agreed. He then told Book he would have to tell the Army recruiter he wasn't going to enlist in the Army and, therefore, couldn't keep the dinner date she'd offered him for that evening.

Book took the fellow directly under tow: "Look, Son -- if'n yu're a-goin' t' be any kinda real sailor, yu tell her in th' mornin'!"

Marcie Niles, my on again-off again secretary, did a creditable imitation of somebody who gives a damn when she answered the telephone before I could grab it off the hook. "You got a call, Master Chief. But not the conference call. You want it transferred to you?" she screeched through the squawk box.

No, I wanted her to transfer it to Pago Pago. I bit my tongue. "Punch it to the two-oh-eight line and put the conference call on the other line when it comes in."

She transferred it to the other line.

"Master Chief Berkeley speaking. May I help you?"

"Good morning, Clay."

I slammed upright in the chair, banging my knee on the edge of the desk. "Patty?"

"Yes, Clay. I want to ask you something."

"My time is your time, Patty. More questions for the interview?" I hoped she was going to ask me to join her in conducting perpetuation of the species drills.

"I have already blue penciled our interview. I called to invite you to dinner tomorrow."

Her soft voice transmitted her face right in front of my eyes. It was a cute face . . . I jerked myself back to the real world. "Dinner? Sunday?"

"Yes, Clay. Mommy and Daddy would like you to visit."

Eating with her wasn't what I had in mind. We'd already done that. Still, NRD really did need free advertising.

"I usually take my animals for a ride and a run on Sunday. Jarhead enjoys them, but Blue Suit won't get out of the truck. Too many wild bugs outside. But, as I told you, Jarhead fell from grace when he ate Missus Post's mums. I held captain's mast and punished him. No ride this week and only water and dried dog food for three days. No Mighty Dog. No beer. Blue Suite can't watch TV until Monday. So, Patty, I'm pleased to accept. When and where?"

"You are bad to punish your little dog and cat -- especially the cat that did nothing."

"Guilt by association. Group punishment. We're big on that in the Navy. Seriously, I suspect Blue Suit of being the mind behind the throne."

Her warm, rich laugh rang through my earpiece. "One for all -- all for one!" The D'Artagnan thing, is that what they do?"

"Crossed paws and all."

"Good for them! Listen. You do not know where we live and it is way up an old gravel road. Meet me at nine forty-five at Indian Run Baptist Church. Do you know where it is?"

"I know where it is, but you don't have to meet me. Recruiters always find their man or woman."

"Yes, you could find our farm, but you are going to services with us, aren't you?"

"You mean -- like in church services?"

"Of course. It is the Sabbath. We will attend services before dinner. OK?"

"Uh, yeah. Sure." I said, weakly. "I . . . er, go to church all the time."

"Wonderful! See you tomorrow. Goodbye, Clay."

Sandbagged! I added her ploy to my list of things that made me suspect Patty was not exactly what folks said she was. I was beginning to wonder if her outward innocence was equally shaky. I hoped so.

After the conference call, I called all my RINC's and knocked the recruiters off a couple of hours early. I then stopped at Marcie's cubbyhole to tell her to secure for the day and that she was welcome to accompany Angie's recruiters and myself to Moe's

"People who inhabit such places are going to Hell!" she sniffed, looking at me like I was the Duty Demon.

"Sorry, Marcie. I didn't know you felt so strongly. Say, what church do you attend?"

"The Church of the Everlasting Redeemed Faith and Saviors All. We would love to have you attend, Master Chief!" Marcie probably thought she'd get twenty or thirty Gold Stars on her halo if she managed to drag me in out of the cold.

"Sorry, Marcie. I promised to attend another church." I'd never heard of her church. They probably picked up live copperheads and rattlesnakes, drank hemlock laced with lye and took turns beating each other over the head with pissed off wildcats.

"Book, you numbskull! That's not how you makes a Gee!" Angie was yelling as I walked through her hatch. "Master Chief, you tells Book this ain't no Gee!"

Book had apparently talked Angie into typing his Request for Recruiting Aids and she was having problems with his printing. Book couldn't do cursive or much of anything else, for that matter. She was correct. The letter wasn't a G. It didn't resemble anything I'd seen before and I'd been reading Book's RINC Reports for months, not that I ever really understood them.

"Angie's right, Book. That's not a Gee."

Book studied the paper while scratching his wavy, corn colored hair. "Then what I want t' know is how th' hell yu' spell Gee!"

It took a while before the seven of us, less Book who didn't understand the funny, recovered enough to secure the office and get underway for Moe's. After I'd bought the troops a couple of drinks, I trapped Angie in a booth and asked if she attended church.

"Course I goes to church, Master Chief. Does you?"

"Is it a regulation church?"

"What you mean, 'regulation?' Us black folks go to the same churches you white folks does. It's Southern Baptist. What you think black folks does in church? Rubs goats?"

"I don't know what anyone does in church, Angie. That's my problem. How does one act in a civilian church?"

"When? When you gets buried. When you gets married. When?"

"The usual thing. Sunday services, like."

"You gets hit with a lightening bolt, like Gary Cooper in the Sergeant York movie?"

"No, Angie. I'm not a complete heathen. I went to church when I was a kid, but that was Methodist. They probably have a different technical manual than Baptists."

"Why you needs to know?"

"I just need to, Angie. Will you hook me up?"

"I don't know but what this ain't something like having to wash the boss' car."

"Look, Angie. I'll buy you drinks with umbrellas floating inside and pictures of Admiral Grace Hopper on the glass all day -- all night too. Just write me a point paper on how to act during regulation church services. OK?" I was prepared to beg.

Angie sighed. "I'll do it, Master Chief, but you owes me. Big Time!"

"Thanks heaps, Angie. I really do appreciate this."

"How many times does I gets to hang in a sleazy slop chute with a pack of horny sailors and a bunch of drunk, dirty, old barflies and writes up a point paper on Southern Baptists so my master chief won't makes a complete fool out of hisself when he goes and does whatever it is he's going to do -- and won't tells me about?

"Hey, this ain't nothing like them travel claims, is it?"

I went to the bar and laid my forehead on my arms. Given a choice, I would rather have had leprosy!"

I'm not certain what happened. Some were drinking because they were going to make goal and some were drinking because they were not, but we were all drinking. I remember Angie resisting mightily when the Army, Navy, Marines and Coast Guard recruiters decided to make a unified landing at Pearl's Topless and dragged her along. I remember her going off on us at the top of her lungs and storming out after Book tried to fix her up with a patron who had been eyeballing her. I lost the bitter end at that point and didn't remember much more until I woke up in a hotel room around six a.m., dying of thirst. There was a female beneath the covers who I hoped was Claire, a lady friend who worked at Pearl's, rather than one of Pearl's second string girls.

I managed to stumble home where, with the aid of two bottles of Dr. Pepper, I partially drown the gremlins stoking forges in my belly. Jarhead was not happy with me, neither was Blue Suit. I couldn't find Angie's point paper anywhere. I was afraid to telephone her and ask that she brief me, so I said to hell with it and hit my pit for a couple of hours.

I didn't feel a great deal better when I crawled out of my rack. I'd once felt worse, but that was after the VC mined me. There were several faces in the mirror, so I shaved them all. My teeth itched and there was a gaggle, flock, herd, deceit, whatever, of frogs hopping around inside my stomach. It felt like they were conducting breeding drills, which was likely more than I'd accomplished the previous night.

There was no doubt in my military mind that I had sipped far too much of the devil's brew.

CHAPTER NINE

CHURCH CALL

By the time I arrived at Patty's church half my brain was telling me I was going to survive and the other half telling me I should muster in at The Big Receiving Station in the Sky and have done with it. I realized I'd killed a multitude of brain cells the previous two nights. I hated killing them. I had so few to begin with.

I wasn't late, but Patty was pacing about beneath a leafing oak tree like a mama cat looking for a place to have kittens. She was decked out in a dark blue outfit with a white, lacy blouse and wearing a tiny, white hat perched on her wavy-curly hair. Her legs, supported by shiny, black high heels was not what I needed to look at before going to church. It was good I couldn't see much leg below her hemline, but their outline beneath her skirt still produced disturbing thoughts.

My compliments worked fine. She went pink and flashed a smile that would have destroyed a monk's outlook on life and caused him to suit up and head for the nearest body exchange.

"You look very nice too, Clay." She laid that strange look on me again as she caught my arm in her gloved hand and led me

84

toward the steps at the other side of the churchyard. "You appear a bit pale, though."

"A slight bug, I think."

"I hope you didn't catch it . . . last night."

Her preacher was one of the old-fashioned, "sock it to 'em" sort. Every time I dozed, he'd let out a whoop and yell something like: "Friends, there are Sinners among us!"

No doubt in my military mind there was at least one.

Patty's mother didn't say more than hello at the church and didn't say hardly anything during what I considered an outstanding meal at the Patterson farm: pot roast, mashed spuds and fifteen to twenty side dishes with mince pie for dessert. She kept looking like she suspected me of committing obscene acts with sheep. I felt about as comfortable as Patty's preacher would have felt in an Arab cathouse.

Mister Patterson didn't exactly greet me with open arms, but was positively friendly compared to his wife. He made a few comments about how hard it was to make a living by farming and how he'd been in the Army in World War Two. He didn't like the Army or Europe. He also said he had known my parents and had attended their funeral.

I must have said something before he hitched up his trousers and headed down to the general store to loaf. I wished I had gone too because Missus Patterson had shifted from the suspicious mode to looking at me like I was drooling. Since my chances of escape equaled that of Charles Manson, I girded my loins, or whatever, and prepared to hang in there.

"Clay, Patty said, after her dad fired off a vehicle somewhere outside. "Did you get the yellow rose bush for Missus Post?"

Great John Paul Jones! I'd forgotten all about the damned rose bush!

"No, Patty. It got sort of busy yesterday and --"

"So I understand. I was telling Mommy, just yesterday, that the shrubbery is simply taking over the yard. There is a yellow rose bush in the far corner of the side yard. I want that spot for . . . Oh, mums. Please uproot that bush while I put dinner away. We will then transplant it in Missus Post's yard. It has been ages since I've seen her!"

I tried to talk my way out of it, but I think Patty had some plantation-owning ancestors.

Sweat drenched my body by the time I'd dug down six inches, even my socks were wet. I could feel beer oozing from every pore. I had removed my jacket and necktie, but my light blue shirt and flannel trousers disintegrated by the minute. I figured the shirt might survive, but the trousers' prognosis was poor. The knees drooped and bagged like I'd bought them second handed from a Goon. There was a buzzing in my ears. I felt like fainting, but I didn't have strength enough to fall down. When I struck a rock with the mattock, my head felt like someone slammed it with a bosun's tool. The damned taproot seemed headed for China or whatever country is directly opposite Jessie's Run.

Marines treat brig rats better than I experienced at the hands of Patty. She was one sly taskmistress; one who brought me glasses of iced tea so she could check up. I really enjoyed her comments.

"Is the ground really that hard, Clay?"

"Try putting your weight on the shovel with your foot, Clay!"

"I would get Daddy to sharpen the tools if he were here."

"Do you think you will have it out by dark, Clay?"

"'I understand excessive drinking and . . . you Know, weakens a person. Do you believe that, Clay?'

I wondered, when what brain cells I had left fired, if her treatment of me related to the innuendos she's whipped on me concerning drinking and sex. And why she seemed to resent that I'd fallen from grace, if she really did know of the previous night's escapades at Pearl's and beyond. I could think of no reason why my running amuck should concern Patty.

I didn't think anything could be worse than digging up that bush, but it got worse when I started to plant it in Missus Post's yard. The soil where she wanted it planted was about as soft as the skin of a battleship.

"Dig a hole twice the depth of the root, mix one shovel scoop of manure with the bottom foot of dirt and that bush will reach for heaven!" Missus Post directed, during an early critique of my work. I suspected the manure was still encased in a deceased elephant, considering the depth of the hole she wanted. I kept chipping away and she kept bossing from the porch where she was chatting with Patty. The porch was too distant to hear what they were discussing with such interest -- the latest edition of *Indentured Servants for Fun and Profit* most likely. I didn't care a whole hell of a lot for the giggling when they looked my way. I felt they were plotting something.

"Clay, I've been wondering . . . why did you wear good clothing to plant a tree?" Missus Post asked, when she finally brought me a cold drink and a piece of spice cake.

I didn't answer. Her knowing smile told me she knew exactly how Patty shanghaied me. I suspected she approved of Patty's sneaky tactics too.

I finally got the bush planted, buried, dug in, whatever, with Patty's sole contribution being critique and supervision. I was covered with dirt. I looked like I'd spent the night in a Dempsey Dumpster cuddled with a jug of Mad Dog Twenty-Twenty. I decided my trousers were salvageable, provided I took up golf at a club where they still wore knickerbockers.

"Patty, I have to change clothes before I take you home. Let's stop by my place just up the lane so I can clean up." I tried to sound beat down as a coolie who had spent the last twelve hours lugging bags of cement into a high-sided ship, but Patty didn't look the least sympathetic.

"Well . . . I do want to meet your unique animals, but I cannot go inside the house."

"Why not?"

"Henry Clay Berkeley! A lady does not enter a house alone with a man to whom she is not married."

Strange I 'd not run into that situation before . . . .

We compromised. She agreed to wait on my front porch where God and everybody could see her and where, I suppose, if necessary, she could scream for help.

Jarhead made a complete ass of himself. He sniffed her legs, rolled his bloodshot eyes up at her like he was seeing the Big Mighty Dog Factory in the Sky, then laid his ugly head across both of her feet and slobbered all over her white tennis shoes. When I tried to pull him away, he snapped at me.

Blue Suit plopped twenty or so pounds onto her lap and purred like a dynamo under heavy load. He'd never before purred around a stranger. He didn't want to look overly friendly. Strangers were always katnapping friendly kitties.

Patty seemed delighted to have fifteen pounds of wrinkled dog head on her feet and a bobcat-sized Persian on her lap, wood rasping her fingers. It was good she had changed into jeans before we left her house. She'd done a lot to enhance her church suit, but she was even better in jeans. There wasn't a whole hell of a lot there, but what existed stuck out nicely -- and in proper proportion to the rest of her too. I'd hung back a bit when we walked to the porch so as to walk slightly behind her. Her sway had to be natural!

I felt considerably better after I got rid of my soiled clothing, showered and changed into some knockabout gear. I felt so good I considered asking Patty if she'd like to see the house, specifically the master bedroom, but thought better of it. I didn't need a woman screaming in my house on a quiet Sunday afternoon. With the poor luck I was having lately, a dirty-minded ghost would probably grab her by the stern and/or superstructure.

"Patty," I asked, as I pried Jarhead and Blue Suit off her. "I'm all out of soda. Let's go get something cold to drink. I'm hotter than a fresh . . . uh, a fox in a forest fire."

"A beer would be nice."

"A *beer*?"

"Certainly. There is nothing wrong with drinking beer if one does not overly indulge. 'Take thou a little wine for thy stomach's sake.' Oh, sorry. I do not expect you are familiar with biblical verses."

Things ain't always what they seem, Shipmates. Maybe she wasn't a puss, press, priss, or whatever Gunny had called her.

"There's a lounge in the Holiday Inn. Is that okay?"

"Let us go to one Joan spoke of. Moe's Mote."

"Uh, you don't want to go there. Moe's is a slop chute . . . a common beer joint."

"I am not unworldly! I drink! I drank a whiskey and Coke on the bus when we traveled to Washington for our high school graduation trip. We sneaked a bottle of vodka into the YWCA too -- both nights!"

Princess Anne wasn't unworldly. Princess Caroline wasn't unworldly. Princess Margaret wasn't unworldly. Patricia Lane Patterson ranked with Snow White.

I tried to steer her to a lounge where normal folks hung out, but that was like changing the direction of an aircraft carrier with a single yard tug. I felt pity for the man who had to formation steam with her for a lifetime. She was flat stubborn, something on the order of Sir Winston Churchill.

Barflies and hung over recruiters lined two deep at Moe's bar. Booths and tables were filled with seedy civilians, most of them older than rocks. It looked like a mandatory muster for the *International Order of Barflies -- Middle Atlantic Branch*. I feared the worst.

"Hey, Boot Camp! Is thet Purty your'n, or did yu borrow her so as yu could 'press us?" yelled my favorite 'fly, a retired ship's cook, vintage USN, WW II.

His running mate, a retired railroader, vintage USA, WW II, got into the act. "You sure traded up, if she's your'n. She's terrible fine goods. Where did *you* find a lady?"

Patty went red and clutched my arm. I'd have jumped had the bar had a second floor.

Gunny Thornton and Sergeant Price, his top recruiter, made room for us at the bar. I wasn't naive enough to think my rank had anything to do with them giving up their bar stools. I knew the buggers! Gunny wanted to satisfy his curiosity as to why Patty was steaming with me. Sergeant Price thought he'd get a chance to put a run on her. Moe, hoping he'd get some fresh dirt on me, hauled down the bar like he couldn't wait to serve us.

Moe inspected Patty until she blushed, then reached across the bar and touched her face. "It won't come off! That blush is real! You're in trouble, Boot Camp. That blush'll reduce your talkin' by sixty-five percent.

"You're in the soup too, Missy. You'll set yourself a-fire with your face if you hang with this sleaze bag. You want I should fix you up with a barfly? They all got more class than Boot Camp Berkeley."

Patty got some kind of red, but giggled. Personally, I didn't see anything to giggle about.

Patty got sort of loose after a few sips of her beer. When Moe told a funny story he had serious trouble keeping clean, she even slapped me lightly on the forearm. Things were looking good, then Angie came tearing into the bar with a bone in her teeth and fire flickering in her eyes.

"You lowdown sons of bitches done got me drunk and taken me to a titty bar! That sucked The Big One! Then you mother . . . Oh, hello. I'm Angie Wallace."

"Hello, Angie. I am Patty Patterson. I have heard of you. You are that wonderful recruiter Clay spoke of."

"Aw, he's just an old fool. Aw, heck!"

King Angie, embarrassed?

"Master Chief, Angie yelled, although I was less than two feet away. "The skipper called and axed me to tracks you down and has you calls him at home. I knowed you'd be here suckin' on a beer bottle."

Thank you, Angie. I needed that so badly.

I headed to the phone, but not before Angie snatched Patty off her bar stool and ordered, "Come on, honey. Let's chase some drunks outta booth. We gots lots to talk about."

No so very good, Buccaneer. Angie had a mouth into which an incompetent coxswain could steer two whaleboats lashed port to starboard without scratching paint on either.

The skipper and chief recruiter had received a Call from Above to drive to Winchester for a two-three day brief on CRUITCOM's latest scheme, whatever that was. I was to play chief recruiter, milk the cows, make sure the chickens were locked up at sunset and keep weeds out of the garden.

"Damn it, Gunny, what do you suppose they're taking about" I was on my next beer after the phone call and Angie and Patty were still jacking their jaws. And I was drinking slowly because I had to drive.

"You, Shipmate."

"I was afraid of that."

"Angie is probably discussing female admin officers, TV news bunnies, state fuzz, high school counselors, topless dancers, regulation women. Such along those lines."

"I was afraid of that too."

"How'd you latch onto little Saint Patricia? You said she wouldn't date you again. Don't answer that!" Gunny snickered. "You'll start sounding like Book again."

"Cork it, Gunny! I'd have been shipshape Friday night if you hadn't lit me off by prodding me about virgins and other rare items. I get a little tongue tied when I'm upset. I'm not used to hard stuff either."

"I never saw you garble before and I've seen you upset. Plenty of times."

"It happens on occasion."

"Maybe, but I say it's because Patty is way, way out of your league and you're bad confused. You've never experienced nothing like her. She's better than that posh English lass you thought you'd knocked up when we were sailing the Mediterranean. As much class as that gal had, Patty's got more and Patty doesn't push it like that stuck-up witch. That Brit's 'My direct ancestor dried King Canute's balls' attitude used to flat piss me off!"

"Gunny, I --"

"Stow it, Master Chief. You garble when you talk about Patty. Let me talk. I can handle it. I ain't in lust. Love neither."

No one in the entire USA would believe I heard a Marine giggle!

"You notice how Patty hits you as being so fine looking when she ain't no where near beautiful? She's to . . . to . . . I don't know what the hell it is, but it ain't beauty. Not that she's ugly, or even plain. Real shapely hull for her size, but she could use some additional superstructure. You said it. Tea Cups."

"I got shanghaied today. She's not going to snatch me again. She's a kid! I got to get it all in one sea bag if I want to conduct bumper drills with Irene. Can you grasp that?"

"I can understand it, but she's got Irene beat all to hell, except in T ampersand A. Patty received an issue of top of the line gear, but God's people fitters likely had to special order parts to match her little hull so all her stuff would meet specifications."

"There's nothing wrong with Irene." I said, defensively.

"No, nothing wrong with Irene. She's one fine-looking woman. But you got to admit she's wore out more chief and officer recruiters than Elizabeth Taylor has husbands. Now, don't puff up on me! I said she was worthy. She fills out a real fine travel claim and she --"

"I steam with Irene because I like her, not because she fills out my damned travel claims! Yeah, she's slept with some men. What woman hasn't if she's normal?"

"I like Irene, but I'm just trying to get you to see none of your women compare with Patty. Patty is the real goods and you ought not mess her up."

"Have you gone completely overboard, Gunny? You keep laying course recommendations on me like you're my navigator!"

"We all have our crosses to bare. You're mine. It's my duty to keep you bow-on to the waves, carrying my burden with which the Lord seen fit to saddle me." Gunny said, piteously.

When I didn't think it could get worse -- it did."

Irene came steaming through the door, sleek as a destroyer breaking smooth seas. I couldn't see any way out of offering her my seat. At which point Angie and Patty chose to return to the bar. I was aware I'd not been a good boy, but I didn't think I'd been that bad! I was in the deep, dark kimchi.

Gunny saved me by giving Patty his seat and jerking Sergeant Price off his stool for Angie. He made the introductions too. I felt quite relieved when the three women lurched into Mark One - Mod Zero girl talk. Irene didn't seem inclined to take her mad out on Patty. I couldn't see problems in the other direction because Patty had no reason to dislike Irene. I felt so good I ordered everybody another round of drinks, the second for Patty, who probably reached her limit on beer number one-half.

"So, Patty," Irene said, sweetly, during a lull in their conversation. "I understand you edit the college newspaper. You must meet interesting people . . . usually. I'm quite surprised, though, that any paper -- even a tiny one, would want to interview Clay. You are still doing that, I suppose. Interviewing, I mean."

"Not really, Irene. I understand you are an administrative officer and you fill things out. You're still doing that, I suppose. Filling out, I mean."

Irene snapped back like she'd been hit in the face with a wet bar towel.

"Time to go, Patty! See you later, Irene. Everybody."

"Bye, Patty." Angie bellowed after us. "You holds that fool master chief down like I told you 'til he falls in line! You hear now?"

Patty turned the color of an October pokeberry.

I didn't mention the Irene-Patty exchange during the drive to the Patterson farm, but noticed several small, satisfied smiles. Despite Patty's alleged inexperience level, she had her qualifications sheets signed off in cat fighting.

I intended to thank Patty for spending the day with me when I walked her to her doorstep, but it didn't quite work as intended. She folded my arms around her, raised on her tippy toes, nailed herself firmly to my chest and hung a lip lock on me that'd flat blown the socks off an eunuch! I was half way back to Moe's before my lips stopped tingling. I suspected an excess of suds on her part.

Despite my best efforts, the waters remained Force Eight - typhoon rough. Irene called me a bunch of names, then refused to talk at all. After what seemed hours, she collected her gear, bitterly bad-mouthed me again, blessed Angie, Moe and Gunny, for good measure, then hauled stern out of the bar.

So, with Gunny's able help, plus assistance from the barflies, I ended drunk for the third night in a row. And I again dreamed of that old woman smiling beside my bed. I might have dreamed more about her had not stupid Jarhead woke me with his whimpering and whining. If that wasn't enough, Blue Suit zipped beneath my arm and hissed into the darkness of the room.

CHAPTER TEN

SHOALS IN THE FAIRWAY

April rolled out with more of a low velocity pop than a bang. My zone made goal plus five, which the chief recruiter grabbed to help District creak through.

Patty and I went ramp hunting in the old sugar orchard on my farm the first Saturday in May. Patty wanted to freeze ramps so she could eat them after she completed college. She said ramps were absolutely delicious, but no one could stand a ramp eater's breath, unless they had eaten them too. She said ramps made a person's breath smell like wet carbide fumes -- like garlic, only worse, for about three days.

She explained in four or five hundred words, that the folks who settled Appalachia suffered from scurvy near the end of winter because they had no means of obtaining fresh vegetables in winter. So they eagerly gobbled ramps, the first eatable greens to appear in early spring. She said ramps looked something like a green onion with broad, dark green leaves, but the ramp was really a member of the lily family. She further explained they could be eaten raw, but were usually prepared by parboiling, then frying in bacon grease and that sassafras tea was the drink of choice when eating ramps. I could almost see her mouth water as she lectured.

She knew ramps grew best under sugar maples on the south side of mountains. She'd forgotten that, although they are the first plants to peek their shoots through melting snow, they go to seed and disappear at the first sign of hot weather. What few ramps we found were brown and scraggly and unfit to eat

We attended church on Sunday, ate brunch at the Holiday Inn, viewed an afternoon movie during which Patty snuggled nicely, then spent a nearly temperate evening at a sissy pub she suggested. We capped the night with a nerve-shattering salvo of kisses. I lost another pair of socks and part of one shoe. It had not been my usual balls-to-the-wall weekend, but for reasons I couldn't fathom, I didn't feel I'd missed anything. I couldn't remember when I'd felt so lighthearted.

Monday started well when the chief recruiter called to report my zone won Zone of the Month, out producing the other four zones in our District. Calls to my RINC's indicated the number of warm bodies they were working might permit us to make May goal early on. I, a Mark One - Mod Zero pessimist, became very uneasy

Senior Chief Storekeeper "Keys" Armstrong called, midmorning, to ask where I wanted sixteen square, glass-fronted display cases measuring two feet by four inches deep. I informed my drinking buddy I'd ordered no such animal.

"I know you didn't order them, but UPS delivered a van full of the mothers to my loading dock this morning, one for each station in District. Area Supply said they are a new recruiting tool. I can't see what we're going to use them for. They're not near deep enough to lock applicants in, less'n there's a quota for bunnies or snakes."

"I don't want to throw the monkey back on you, Senior Chief, but I don't want them. Ask the chief recruiter. Maybe we are going to have a quota for snakes."

"He's hard to live with lately. Kinda cranky. Well, I'll get back to you depending on the Big Stick's decision. See you at Moe's tonight, even if Dottie won't issue my liberty card."

"You'll be on restriction for a month if you go AWOL. She might calibrate your head a bit too."

"She's done it before!"

I'd gotten almost through the daily stack of guard mail when I came across a quarter inch thick CRUITCOM instruction. I knew, after reading it, what the display cases was for, but I didn't believe it! I'd sooner believed the Pope had taken up with the Hare Krishna Clan and hung around airports flogging books with pictures of purple gods and spitting pumpkin seed residue on the deck. It was time to confer with my neighborhood chief recruiter

"Yeah, Clay. That's the reason the skipper and I got hauled to Winchester." the chief bush beater said, after I'd broadsided him about the CRUITCOM instruction.

"Was there some reason you kept it a deep, dark secret from the rock packers, like maybe you were afraid we'd request immediate transfer to the Salvation Army?"

"Not quite, Clay. I had to wait because the skipper pitched a bitch about wasting recruiting time, which pissed the commodore off. The admiral visited the last day we were there and the skipper hit him smack between his running lights with his objections. The admiral obviously finally decided with the commodore because the damned cases arrived this morning, along with instructions for their care and feeding. I was studying how to put the word out without everybody going over the hill when you arrived."

"Listen, John, Here's how I understand the thing. The idea is, and I quote in part:

"'Purpose: To ensure every recruiter understands thoroughly the demographics of the area in which he or she recruits.

"'Action: A map, the size of the inside of the case and outlining in detail the geographic area for which the recruiting station is responsible will be obtained. Maps can be procured from commercial sources, surveyors or drawn free hand if such talent exists locally.

"'A colored pin will be inserted into a clear plastic overlay to show each accession as follows: Blue - Nuclear Power; Red - Advanced Electronics; Green - Advanced Technical Field; White - Male High School Graduate, Majority; Black - Male High School Graduate, Minority; Orange - Non-High School Graduate; Pink - Females.'

"John, NAACP and NOW are not going to like the color scheme one damned bit!

"'Stations will prepare overlays showing, by use of colored grease pencils or other erasable marking devices: population density; schools; colleges; major industries; military installation; employment centers. Each category requires a separate overlay.'

"John, it would take a demographic expert a year to round up the information required, a sea bag full of commercial artists to get it right, and a CETA worker in every station just to stick pins and keep overlays up to date!"

"We have until the end of the month, Clay."

"You mean, like *May*?"

"I mean like June, so we've got a little slack. The skipper intends to put the arm on surveyors to get maps. Keys just charged out to get acetate, colored pins and grease pencils."

"John, how are we going to make goal and cut and paste and stick, to say nothing of hanging around court houses dredging up enough information to make Confident Claude happy? Can you

99

imagine Book Arnet trying to figure out that instruction? Can you, John?"

"To your first question. It'll be rough. To the dumb one. Not only no, but hell no!"

"Can I quit, John? I'll give you my old Power Wagon pick-up and my GSA Pinto what won't pull a tired hooker off a bar stool. If you hold out, I'll share my pay, sweeten the pot with some addresses in the Far East and maybe even a beautiful topless dancer right here in town."

"The topless dancer sounds good, but Charlene would never go for it. You can't leave until the skipper and I get fired. That doesn't look far off. The commodore is some kinda bad pissed at the skipper. It's not necessary to discuss how much he loves you!"

I had Marcia initiate a conference call to my sixteen stations. I had to redo it myself when the call connected with ten of sixteen stations, a Logan bank, a Walmart in Elkins, the FBI down the hall, a woman asking if I'd been saved and requesting a love offering, a coal company in Valley Forge and a country store in Johnstown.

It took the better part of an hour's hard selling to quell a potential mutiny on the part of my recruiters.

Finally, the workday ended.

I stumbled into Moe's, feeling like the fleet tug that challenged an unknown ship in a fog bank and received: 'This is the United States Battleship Iowa. You may fire when ready!'

I was down two beers and working hard on the third when 'Keys' Armstrong elbowed his way to the bar and ordered: "Triple Turkey. Straight!"

"Having a good day, Keys?" I asked.

Key's polarized look like to melted my collar devices. "It's been twenty-six years since I told a senior to take a flying leap at a rolling doughnut, Master Chief. That cost me three days in the brig on bread and water -- good ole piss and punk! This new tool has more sucks in it than Deep Throat!"

"I hope for the sake of your stern, you got the stuff sent to the stations."

"Yes, Sir, Mister Master Chief, Sir! My storekeeper's got a loaded truck, travel orders with no end date and advance travel money, a GSA gas card and toll tickets. She is, as we speak, en route to each and every station in NRD. Those damned pins was one hairy-assed problem. No company had them, not umpteen thousand in umpteen colors!"

"You didn't get the pins? Confident Claude will go banzai on us!"

"Oh, I got 'em, but it took one hell of a lot more effort than I wanted. I had to sweet talk an awful plain woman at Kerry's Office Supply into rushing them from a warehouse in Pittsburgh. I did say she was ugly, didn't I? She is too. Book wouldn't jump her bones if she was naked and toting six fathoms of dog chain, two dildos, a vibrator and a horsewhip!

"I had to promise I'd take her out on the town if she'd get the pins for me, even if it would ruin my reputation and get me killed by my wife. But the Big Storekeeper in the Sky blessed me. I got saved when she asked me what I really wanted all the pins for. I told her good pain meant good sex. I said pins made a big difference when they were stuck in the right places, but it got even better with an ice pick and vice grips!"

It was nearing twenty-two hundred and four beers later when I felt a soft hand on my shoulder. I turned, knowing it had to be Irene wanting to complain about Patty, my inattentiveness, my failure to act like her other puppy dogs, or all three. A dazzling, broad tooth smile whipped directly upon me somehow made the day fade away. "Patty! Don't you have classes tomorrow?"

"A late one." I just approved the layout of the last edition of the newspaper to be issued with me as editor. It will be a great edition, thanks, mainly, to our interview.

"Sure hope it's good. There are Slimy Creatures who'd just love to see me step on my cran . . . er, say the wrong thing to the media."

"You mean Curtis?"

"Among others. Sorry, I forgot he is your cousin."

"That is *not* my fault. He really dislikes you, Clay. Why?"

"Probably because I like him about as much as a case of the bullheaded gleep . . . er, never mind. He's hated me since grade school. Why? I don't know."

"Be careful, Clay. He is very sneaky. He has done some awfully mean things."

"When I start worrying about a no-load like him, I'll hang up my anchor."

"Just be careful! He is a vicious conniver. I am not fond of him, even though we are closely related."

That made two of us, except for the closely related part.

"Oh," Patty turned pink. "Curtis said we deserve each another. What do you suppose he meant by that, Clay?"

"Either you misunderstood him, or he's lost his rudder. Curtis would never wish anything good on me. Certainly not you! You're far too pretty. Sweet too -- especially your lips."

Those statements caused a bonfire on her face. She didn't say anything, but she whipped that look on me, then a broad toothed smile to go with it. "Clay, may I have a beer? Please."

"Huh? Oh hell! Sorry, Patty, it's been a bad day."

"Yeah," Keys piped up. "Noah had it better when all his animals came down with the screamin' shits!"

After giving Keys Disappointed Look Number Three, for use of vulgar language, I told Patty sorry again, for not introducing Keys. I then gave her a quick and dirty on the display boxes. I fear I used slightly nasty words while explaining.

"Are your recruiters terribly angry, Clay?"

"Here is a partial synopsis. King Angie won't talk to me. Book thinks the Air Force is behind it. The guys in Pickens are going to pis . . . er, desecrate the Civil War statue and get fired. Petty Officer Lewis of the Weston Station is going to have his Sicilian wife put a contract out on everyone in the chain-of-command, including me. The others have worse planned for me!"

"Oh, Clay!" Patty giggled. Your people are terrible to treat you so."

Conversation damned near ceased after Patty arrived. Her presence cut my running mates' vocabularies by at least twenty-five percent, so I took her to a booth to let them exercise their God-given Right of Free Speech in a Male Oriented Slop Chute.

"Clay, have you ever gone steady with a girl?"

"Not really."

"Then you had . . . more than one girlfriend at a given time?" That question turned her face the color of a Catholic Cardinal's Sunday-go-to meetin' attire.

"I'm a sailor. I know a lot of women. None were serious."

"If you do not consider your relationship with Irene serious, then she was never your steady. She was just someone to . . . you Know!" She raised a fine crop of beets on her cheeks that time. I was wrong about her being a little hardheaded. She had Sir Winston Churchill beat all to shucks.

"Irene is not my steady and I am not serious about her. Now, can we change the subject or do I start asking you about your boyfriends?"

"You may if you wish. I do not have any . . . one, Clay. I never did, not that counted. I would like to have one. One I really liked. I will tell you one thing. I am happy you had Irene only for . . . Oh, you *Know*!"

In absence of knowing how to respond, I gave her a low voltage, I'm a Master Chief -- and I am displeased, look.

"I am sorry, Clay. I do not know why I keep pestering you about your . . . women. Let us change the subject."

Patty responded well to visual rudder orders. I liked that in a woman!

"Clay,' she said, in a little girl type voice. "Do you like children?"

"Pretty well -- roasted."

"CLAY" she cried, something between a loud gasp and a scream that got the barflies glaring at me.

"Just joking. W. C. Fields said something like that."

"Who is W. C. Fields?"

"An old movie star."

"He must have been a horrible person!"

"Yeah, several folks thought so."

"Did you?"

"I didn't know him personally."

"Not that. Do you like children?"

Sir Winston was sucking hind tit.

"They're okay, I suppose. I don't have any. I don't want any. They cry a lot. They bar . . . er, spit up a lot too."

"Their parents love them, regardless of their crying and spitting up."

Not necessarily, Buccaneer.

"If, and this is hypothetical statement, Clay -- if you were to marry, you would have to have children."

"Why?"

"Because . . . you Know!"

"Maybe once, but not anymore. People usually only have kids when they want. You do know why? Don't you? Sure you do!"

If she didn't know about birth control, it was time to grab some sackcloth, some ashes, shoulder my sea bag, and head for the hills. Once I got set up in a dank cave, I would thank every Power I could think of, for keeping me from jumping her little bones.

She shifted her crop from tomatoes to beets. "Supposing one partner did want children and . . . forget it, Clay. I'm upsetting you again. I have to leave anyway. Are you going home?"

"No, but I'll walk you to your car."

I didn't think she'd want to kiss me in my somewhat less than sober state, so I opened her car door and gave her a friendly peck on the cheek."

"Please get into the car, Clay. I will drive you home."

"I don't drive when I've had more than a couple beers. I'll call a cab when I'm ready."

"I want to talk to you. Please get into the car."

Patty whipped right up my graveled lane like she didn't give a damn who owned it. The night air had helped me a lot. I felt ready for one of her sock destroying kisses. She was willing. She was too willing! It got right friendly. It got way, way too friendly, considering Patty's knowledge of birth control seemed limited to locking her knees together to prevent storks from landing. I needed to question her further, or get Angie to do it, if she would.

"I'd better go, Patty. You have school tomorrow."

I gave her a final tiny peck on the lips, opened the car door and set my foot on the gravel, only to be jerked inside. It was a strong, practical leadership type jerk too. Her shift from prissy schoolteacher striker to hillbilly female surprise me greatly. So did the two little tears coursing down her cheeks.

"Did I do something wrong, Patty?"

"Yes! No! . . . Oh, damn in hell!" She yelled. "You want out of the car, Henry Clay Berkeley? Then, get out of the car. Right now!"

I stood there in the swirling fog, watching her tail lights fade in the distance. I hoped the trolls weren't out tonight; she was making like a Formula One race car driver.

I dreamed that night of babies with wavy-curly hair laying in roasting pans, held toward me by the same old woman as before. She had a real mean look on her wrinkled face. Jarhead woke me, whining and trying to force his fat body beneath the bed clothing. Blue Suit hissed and dived beneath the pillows. I felt a bit uneasy myself. It was a strange, frightening dream.

CHAPTER ELEVEN

THE LONG, GREEN TABLE

Patty and I talked on the phone throughout the week, but she always had an excuse for our not meeting. When I finally decided our relationship was a dead issue, I felt both loneliness and relief.

The week ended well. My recruiters obtained sixty-eight accessions. That put us well ahead of the power curve. I suspected we'd make goal within the next week, giving time to get a jump at June's goal. I was pondering this and the Patty/Irene/display case situation when Marcie informed me the chief recruiter was on the two-oh-eight line. He was on the other one.

"Say, Clay, Slayer of Dragons and Defender of Virgins, what's your plan for field boarding your failures who have now missed goal for two months?"

Recruiters who failed to make goal two months in a row were hauled in front of a field board to determine the reason for failure. The basic idea was good. Senior recruiters, who comprised the board, could sometimes find flaws in a recruiter's techniques and provide valuable recommendations for improvement. That was the way boards once worked.

Unfortunately, field boards, thanks to changes ordered by Confident Claude, turned punitive in nature. Confident-baby had directed boards to administer a severe reprimand and also issue a Letter of Possible Termination from Recruiting Duty. The letter had to be issued, regardless of how the board felt about a recruiter's potential, or what caliber record a recruiter established prior to the period of failure.

Recruiters who did not come on track by the sixth month were fired. If the board deemed the failure to be the recruiter's own fault, captain's mast was imposed for dereliction of duty and the recruiter was punished. I agreed with this, if accomplished fairly. There was, however, considerable pressure from Area to find the recruiter had, in fact, been at fault. Confident Claude did not like simple executions. He liked a little fanfare with his hangings.

Recruiters who wanted and needed relief from the pressure and shame of letting their shipmates down did not get relief from Confident Claude mandated boards. Such boards only reinforced feeling of failure and recruiters returned to their respective station with an even bigger monkey on their back. Instead of returning with a feeling of reassurance and a burning desire to succeed, they felt panic and fear.

"I had only two make the hole, John. Chief Bryant and Petty Officer Skidmore."

"I've seen none of your people before a board in months. You've had other failures."

"All have seen the light and are back in the fold. I believe both Bryan and Skidmore will make goal next month."

"The problem is the computer readouts make it look like they are not prospecting."

"I'll decide when someone is not prospecting, not a sea bag full of numbers anyone with half a stern can gundeck. I seriously frown on gundecking, but if I allowed it, both failures would look like prospecting hero's instead of the duty goat."

"Hold on, Clay. Your stations are making goal, but those two recruiters are not. CRUITCOM lives by what those sheets say. We've got to stay in sync with CRUITCOM."

"Boards are no longer effective. You'll recall I boarded a recruiter in November. His attitude got worse after that, a whole lot worse. I had to fire him in January after he went on a bender, wrecked his GSA car and beat the caulking out of his girlfriend's ex-husband."

"Master Chief, we've worked well together and I don't want our relationship ruined, but we are going to board your people, along with those from other zones! Do I have to make it an order?"

"Yes, you do."

"Master Chief Berkeley . . . tomorrow morning, Saturday, at oh-nine hundred I want those who failed here!"

"I'll have the guilty there. Confident Claude and his Band of Super Salesmen are breathing heavily on you. Right?"

"Goodbye, Clay."

Master Chief John Downes was a fine man and a sailor to emulate, or had been until selected for the Career Recruiting Force. He'd since spent a portion of his time protecting his CRF billet so he could remain ashore until retirement. It was too damn bad he put sleeping alongside his wife ahead of his principles and caring for subordinates as the United States Navy decreed. He no longer acted like the man who once quelled a panic, slapped sailors back to their senses, then led them to success in extinguishing a flight deck conflagration that threatened the life of his ship.

I mustered at District at ten of nine, a little hung over and angry as a monkey caught in a thorn patch. At nine-zip-nothing, I knocked on the conference room door, entered, marched forward and halted, centered before The Long, Green Table -- a location that strikes fear into the hearts of strong men. Mine too.

That was when I saw the commodore, flanked by the skipper and Area's chief recruiter. There were two other Area slugs at the table, along with my chief recruiter. The commodore had never before attended our field boards, although I'd heard rumors of him having done so in other districts. I had not only stepped on it smartly -- I had mashed the pink part!

After a second or so of silence, my Chief Recruiter said, angrily, "You are not supposed to report, Master Chief, you're a standing member of this board. Where are your failures?"

"I'm here. That should be sufficient. I'm obviously the one at fault, not Chief Bryant, not Petty Officer Skidmore.

"Gentlemen, I thought it over and decided someone must be at fault, or you busy individuals would not have taken the time and interest to grace us with your presence. I can only say a flaw in my training ability must have caused two of my recruiters, neither who failed before, to fail twice after prospecting twelve to fourteen hours per day.

"Gentlemen, I stand ready for group criticism!"

"That's enough!" screamed Confident Claude, his face as red as a pig's stern in pokeberry time. "I've listened to your bilge since your captain promoted you to supervisor of my largest Zone, against my better judgment . . . and all I hear is bilge!

"You complain openly of initiatives we implement. You shield poorly performing recruiters and you threaten members of my staff. You're no longer command master chief of a battle group. You are no longer the fair-haired boy prying into command policies, then convincing your admiral to support a mere enlisted man's accusation against his commanding officer. Can you provide a reason why I should not order your captain to punish you at captain's mast, for disobeying a direct order?"

"I didn't disobey a direct order. I was ordered to have the failures here. I failed and I am here. You could have charged me with 'Silent Contempt,' except the legal beagles scrapped that article when the Uniform Code of Military Justice superseded Rocks and Shoals as the Navy's judicial bible long about 1951. That charge, now history, permitted a senior to punish a subordinate who did not outwardly express contempt, but who was suspected of having contempt."

The commodore looked like a boiler about to lift safeties. The skipper was smiling slightly. My chief recruiter was pale.

"Commodore, Captain, Gentlemen, I am guilty of that charge. I do have contempt. I have contempt for an organization that jumps stem to stern in a vain attempt to make goal in a market gone sour, and does so at the expense of outstanding sailors. Our recruiters no more than master one 'Tool' that 'will ensure goal by recruiting smarter,' than another outfit sells us an 'Improved Sales Technique,' or an advertising firm lobs a 'New Approach' across our bow."

"Master Chief Berkeley! That is enough!" The Commodore gave a right good bellow that time and jumped out of his chair as though he intended to subdue me.

Fat chance, Buccaneer.

"No, it's not, Commodore. With all due respect, I intend to explain how every recruiter, not only in this District, but across Area feels. They can't tell you, Commodore. You can hurt them. There's no way you can hurt me more than I already hurt at having to work outstanding men and women like coolies, maybe ruin their careers, to achieve a number we can present to congress to obtain more money.

"Here's what is laying on the deck plates.

"Gentlemen. I am going to continue to run my zone as best I can within guidelines of CRUITCOM instructions. If you disapprove of my intentions . . . fire me and I'll transfer to the fleet laughing."

Confident-baby choked like he'd chug-a-lugged a shot of West Virginia's best stump juice without a water back. Others behind the table, except the skipper, were blinking like a sexually inexperienced sailor watching his girlfriend unbutton her blouse

"Taking me to captain's mast won't work, Commodore, because you have moved out of your ordained place in the chain-of-command into areas rightfully the realm of zone supervisors, chief recruiters and CO's. You've constantly contacted people far beneath you in the chain-of-command and gave them rudder orders their seniors knew nothing about. How can you punish anyone for failure when they carried out your orders, your techniques and your policies?

"Commodore, according to the UCMJ, you are Reviewing Authority for punishments imposed by Captain Markham. How are you going to exercise an unbiased review of any punishment he might impose after you, yourself, ordered him to discipline someone? Captain Markham can't discipline anybody on your orders without it being thrown out in review. It's illegal. It's called something like 'Undue Influence.' Navy lawyers just love it when they are defending. Cruiser-Destroyer Group Twelve's Judge Advocate told a funny story about an admiral having to retire because of that. It seems --"

"I believe we should leave that story for another time, Master Chief." the Skipper broke in. "Are you finished?"

"Not quite, Captain. I want to review the ratios the CRUITCOM computer says Chief Bryant must accomplished next month to make goal. I trust Area staff can tell me how to accomplish this amount of work. Skidmore's ratios are a bit better.

112

"The ratios say Chief Bryant must do sixteen hundred phone calls to get four hundred fifty-two contacts to get eight interviews that will result in one accession. He would have to do six thousand, four hundred calls next month, two hundred and twenty-eight per day, to enlist four people into the Navy. He would have to make one call every three-point-two minutes for a solid twelve hours for the entire working month. That leaves him no time for any other type of prospecting, interviews, filling out enlistment kits, chow, or even head calls

"The computer is only as good as what we put into it. It doesn't lie. It just doesn't tell the truth because we don't. It provides workable data only when a recruiter is successful. Every half-bright recruiter is padding their figures downward to keep the computer from spitting out an impossible task. How many people are we *really* working to put one person in the Navy? How much trash are we digging through to find that one person?

"Commodore, Captain, Gentlemen, I thank you for your indulgence."

The Chief Recruiter grabbed me as I was exiting the hatch and ordered me to await the captain's presence in the CO's office.

"Master Chief, you sandbagged us and I should eat you out like a boot seaman. Wait!" The Captain held up his hand. "The chief recruiter admitted you knew nothing of the commodore being here, but he does think it wouldn't have a difference had you known.

"The commodore is livid. He does not now just dislike you. 'Hate' is the operative word! Since he disliked you from Day One, I suspect you once created problems for one of his friends when you were Admiral Grayson's command master chief. That aside, he is in no way fond of your implied threat concerning his tactics in disciplinary matters.

"The chief recruiter is less than happy with you. He feels you shuffle-footed him when you turned his order around and took the heat yourself, rather than your recruiters. He thinks we should fire you.

"I should be less than happy with you too, but I'm not." The Captain held up a blue folder. "This is a project I took upon myself. It condemns very badly, I'm afraid, our recruiting system. This document includes some of your complaints and the tactics you employed to improve not only production, but recruiter quality of life.

"I forwarded it via the chain-of-command. It has traveled all the way to CRUITCOM, but no one has yet provided feedback. Hopefully, someone will recognize the most important part of this document is that people can be doomed to failure by the system. I believe my research proves many recruiters who fail could not have succeeded in the area assigned.

"So, Master Chief, we've both climbed on you soap boxes and cleared the decks. Now, I'll let you buy the chief recruiter and myself a beer at Moe's, if you promise not to talk shop with either of us. We've had enough of that for one day!"

CHAPTER TWELVE

ESCORT SERVICES

After the captain and the chief recruiter quaffed a beer and departed Moe's for better company, I once again realized the skipper was exactly the type of officer who should make admiral. The military had one hell of a lot of managers, but no abundance of leaders, except in the Marine Corps. Even the Corps wasn't totally free of manager types who subscribed to peculiar, nonmilitary methods espoused by Robert S. McNamara, a man who during his tour as Secretary of Defense, preached graphs and computer readouts would win wars

Getting subordinate commanders to put their troops and ships in harm's way is not something that can be accomplished by a manager. Getting troops to charge a hill under fire takes strong, confident leaders who do not outwardly show fear. It is extremely difficult to manage men to proceed onto a deck where projectiles are exploding, or to manage them into a smoke-filled compartment with paint blistering all around them. It is also difficult to manage them to put loyalty to shipmates and duty to country ahead of self. Managers manage. Leaders lead.

I lifted my glass and made a toast. "Cheers, Robert Strange-baby."

"Did Mister Strange do something for you, Clay? Paid for a hotel so you could rip into his wife while he watched, maybe?" Moe asked.

"Do you know anybody who might? I'm about to go into Condition Whiteout."

"You might get taken care of. Here come Irene and that fellow Longly. Be a good little boy and she might play doctor with you again. Notice I said might. I'm surprised you didn't need a proctologist the way she jumped you that Sunday she caught you in here with Patty."

I turned my head slightly to the right. They were coming up the street, arm in arm, breaking the shafts of sunlight that streamed through the sycamore trees. I was reminded of hungry jackals stalking a lame zebra.

"Hello, Clay. Celebrating your pack out next week?"

"Am I going somewhere, Irene?"

"Transfer is imminent when one is relieved for cause." She smiled, bitters honey dripping from every word. "Big Otter's Pixie will be so lonely when the only man dim enough to date her departs. Oh, I can see it now! Mister Know-it-all-Berkeley stuck ashore in a command that does nothing significant. You've had your last important job in the Navy. You brought it upon yourself. If you'd paid more attention to what, your superiors wanted and less to Saint Patty while trying to --"

"I'm not leaving here."

"You are too leaving!' Curtis shrieked. "You're history!"

"I didn't get fired and I'm not in the mood for a bunch of flak. I intend to sit here until a Real Sailor comes in. I then intend to get snot slinging, hand walking, head hugging drunk. I recommend you not remain within range when the serious drinking starts.

Why? Because I had to talk to that ass of a boss of yours today, that's why.

"Irene, I don't want you spouting at me either. All you've done lately is make snarky remarks, chew me out and bad mouth a girl who did nothing at all to you."

"Jesus, Clay. She is as plain as soap!"

"If you believe Patty is plain, you have a severe vision problem!

"And you, Curtis. You whined to the commodore about our little talk by the head the night of the interview. You told him I threatened you. There is only one thing that keeps me from jerking out your rectum and strangling you with it. It is unseemly and highly frowned upon for a senior to kick the crap out of a junior. It keeps This Man's Navy on an even keel. So, Curtis, all I can do is tell you what I think of your sneaky carcass.

"You're slimy. If you wonder why no one associates with you, except other Slimy Creatures, it's because no one trusts you. You probably believe people are standoffish because of your closeness to the throne, that some of the power rubbed off on you and they're afraid of you. Not true! You're nothing more than the NRD joke, Curtis. You are a total a total disgrace to the CPO Brotherhood."

"You son of a bitc --"

"Don't even think it, Curtis! You call me that and the dental surgeon is going to be mule haulin' into the dead of the night. I strongly recommend you get your no-load stern out of here before I forget I'm senior and lay a direct shot to your snot locker."

Curtis stepped back and swung a clinched fist to his extreme right as if he was going to lay one on me.

"Puff up and get huffy, Curtis, Some on, Sissy! You're bigger than me. You might get the biggest slice, but I'll dot you between

117

your running lights so hard your stern will pucker like you've had an alum enema with a fire hose!"

"You shouldn't be allowed near recruiting duty. You're a horrible example -- whoring around, drinking, playing the fool!" Curtis screamed. "You should be court martialed for the things you said to the commodore. He absolutely despises you. He's been praying for you to foul up. I don't understand why he didn't fire you today, but he will get you. Count on it!"

Curtis drooled spit from the corners of his mouth. His face was flushed and his hands shook. He looked as if he was having a fit of some sort. Who would have thought the commodore's ranking Slimy Creature would have guts enough to take a strong stand. I even respected him a mite . . . naw, not really.

"Actually, Curtis, the commodore and I found we have something in common. We agree you're a douche bag."

I liked the way Curtis wilted.

"Irene, I apologize for the bad language, but it is impossible to express things clearly to Curtis without resorting to deck plate vernacular."

"You've no room to speak of Curt being a joke!" Irene spat at me. "The entire town is snickering at you chasing that oh-so-proper midget. You are the sickest man I know, chasing after a girl that young. You idiot! She lets you pant after her only because she can't get a date with anyone her own age. If you were a man, you'd be ashamed. You're not a man! You're a skirt chasing, unfaithful fool who would sleep with anything on legs and brag about it to that stupid Marine rhinoceros who is no better than --"

"Do you consider yourself proof, Irene?" uttered a soft, clear voice with a slight hillbilly accent.

"Proof of what?" Irene whirled toward Patty, who had joined the fray unbeknownst.

118

"You said Clay would sleep with anything on legs. Are you proof?"

I thought Irene was going to choke on her bridgework. I hoped it wouldn't get violent. Irene was twice the size of Patty anyway you measured her, except vertical.

"You little *Bitch*!"

"I have firsthand proof that he is a man, Irene and a darned good one too. Neither am I a bitch, nor do I think you are one."

Irene looked confused. That was new. Irene was a confident woman not given to uncertainty. Maybe a soft voice really did turn away wrath better than dried kitty cats.

"You're too young to understand." Irene said, after she got her gear locker restowed. "Don't trust him. Let me tell you something else. He's almost impotent."

"That is not true, Irene."

"How would you know?"

Patty blushed brightly. "I do not find him that way. Anything but!"

Irene whirled and sprayed me from hair line to neck "Pervert! Child Molester!"

After Irene and Curtis charged out of Moe's like dopers heading for a vacation in Amsterdam, I stood up and dinged my bottle with a quarter. "What Patty said about our relationship is not true. She opened fire on Irene to protect me. She provided great escort services. Her salvos hit right on! She can sail shotgun for me anytime."

The barflies clapped.

Patty really lit her lamp that time. In her urgency to protect me, she failed to consider there were people listening other than our immediate group.

"Well, Patty Lane, you just as well take up drinkin' hard liquor, smokin' seegars and cussin,' now that you' sneaked in here and established yourself as a Woman of the Town."

She flickered again. "Really, Clay. I had to speak out. She insulted us."

"And I thought Aquarius types didn't pick fights. I thought they were mellow, forgiving folks. Remind me not to get into arguments with you. You're pretty damned sharp"

"I have many hidden virtues. Are you interested in learning of them, Clay-dearest?"

"Ask a foolish question, Patty, and --"

Patty threw a lip lock on me that would have melted a snowman. The fact that she whipped a heavy, totally unexpected endearment on me for the first time didn't aid me in maintaining an even keel.

After a respectable time, the barflies cheered, stomped their feet and clapped.

Patty's face almost set the establishment on fire. Moe leaned across the bar and felt her face with the back of his hand. He didn't say anything, just shook his head and popped her a free beer. I'd never seen him do that before.

We had a couple beers -- her one, me two, while she grilled me as to what caused Irene to light her boiler. Then we did a little purring. I was totally enjoying myself when she informed me we would attend church the next day and hauled me out of the place. I kicked and screamed, but that didn't help. She had her hawser secured and I was firmly under tow.

We devoured a fine supper at the Foxfire. I had the county ham platter again. Patty tied into a chicken breast, a pile of mashed potatoes, peas, fried okra, corn bread and a salad. That made me wonder if she'd read my thoughts about her slight figure the last time we were in Foxfire. The other possibility was that hair pulling gave her an appetite.

Missus Moore really fired some eye rockets at me. She didn't smile at me once, but gave Patty several sad, little smiles. I think she believed we had committed the Ultimate Act what with Patty giggling at everything, petting the back of my hand every so often and once even on the cheek. Customers were casting glances at us and smiling. Providing amusement for the other patrons didn't seem to faze Patty but I was embarrassed as a wet cat. Patty was just too tiny to hold her booze.

Missus Moore shackled onto Patty after a while and hauled her off to the head. I figured she was going to get Disappointed Lecture One through Eleventy-eleven.

Missus Moore whipped a big smile on me when they returned. She patted me on my head like was I a puppy or some such, then said I was a 'Gentleman of the First Water.' That really caused giggles from the customers. It had been a weird day. Damned strange goings on.

After supper, we sat in Patty's little Chevy for a while before we left for our respective homes. We talked mostly, but there was a certain amount of rubbing and purring -- more purring than rubbing. Still, what little rubbing that did occur was enough to ruin me. I badly needed to prime Angie to find out when she was going to discreetly instruct Patty in Accomplishment of Sexual Fulfillment Without Child Bearing.

CHAPTER THIRTEEN

STEAMING IN CLOSE COMPANY

Gunny came into my office Monday evening near knock-off time, carrying two cans of Coke that reeked with the nectar of spiced rum. "Thought you might like a little snort at the end of the week's beginning. How you doing?"

"Finer than fish fur. I'll probably make goal by Friday." I took suction on the cold, damp can. "Ah, the Corps really understands the basics of life! You making goal?"

"Not doing too shabby. We've got enough in our ditty bag to make goal next week. It's tough. Everybody wants to be embassy Marines and parade around in their pretty blue uniform with the shiny brass buttons. It's like you said about the Navy's applicants wanting to strike for computer expert or some such. No one wants to do real work: chip paint, clean compartments, maintain gear, stand sentry, handle lines, police the grounds, mess cook, crawl in the mud, get shot at -- the good stuff.

"Yeah, Gunny, damn shame how soft this generation is. The old ways are gone. It has been years since we keelhauled or cat-o-nine-tailed anybody. Not that some don't need it."

"Say, you hear from Confident Claude?"

"I was severely lashed with a Letter of Reprimand."

"The hell you say?"

"The skipper lashed me firmly to the grating and presented it formally. Captain Markham signed it himself, but I know the commodore ordered him to issue it Pretty good letter, Gunny. It says, among other things, that I've been less than diligent in my application of Area directives. Navy Regulations and the UCMJ are conspicuous by their absence."

"In other words, it's not worth diddly squat."

"Correct, Gunny, and to top it off, it's self-canceling. It's to be removed from my service record if satisfactory improvement is noted within ninety days. Confident Claude forced the skipper to lay a reprimand on me, but the skipper done one fine job of cooling it down."

I leaned over and whirled my safe tumbler, roughly four turns in one direction and four turns in the other. "Grab your cover, Gunny. It's time to meet Patty and Keys at Moe's. Keys had to drag his anchor along, otherwise, she wouldn't issue his liberty card."

Apparently some sort of benefit check had just hit the mail boxes because the 'flies were treating folks to drinks and talking louder and louder and filthier and filthier.

The sole female barfly, a Korean War era WAC, was going at it full-bore with a county official, arguing about females using sex as bribes. Patty was making like Rudolph with her color intensity increasing in direct proportion to the 'flies language. So after a short planning session, Keys and Missus Key, Gunny and Patty and I shifted our Flags to Holiday Inn.

Gunny started telling his funny sea stories as soon as we were seated. He soon had us rolling on the deck. Keys and I sounded like two wart hogs in a plum thicket. Missus Keys melted her makeup and Patty almost lost it altogether. He was nearing the punch line of a story about a city boy Marine waking in a Vietnamese hooch with a chicken roosting on his forehead when he halted in mid-sentence. He stood up and excused himself, then hauled toward the far side of the lounge at a floor shaking trot.

"Where is he going, Clay-honey?" Patty asked.

"I do believe Gunny is about to make a beachhead on that woman who just walked in the door, the big one in the dark green skirt and tan blouse with the gold badge. I suspect she's the deputy sheriff he's been blabbering about."

Patty grabbed my arm. "She is almost as huge as Gunny -- and he's a giant!"

"She's right good sized. A bull alligator could sleep beneath her blouse with room left for a wildcat and a screech owl."

Patty giggled. Good sign, that.

I was looking forward to meeting the deputy, but Gunny waved to us as they rumbled off.

"Gunny likes 'em big," Keys snickered. "He rolls 'em in flour, then looks for the wet spot!"

"I warned you about talking nasty!" Missus. Keys snapped Keys out of his chair and dragged him toward the lobby. "Saying a thing like that -- in front of a young girl too!"

I strongly suspected the six-two, beer-bellied Senior Chief was about to get taken to task by the five-six, one hundred, zip-nothing pound Missus Senior Chief, which would look like a broomstick beating up on a saw log.

Patty started giggling. Her giggles turned into gasping titters and then into laughter. Before long she was hanging in her chair, holding herself below her breasts and whooping: "Flour! Oh, my Lord! Oh, Lord!"

It surprised me that something so crude could light her off.

"Ow, my side hurts! Flour! Oh, I cannot believe it!"

When her laughter subsided to outbursts of tittering, she dabbed at her eyes with a corner of her napkin and asked, "Clay, what did I do for entertainment before I met you and your friends?"

"I take it you're not pis . . . er, mad like Missus Senior Chief who, I believe, dragged Keys off to her cave. That woman has a really bad case of Irish temper."

"Mad? I am having the time of my life! Clay-honey, you will never guess what I was thinking before Mister Armstrong said that. You will never guess."

"Lay it on me."

"I was wondering how they managed to get together." She whispered, between giggles.

"I suspect Missus Armstrong clubbed him into submission when he was a young sailor stationed in Londonderry, Ireland."

"Not them. Gunny and his Amour."

"Oh. She's Chief Deputy Sheriff. Gunny met her while running police checks. He's been staggering around like a pole-axed steer since they met, when he's not bugging me about yo . . . uh, things."

"No, silly, not how they met. How they . . . Oh, you Know!"

"How they jump each other's bon . . . er, make love?"

"Yes. They're gigantic! It must be physically difficult. Normally, I mean."

I had absolutely no idea how to answer her question. I had no idea of what she meant by 'normally.'

"I suspect they're doing more than shining each other's brass. They must be about out of places to shack . . . er, stay. Hotels surely wouldn't let them back a second time. It costs too much to replace the furniture."

"Oh, Clay!" she cried, slapping me smartly on the arm.

Patty was getting awfully loose and frisky. She had made it all the way through her risqué questions without glowing more than a bright pink.

"Did you ever have a heavy girlfriend, Clay?"

I'm no brighter than your average hillbilly, but I seen the snake laying in that question real quick. "Never did, Patty."

"Do you not like large women?"

I saw that snake too. "I've nothing against them, but I'm not attracted to them."

A short silence and then: "To what type are you attracted, Clay-honey?"

It was time to ship over for the benefits. I brushed the tips of my fingers against her cheek while trailing her neck lightly with my thumb. "Small, bright, perky country girls with big gray eyes, sun bleached taffy hair and a slight overbite."

Patty shivered and leaned her head against my shoulder. "Irene is not . . . like that."

"You notice," I whispered close to her ear, "that I'm not with Irene."

She covered my hand with her own, then placed them both in the proximity of her lap and gave me a deep, direct look. The depths of her clear, gray eyes made me lightheaded. "Yes, dearest,

126

I certainly do. I am so glad." She said, reddened, then looked away into the distance

I never knew what Patty was going to come up with she got quiet and thoughtful and it was happening again. It was time to pull chocks before she hit me with something I couldn't answer, or wouldn't want to. She was way, way too hardheaded when she got wound up. She wanted answers right damned now! I suspected that had to do with her schoolteacher striker status. Plus, she had just whipped another endearment on me.

"Come on, Patty. I have to hit the road *manana por la manana*. Zero dark-early too." I put my hand in my pocket, made the necessary adjustments and stood up. Socks and pocket linings were becoming a major expense.

She collected her woman type things and stood up too. "Do you really have to leave for four whole days?" she asked in a wistful, little girl voice.

While walking to her car, I explained a significant part of my job involved inspection and training, for sixteen stations and thirty recruiters.

Patty twisted sort of under my arm and looked up at my face. "Hence, the travel claims?"

"Er -- yes."

Patty looked furtively about the dark parking lot. "Oh, dearest -- I am going to miss you terribly." she whispered, as she slipped into my arms. She tasted of nothing but pure, clean woman -- not a trace of lipstick, or anything else.

Her fingers fumbled a button loose and slipped inside my shirt. When I returned the favor, she pulled slightly away and gave me an odd, wide-eyed stare. She then gently moved my hand on her breast and offered her lips. The rest of her motions came naturally as did mine.

127

She jerked away when I stroked her hard little nipple through her almost nonexistent bra. She fumbled her car door open, jumped in and slammed the door. She tossed her hair back with both hands and tilted her head back on the head rest. There was a light sheen on her forehead. She was gasping slightly. "Oh, Clay-honey." She shuddered, as she started her engine and began to roll slowly away. "What in the world am I going to do with you?"

Damned good question, so I ditched my original sail plan to go home and steamed for Moe's to ponder on it.

CHAPTER FOURTEEN

COUNSELING SESSION

I heard Gunny ordered me a Fall City beer as I edged past a herd of barflies exhibiting dance steps from the 'Thirties. One old codger threw another's feet into the air at about a point-nothing degree angle, yelled "Bee's Knees! Hotsy! Hotsy!" after which they fell giggling to the deck

People of the 'Twenties and 'Thirties were surely strong, healthy folks. The weak could not have managed such wild dances after walking two miles from school, shearing a flock of sheep, painting two outhouses, milking eighteen cows, then completing four hours of homework. I'm certain they did these things. People told me so when I was growing up and the 'flies confirmed such evolutions were daily routine in their youth.

It surprised me to see Gunny there, after the way he'd hauled sternly across the lounge to maneuver starboard side to the chief deputy, so I queried his presence at Moe's.

"Elizabeth has a fourteen-year-old son. She can't get away at night, except when he goes to a movie. She'll only steam with me on the weekends when his dad gets him. Otherwise, I'd be locked onto her every night like a mongoose on a cobra. I like the way she treats me."

I was glad for Gunny. It was time someone was satisfied with this hard world. Not that I could whine much about my own life, but my relationship with Patty had me frustrated as a French gourmet forced to eat at a New Orleans Lucky Dog wagon.

"Lash yourself firmly, Gunny. Hang on 'till she sinks."

"Going to hang on for a while, but I don't much like sleeping with my teddy bear five nights out of seven -- seven out of seven some weeks. It'd be better if she could get out more. Say, Clay -- you decide what you're going to do with Patty?"

That was the first time Gunny had called me by my given name since he was senior to me some long years ago in an AMPIG in the Mediterranean. I was now senior to him by two pay grades and had repeatedly asked him to use my first name, but he refused. Gunny was big on observing the proprieties.

"I'm not going to do anything with her, Nosy Person."

"Then why are you keeping her around? Because she's cute, or because she dresses your arm so well?"

"Aw, hell, Gunny, are you going to bug me about her again?"

"Answer the question. It's polite."

"The truth is I don't know what to do with her. Now leave me alone about her!"

"Take her to bed and practice making The Beast with Two Backs. People have been doing it for a good, long while now. Anyone can learn to do it. It's fun."

"Not at the price you quoted! You said, right here in this bar, I'd have to marry her to sleep with her. You said that, Gunny. Don't try to slide out of it."

"Yeah, I said something like that, but I missed something that impacts the situation."

"Like what?" I questioned, warily.

"I forgot most any woman will spread 'em for the man she thinks loves her."

"Patty is different, Gunny. She's a lot younger than I am, which is sort of embarrassing, mainly because she looks so much younger than me. Anyway, I've never told one single woman in my life that I loved her. Not a one! Plus, I am not in love with her!"

"Naw, I don't buy any of that her being Young Stuff bugging you. You're afraid of Patty because she's a virgin!"

I whipped the International Signal of Extreme Displeasure on him. "How do you know Patty is a virgin? Your sister tell you?"

"I don't know that she is, but you think she's one, don't you?"

Given a choice, I'd rather have been ship's company in a rusty, dirty AMPIG . . . "Yeah, I do. She's hot as a boiler -- up to a point. She gets all heated up, then she quits."

"I don't want to give you the Big Head, but you've encouraged lots of girls to make a full power run with you. Patty is almost certainly a Tight Fitting, but she probably wants to spread 'em as much as you want to crawl between 'em. I say go for it!"

"Why not Patty? I don't know. I keep saying that, don't I? I just don't feel right about it. What if I were to hurt her, or even get her pregnant. She's so tiny!"

"This isn't like you, Clay. The crack of a rifle isn't safe around you! In case you missed something in Practical Sex Education - World Wide Course, I don't think you can hurt them, except the first time. A woman once told me that was just a quick, sharp sting. You do know how babies are born, don't you?"

131

"I've never slept with a virgin, Gunny. I've likely not seen but one in eleventy-eleven years. I'm sure, though, it hurts a regulation-sized girl. And, if worse should come to worse, how can a tiny, little thing like Patty give birth to a baby? Where'd she put it? Her waist is no bigger than my thigh. Why, it'd kill her!"

"I never thought I'd see the day! You don't even know the basics. Believe me, their equipment stretch. It's one of their design features. I don't know why you're so worried about knocking her up. You must know how to prevent rug rats!"

"Gunny, I don't know where you're aiming, but get off my case about Patty! If you need something to write in your log, suffice it to say she's a sweet girl and I can't see any reason to foul her up. Not when the town's full of women who've been laid more times than me and --"

"Oh, really?" Gunny smirked. "Only women who've shucked their skivvies more times than you are hookers. Old ones too."

"For that you can buy me another beer."

"Yes, Sir!" Gunny gave a mock salute, then yelled for Moe. He then set the anvil he called a chin in the heel of his hand and whipped a look on me almost as strange as those I'd been receiving from Patty. "You know, Clay. Patty Lane the Virgin has got the hook set just about where she wants it. You make one wrong jump and it's going to set. Securely too."

"WHAAAT?"

"She's in love with you."

That statement caused me to slop a perfectly good glass of beer right on my crotch. "Damn it, Gunny, now look what you made me do! Stupidest damned statement I've heard. Worse even than Book when his read head it hitting on bad clusters."

"If you'd pay a little attention, you'd see how Patty looks at you. She watches you all the time. No matter what's going on around her, she's got her big, gray eyes locked right on your beat-up carcass. You could tell her you have acute gleep and she'd think it was an attribute."

"Tell me, Gunny -- do you have a policy with Lloyd's of London against me going out of my mind? What is it with you? You need a new bore sight, or something?"

"I'm not kidding. Others see it too.   Megan Armstrong remarked on it tonight. And she's about as sensitive as a battalion sergeant major in the French Foreign Legion!"

"Stow it, Gunny! Patty is pure gold, but there's too big a difference in our ages, for one thing.   There are other considerations too. She might, sometime, manage to get her little boon-dockers under my bed. But, Gunny, the first time she starts that ownership stuff she's outta there. You can stake your dress sword and swagger stick on that!

"I know all about marriage, and so do you. Jack meets Jill and she convinces him she has the only matching socket in town. Next he knows is that she's got his whole life in her now fat hands and he's got a mortgage that'd break a Texas oilman, two-point-three nasty kids and a seven-year-old junker, which is all he can afford. As a side benefit, she lies on her stern eating an apple, reading a crotch novel, or something, and lets him hunch at her once a quarter whether he needs it or not. I tell you exactly how it is, Gunny. Look at Megan Armstrong. You marry an Irish Rose and wake up with a POB, a Plain Old Bitch!"

"I'll grant there are marriages like that. Maybe every marriage have some of what you say in them. But if they were always like that there wouldn't hardly nobody stay married."

"That, my Leatherneck Friend, is why we got a thirty percent, or better, divorce rate in this country. The divorce rate oughta tell every male that marriage is not an opportunity to get laid regularly. Marriage is nothing more than a woman-made hell. A fellow's got to be a right idiot to get married!"

"I was engaged once, Clay. Jan was scared silly when I deployed. She just knew I was going to get my stern blowed away and wanted me out of the Corps, which I wouldn't do, so she left. Breaking up with Jan hurt worse than getting shot and the hurt lasted one hell of a lot longer. I ultimately realized I should have gotten out of the Corps like that great girl wanted.

"Man is cursed some way. He's never bright enough to understand what he's got until he loses it. And here you are -- steaming the same route."

"Let's clear the breech once and for all, then you shut up. I have only one question. Why are you so interested in my love life?"

"Patty and my little sister played together since they were small, so I know a lot about her. Heather turned into a real terror about fourteen. She like to drove my folks off pierhead until she joined the Coast Guard. I tell you, she was so wild I'd probably had to horsewhip half the boys in town, if I'd been home when she was a teenager.

"Patty never drove her folks crazy like Heather. Folks on Jessie's Run think Patty is the nicest girl around. She doesn't have one mean bone in her body. You couldn't ask for no one sweeter, Clay. If it bothers you that Patty isn't as good looking as some of your gals, you better get that flat out of your mind and grapple onto her. Patty is too good for you, but it does look like she'll be the one who brings you down. She's one sweet girl!"

"You're going to marry me off because she's sweet?"

"I can't make you do anything, but I'll tell you exactly how this is going to end. I see formation steaming on the horizon. So does everybody else, except you. It'll be good, Clay. A man would have to be a stone ass to foul his anchor with a girl like Patty. I'm so sure of what's in her Annual Schedule I'm going to break out my full dress uniform so I can look pretty when I stand at the altar next to your quaking body."

"For God's sake, Gunny! What are you trying to do to me?"

"It's time, Clay. You've been acting awful bitter lately. You keep going the way you are and you're going to end a drunken old whoremonger. You'll eventually end hanging with the barflies, if they'll have you."

CHAPTER FIFTEEN

SUPERVISE AND DEPUTIZE

I felt rested and alert as my GSA Pinto climbed the steep, green hills en route Pickens, my most distant station. Farmers were out in force, cultivating between barely visible rows of corn and potatoes and other crops I couldn't identify. White-faced, red cattle and an occasional herd of black cattle grazed their way up the hills as the day heated. Horses that had not been caught and put to work in the steep fields were smarter, or not so hungry as the cattle. They were in fence corners on high ridges where breezes blow cool.

I'd discovered early on in the recruiting trade that the best and cheapest food was located by searching for an early morning or noon cluster of pickup trucks. That designated the local folk's eatery and they Know.

I used this technique to find a ten-stool diner just off the winding, two-lane road. The shabby diner, plastered outside with rusted metal signs advertising products of long extinct companies and inside with stained, outdated calendars indicated that little had changed since around the 'Forties. An antique juke box, filled with large, thick records cut by legends of the past played for a nickel. Teresa Brewer, Hank Snow and Hank Williams were still big in these parts. The dingy, not overly clean diner, cared little for the occasional passing traveler. It had only one strong feature, good food. Their biscuits, covered with sausage gravy, were a delight as was the aged country ham and strong coffee that could be sniffed a block away.

Pickens Station was immaculate. The recruiters had taken various Navy insignia and cutouts of ships and aircraft, projected them on newly painted, pale blue bulkheads, traced around them with a pencil, then filled in the images with appropriate color paint. Their display case was about one-quarter completed and was, thus far, a perfect job -- a fact I stated to the recruiters. There was no reason to remain in Pickens Station. Both recruiters made goal every month and their administration was perfect.

Merrifield, the next station on my route was a crippled kitty with a history of low morale and disciplinary problems not expected of the Navy's top people. I'd had a wife beating coupled with a drunk and disorderly arrest involving a Merrifield recruiter shortly after I'd taken over the zone. The judge dismissed the wife beating charge and imposed a light fine for the D and D. It helped that the recruiter's wife had done some of the beating too. The judge seemed to believe she gave better than she got!

The petty officer did not fare so well under the Navy judicial system. The captain fined him one-third of one month's pay, awarded a reduction in rank suspended for six months and terminated him from recruiting duty. It was a light sentence for the charge -- Bringing Discredit Upon the Naval Service. His punishment was light because he had, until then, been an outstanding petty officer in every respect.

Investigation into the root cause of such conduct from a petty officer without a single blot in his copybook, revealed a slave driving, ill-tempered, 'Do as I say, not as I do' RINC whose personality better suited a New York cabby than a recruiter and leader of men. His subordinates detested him and civilians in the area liked him almost as much as they liked a republican or a left-wing democrat I no-faulted the RINC for ineptitude, wrote a less than glowing transfer evaluation and transferred him to sea duty. I then designated the station as a satellite under the Pickens Station because the remaining recruiters were not exactly God's Gift to Navy Recruiting; neither man was RINC material.

I waylaid the next CPO who reported for duty, trained him for a couple of days, then assigned him to shadow Angie. When I thought him ready I transferred him to Merriville and hoped for the best. Merriville improved greatly under his supervision, but four applicants subsequently refused to swear in after their enlistments were approved by the examining center -- a caution light that all was still not right in Merriville.

I commenced my inspection directly upon arrival. I found the administration near perfect. The display case was barely off the ground, but I expected that. The Tracking System showed considerable improvement since my last visit, but Signalman First Class Hinkle's folder showed far too few school visits. I questioned that.

"I don't get much out of school visits, Master Chief. You can barely get one of the snots to talk to you, even after you buy him a soft drink."

Not so very good, Buccaneer.

"Why do you think that is?"

"Aw . . . the lazy bastards don't want to do anything except drink cheap wine and smoke dope. The peace creep teachers don't help either. I have some real poor schools."

"Petty Officer Hinkle, I'm not going to tell you there aren't any, but I've never heard of anti-military teachers in this area.

Anti-war, maybe. I've never met a single soul who is not anti-war. Why do you think the teachers aren't helpful?"

"They're a bunch of stone asses!"

"We'll talk tomorrow and visit a couple of your schools. Maybe Ann Arbor University infiltrated baked banana skin addicts into our school system. Enough of that now. Sailors -- it's Miller Time!"

"Uh, not right yet. You guys stick around another hour and dial some phones." Chief Hagland ordered. "We've got a ways to go yet for goal."

Pouring a few beers into my recruiters served a purpose. It gave them an opportunity to moan to The Big Dog From Out of Town. It was difficult to keep abreast of their needs, considering I was able to visit my distant stations only about once per month. Chief Hagland understood my tactics, therefore, his counter-manding my invitation surprised me greatly.

"OK, Chief," I said, when we'd done the friendlies over a beer. "What do you want to talk to me about?"

"I'm probably going to put Hinkle on report I really need to get rid of him."

"I agree he's got an attitude like a bent trash can, but you can't write him up for that. No-fault transfer him, maybe -- if we can't square him away with old-fashioned attitude adjustment."

"I can live with his attitude. He's a productive recruiter. He usually makes goal, after which I have to kick his ass to get more work out of him. But, Master Chief, a bad attitude isn't the major problem. I believe he is lying to prospects and parents."

That called for a long drink of tea!

Navy recruiters rarely lie to applicants. Most recruiters return to sea following a tour of recruiting duty and do not want to run into a shipmate to whom they had once lied. Also, recruiters learn early on that civilians become more responsive when they realize the recruiter is making his case honestly. Recruiters also realize The Word gets around on a dishonest recruiter almost as fast as the name of a promiscuous girl.

Lying to parents can be terminal. Parents talk to each other, particularly in small communities where a fair percentage are in position to do a recruiter serious harm. A person does not have to be of importance to damage a recruiter. A clerk can drastically slow the procurement of birth certificates, social security cards, police checks and a host of other documents needed to affect enlistment.

"Can you prove it, Chief?"

"Not yet. I suspected he was crooked, but nothing concrete, so I nosed around his schools last week and found he was bending hell out of the truth. I was about to take him to task when I learned he told Mister and Missus Bailey that the peacetime GI Bill is coming back."

"He **WHAAAT**?"

"The Bailey's girl, Janet, is going to be the valedictorian, but she didn't get a college scholarship like valedictorians in previous years. The way they give scholarship is something like how things are done in Russia; you have to know someone with influence. Mister Bailey's is sick and can't work. They're poorer than Job's Turkey, so there is no way in God's green earth they can afford to send Janet to college. Janet is toying with going into the service. Hinkle's been working to DEP her into the Navy. Supposedly, last Friday, he told the Bailey's he had inside information the GI Bill is coming back. Janet got all charged up and was ready to sign the dotted line!"

"Chief, are you sure he told them that?"

"Janet said her folks got it from Hinkle."

"Look, I might have to court martial that flange head, so I'm damn sure not going to drink with him. You make like a bunny, hop back to the station and tell the recruiters I'm tied up with a Center of Influence. I don't want the other recruiters to miss out, so I'll throw forty bucks in the till for their beer. Tell the recruiters I'll meet with them tomorrow and listen to their tales of woe. You get in touch with the Bailey's and make an appointment for tomorrow. I'll meet you in Gloria's when you're done."

Some years after the B&O Railroad abandoned the track through Merriville, Gloria Matthews purchased the depot intact with furnishings and fixtures and converted it into a bar, which she named Gloria's Depot. She kept a couple of the passenger benches, the agent's wrought iron and brass case and an oak cased banjo clock that ticked the minutes away as it had done since around the turn of the century. The highly polished bar was a fifty-foot slab from a beech tree believed to be over three hundred years old, already tall and strong when it observed the birth of the United States. It might have once sheltered Cornstalk, Indian Chief; Lewis Wetzel, Scout, or maybe even George Washington, Surveyor, beneath its wide branches. Gloria's Depot, although a bit cluttered, was a comfortable and cheerful establishment, more like a British pub than a beer joint.

"Look, Everybody! The sheriff let the Head Swabby out of jail!" announced the tall Brunette, perched on an organ stool in front of an old-fashioned, upright pedal organ. "What were you in for this time, Clay -- pandering?"

I kissed the offered cheek. "Goodness! Trade must be rough around here if you've got to pump that organ to earn your bread. I can think of other ways a pretty girl like you could make some money."

"If you are speaking of yourself, there is no girl that hard up!"

141

That really broke the hillbillies' jugs and the bar roared with laughter.

"Come over here, Clay. You ain't a-goin' to get one up on Gloria tonight. She's been on a roll since she beat the Budweiser salesman outta that big mirror last week."

I smelled the clean scent of sawdust and the day's honest sweat as I climbed on the stool beside the small, gray-bearded man. "I don't know if I want to drink with you sawyers, Cletus. You fellows are a mean bunch."

Cletus laughed way back in his throat. "You still a-bitchin' about that Merriville stump juice we fed you? Hey, fellows! You recollect Clay a-tryin' to walk straight the night we wet down my new mill? Weren't he a sight?" That question bought a lengthy round of remembrances from the boys at the bar, none of which made me look too slick.

Cletus, who operated sawmills for the Seabees in the South Pacific during World War Two, had five sons. All of them either served or were serving in the Navy, all in Seabee battalions. He also had three married daughters thought to rank among the best looking women in West Virginia. His wife, far from worn down by the toils of raising eight children, some less than two years apart, was a cheerful, gray-haired woman with as much energy as any thirty-year-old. Cletus looked and sounded like a West Virginia mountaineer and was proud of it. He'd gone to war when called, stayed as long as needed, then returned to the hills. He loved his family, his state, his country and Navy, but their order of priority got a bit confused at times.

His often spoken fondness for Navy folks had not stopped him from spiking a keg of beer with the local pop skull and forcing it on me during the wetting down of a steam powered sawmill he'd just placed into service. I couldn't keep anything down, except vanilla ice cream and potato chips, for nearly a week after I drank that stuff!

"You boy oughta patent that jungle juice and sell it to the government. It'd work better than that stuff the law gives to keep drunks from drinking after they run up a few DUI convictions."

They went hysterical that time.

"We'uns though you wuz a West Virginia boy!" Cletus exclaimed, while he wiped his steel-rimmed eyeglasses on my well-creased shirt sleeve -- nothing shy about Cletus.

"I am, but that stuff would corrode a cast iron boiler!" A New York wino couldn't keep it down."

That set them off again.

During the next half hour, I heard about the price of hardwood lumber (low), the no-count politicians in Charleston and Washington (known crooks and socialists), welfare (kept taxpayers broke) and a whole lot about West Virginia's Junior Senator (coon ass carpetbagger).

Chief Hagland called about nine-thirty to inform me he'd accomplished his mission. Unfortunately, Missus Chief caught him in the office and canceled his liberty. I commiserated with him a bit before telling him to meet me at Rock Ridge Motel for breakfast, after which we'd get underway for Bailey's farm.

"Say, Clay," Cletus rumbled, "I ever tell you your dad came through here the winter afore World War Two with a partner named Reed a-buyin' cattle?"

"No, Cletus, but you did tell me you knew him pretty well when you two were young."

"Your daddy and Mark Reed, who got killed in North Africa early in the war, got snowbound in Merriville and we had us one fine time! We got in two-three fights, got wobbly-assed drunk and chased every girl what wanted chased, and some that maybe didn't. I stayed in trouble with Charlotte Ann for weeks after that. We wuz nowhere's close to getting married neither. Leastways I didn't know we wuz. I thought we wuz in foolin' around times. 'Course the man's always the last to know when some leetle gal is about to bark his tree. Ain't that true, boys?"

That comment lit off the natives again, but it didn't sound all that funny to me, not after the groups Gunny had been laying on me about Patty.

"Clay," Cletus said, after the bar quieted to a dull roar, "We'uns got to go. Civilians got to work for a livin'. You come and see me afore you leave. Me and my boys got a sack of sea stories to tell. Might drink us some stump juice too, if you promise not to go a-fallin' down.

"So long, Gloria. You watch this sailor -- they're quick!"

Gloria was somewhere past thirty. Scuttlebutt had it she was selective in her lovers. She would not sleep with regular customers, married men, or men who wanted to sponge off her. Smart woman, but her own rules must have kept her in a constant state of tension. After subtracting regular customers, married men and possible sponges, here wasn't anybody left near her age, except a holy roller preacher. She wasn't likely to go with him, not when he bad-mouthed her and her establishment every Sunday of the year.

I'd never slept with her, but we'd done some rubbing and purring. We nearly committed the Ultimate Act three times, but something weird happened to prevent it.

The weirdest happening was the night Cletus wetted down his mill. Our high-level rubbing and purring, deep in a thicket by the mill pond, would have surely turned into a full-scale romp, except for bad luck. We were slithering around on a tablecloth I'd lifted from the wetting down area when the bank of the newly dug barking pond caved in and we tumbled into the water. The night went down hill after that.

Around eleven-thirty, Gloria caught me by the upper arm. "Help me lock up and we'll get a drink at your motel. That will make Preacher Jarvis so happy. He can tell next Sunday's congregation I've fallen to selling myself to passing sailors in the Rock Creek Motel

"I intended to cuddle next to you tonight when I heard you'd be in town, but I got into poison ivy yesterday and I am covered with it! That's what I get for cleaning my garden fence row in shorts and a short sleeved shirt. Damn! Every time we contemplate sleeping together there is a tidal wave, or something."

Strange, but I felt relieved we'd not end in bed tonight. There was no doubt in my military mind something odd was creeping into my life. I wondered if age was creeping up.

I bent over and gave her a little kiss. "Don't worry. We'll give it another shot when your skin clears up. You've got to wonder though, when you think of all the weird things that have happened since we met. The week we met, you bit through your lip when your car hit a big chuckhole and you had to get a couple stitches. Then you fell off an icy stoop and cracked your ankle. Next, I caught the flu and spent two days shorted to ground in the motel. That preacher didn't put a hex on you, did he?"

Gloria gave me a crooked, little grin, then said. "He lusts for me in his heart! The poor devil couldn't impress a woman if he was driving a new Cadillac with a hundred-dollar bill stuck on his forehead, let alone me!"

CHAPTER SIXTEEN

KEELHAULING

"That's Bailey's Bald." Chief Hagland said, pointing to a bare, rounded peak above the timbered slope we were climbing. "Turn on the road by that mailbox."

I did and it wasn't fun. "Damn, Chief, a horny buck sheep wouldn't travel this road to breed with the prettiest ewe on the mountain!"

The road got rougher and narrower. Low hanging oak, hickory and maple branches scraped against the sides and roof of the Pinto. I was about to give it up and rent a jeep when the rust streaked roof of a barn appeared around a near ninety degree turn.

"There's Mister Bailey." Chief Hagland pointed to a badly stooped, gray haired man wearing washed-out bib overalls with high rubber boots. "He doesn't look too good, does he?"

"What's wrong with him?"

"Black lung. He's got his claim in, but no money yet. Piddles around on his farm some. That's about all he can do. I don't know what they're going to do without Janet."

"You don't want to put her in the Navy, do you?"

"Janet is way too shy to be in the Navy. I suspect she'd be an attrition from boot camp, worrying about her folks, and all."

"Good morning." Mister Bailey greeted, in a wet, raspy voice. "Mother poured the coffee when we heard you coming up the road."

"I have to tell you," Mister Bailey said, after we were seated in the shabby, but squeaky clean room. "Janet ain't decided on the Navy yet. She's still trying for college money."

"I hope she gets it, Mister Bailey, but that's not what we came to talk about." I said.

"You boys got business for the government, other than being recruiting officers?"

"No, we don't. Mister Bailey did you hear anything about the GI Bill? Recently, I mean?"

"Well, Sir, Mister Hinkle talked about it some."

"Mister Bailey, I'm in charge of recruiting in this part of West Virginia. It is important you tell me everything you recall about what he told you."

"Janet ain't in any trouble with the government, is she?"

"Not at all. This concerns her only indirectly."

"Mother!" he called. "Please come in here and help me a little bit."

"Now," he said, after the pleasant faced woman introduced herself, then perched on the wide arm of his tattered, faded blue chair. "Mother, we're talking about this GI Bill that Mister Hinkle told us about."

"It'd be a blessing!"

147

Mister Bailey didn't look like he thought it'd be a blessing. He looked sad.

I felt like throwing up.

"Let me see . . . Mister Hinkle said, as best I recollect, the Navy was having trouble getting people because the Navy didn't have the bonus the Army had for . . . Combat Arms, I think he called it. He said Congress was likely to approve the GI Bill next year. He said it would pay for four years of college. Is that how you understood it, Mother?"

"Just about. He made it sound very mysterious."

"Mister and Missus Bailey, there is a Navy college program, but it is a contributory program. The way it works is the Navy adds two dollars to each one dollar a sailor contributes. It works out to eight thousand-six hundred dollars per enlistment. That won't pay for four years of college. Are you certain he said GI Bill, and not Navy Campus for Achievement?"

"Yes, Sir. He said 'GI Bill.'" Mister Bailey confirmed, while Missus Bailey shook her head in agreement. "What are you trying to tell us, Mister Berkeley?"

"The GI Bill is available only during wartime. It is intended for readjustment of veterans, not as an enlistment incentive."

"You mean he lied to us?" Missus Bailey questioned, with a hurt look.

"Yes, Ma'am. It appears he did."

"To influence Janet to join the Navy?"

"It appears so, Missus Bailey."

Missus Bailey was a lady, but she had a mean tongue when angry. Hinkle's ears ought to have burned clear to the nubs when she finished working him over.

"Ma'am, I agree completely with what you said. I'm angry too. I emphatically do not condone what Petty Officer Hinkle appears to have done and I intend to take action --"

"I read in the newspaper about the Army outright lying and cheating to influence boys and girls to enlist." She broke in, and clobbered me some more. "Are you going to cover it up like the Army tried to do?"

"No, Ma'am. That's why we're here. To find out what happened. The action I recommend depends entirely on your statement. Otherwise, I cannot prove anything."

"You want a statement from us?"

"Yes, Ma'am, I do."

"We will certainly give you one!"

"Now, Mother. Let's not get mixed up in the government's problems. They might hold it against us and we'll never get our black lung check."

I tried to assure them the situation was in no way connected with any pending black lung claim, but mountaineers tend to trust the government not at all. To mountain folks, one part of the government is the same as another and they suspect all of them are crooked. They argued for a bit with Missus Bailey wanting to provide a statement and Mister Bailey against it.

In the end, I didn't get a statement, nor would they agree to discuss it with the Navy Criminal Investigative Service. I thanked them for their time and again apologized for Hinkle's lie. I told them we would not contact Janet again unless she initiated the contact. It was bad enough HInkle lied, let alone to a family who didn't have much to look forward to. When I left them, I felt lower than a brig rat on his second day of a three-day sentence on bread and water.

Back at Merriville Station, I read Petty Officer Hinkle his rights, questioned him briefly, then informed him he was relieved of duty pending further investigation. I told him he was to consider himself Confined to Quarters in his apartment until I could get back to him with further orders. I then told him to get the hell out of my eyes!

After Hinkle left, looking less worried than he would when I ultimately finished with him, Chief Hagland said, "Master Chief, I expected you to ream him to the bone. You were madder than an alley cat raped by a poodle dog after you talked to the Bailey's."

"Chief, as we speak, I'm madder than a male alley cat gang banged by a big rat, a sausage dog and a wild monkey. I'm too mad to chew on him without totally dropping sync. Well, that puts the squelch on the rest of this road trip. I'll confer with the chief recruiter and let you know what we decide. Hanging him by his cojones doesn't look possible right now."

"I've got to keep that squirrel? No way!"

"Consider him gone, Chief. He's haze gray and underway! I still want NCIS to have a crack at the Bailey's. They probably won't talk to an agent though. Once a hillbilly makes a decision, you can't change it with a white hat of blasting caps and a barge load of Hercules Powder."

I worked up a plan of action en route Big Otter and stopped in my office to bang it out on paper before proceeding to NRD. I had to have my duck in a row because I could see no way to punish Hinkle within the judicial system without a statement from Janet's parents. The commodore wasn't going to like my recommendation either!

The captain, chief recruiter and I studied the UCMJ and the Manual for Courts Martial for a fair part of the early afternoon before deciding, tentatively, that a low performance evaluation and a no-fault transfer was the only way to go. I thought it resolved, at least at our level, until the chief recruiter cracked the knuckles of his scarred, engineer hands, laced his fingers behind his head and leaned way back in his chair. "Captain, the commodore is going to fight you for not punishing Hinkle at mast."

"I am quite aware of that, but unless NCIS can obtain a statement, which they will not, we cannot punish him. All we can do, legally, is place him into a position where he causes no further damage. As Master Chief Berkeley once pointed out, the commodore cannot dictate punishment and I am not going to impose illegal punishment on anybody. I command this NRD and it is my decision. It is settled."

"Captain, I don't like to see a liar and a cheat treated almost like a normal transfer. We ought to hang the bastard anyway we can!" the Chief Recruiter said, sullenly.

"If you have a better plan, a legal one, please be so kind as to enlighten us." The skipper looked hard at the chief recruiter, probably wondering where the man's loyalty lay.

Me? I'd been wondering about the chief recruiter's loyalty for some time.

"I don't think we should make waves with the commodore, Captain. If Clay had kept an even strain on his Zone, he'd have known Hinkle wasn't squeaky clean and we wouldn't be in this situation!"

"That was a petty and not a particularly intelligent statement! Master Chief Berkeley has, as you, yourself, stated in his last evaluation, turned around Southern Zone. Production is up, morale is up and disciplinary problems are few. If you are aware of something he has done wrong, or is not doing properly, it is your duty to correct him. Until you do, I strongly recommend you cast no stones of an unfounded or personal nature!"

The chief recruiter's worn, seamy face turned a dull red, but he said nothing.

"I must notify the commodore of our nasty situation and of our decision. I anticipate telephone failure due to deceased felines on the wires." the captain said, smiling.

"Master Chief Berkeley, notify Chief Hagland no disciplinary action will be taken until we resolve the statement issue. Have the administrative officer prepare the appropriate letter notifying Hinkle of his imminent termination from recruiting duty. I want it in tomorrow's guard mail."

"Chief Recruiter, please remain."

I had strong suspicion the skipper was about to flush the head on the chief recruiter. I felt sorry for old John, but lately his bunting was bad ragged!

The administrative officer was less than enthusiastic about preparing the letter. She shot up a smoke screen a high-powered searchlight would have had difficulty penetrating.

"Irene," I said, tiredly, "I don't care how many envelopes your people have to stuff for advertising and I don't care how many beans you have to count for an Area report. This letter will be in tomorrow's guard mail! The XO will authorize overtime if you need it. Should I ask him?"

"No, Clay. The letter will go in tomorrow's guard mail. Did you just return from a trip?"

"I started one. I'd be in Palace Valley today, except for this."

"Let me remind you, Clay, travel claims must be completed within seventy-two hours."

"I've heard that."

"Watch the little errors. Recruiting travel claims are tricky."

I was reminded of a black widow spider about to copulate. "Irene, I'll write the letter myself, if it'll make you feel better. Give me a serial number."

"It's not the letter, Clay."

"It's damned sure something. We've been butting heads for weeks now. Tell you what -- let's meet at Moe's tonight and sort this thing out."

"Won't your teenaged shack job get angry?"

"She's not a teenager! She doesn't own me. She doesn't tell me what to do. She doesn't tell me where to go. She surely isn't going to tell me who to go with. She's not a 'shack job' either. I've never laid a hand on Patricia Lane Patterson, no matter that she told God and everybody in Moe's." Not strictly correct, but close enough. "Irene, I might be a little stupid. I might even be a lot stupid, but I can't understand why you're so angry with me for having a few drinks with Patty."

"Did you ever accompany me to church?"

No secrets in this town.

"Did you ever invite me? Do you go to church?"

"That is beside the point! You've been running around like a lovesick fool since you met her. It is disgusting!"

"Irene, I'm not repeat not tied up with Patty."

"Aren't you?"

"No, I'm not!"

"Clay, I have to make a decision that, to use one of your phrases, has been 'hanging fire.'"

I stepped back and closed the door. Her secretaries had heard enough.

"This means, Clay, you too, must make a decision. Cease seeing her and I'll consider dating you again. There can be no other women. None at all."

"You mean, like. Forever?" I gurgled.

"Something like that . . . if I decide in your favor. I give you no guarantee, except I will reconsider a decision I believe I have already made."

"Irene," I said, after I considered her statements. "I don't intend to stay with any one woman on a permanent basis, ever! Can't we go back to where we were?"

"No, Clay, we cannot. Even before Patty, you had become an embarrassment to me what with your catting around."

Say **WHAAAT**? Me catting around? She'd have given birth every few weeks if she'd been a pussycat and I wouldn't have been the daddy of most of the litters!

"And you didn't sleep around, I suppose?"

"Not to the extent you did! I didn't complain about the cheap office workers, that media doll or that state policewoman. I never even said anything about the tramp from that topless bar. But, when you started lusting after Patty, a woman just like me, the type woman men marry, then rubbed it right into my face, it was too damned much!

"Now, are you going to give up Patty, or do I make a decision I've been putting off?"

"You are an intelligent and a beautiful woman, Irene. You are a nice person too. But not full time. No with anybody."

"I'm sorry, Clay. I'm sorry you are a man with no desires, save getting blotto and laid at every opportunity and staying in the Navy until you die.

"You've made my decision for me. I believe it was really the decision I wanted to make all along. I want a man who wants to sleep with Irene Johnson because she is someone he loves, not because Irene Johnson is good in bed and he needs to satisfy an urge. I have, colloquially speaking, another ax to grind, Clay. One I can keep for my own."

"I wish you luck, Irene." I turned, opened the door and scared the liver and lights out of a gaggle of women milling smartly just down the hall within easy listening distance.

CHAPTER SEVENTEEN

HOOKUPS

Back in my office, I phoned an old running mate from *USS King*, now a senior chief yeoman stationed at the Bureau of Naval Personnel. I asked if he and other former shipmates stationed in Washington had cornered enough government gulls to get help from various agencies.

"Clay, I don't want to sound like I'm bragging, understand, but we can operate inside any office in Washington, except, maybe, the Treasury printing room and the CIA. Well, maybe only the printing room. What sort of hook up you need this time? Your service jacket cleaned up so you can apply for an officer program, maybe?"

Frank "Pens" Larson had no problem with checking into obtaining a set of bad transfer orders for Hinkle, but he had a little trouble believing I wanted him to locate and expedite a black lung claim. He accepted the black lung tasking though, saying he'd run the problem by a fellow yeoman who had a girlfriend with contacts everywhere that counted. Pens clicked my call on hold while he looked into the Hinkle situation.

There were no known bad ships available, but Pens got Hinkle the next worst thing. Port Services, Guam was in Hinkle's future. Pens said my tab had now increased to where I owned our shipmates and the gulls a tank truck of beer, a U-Haul full of roses and five gallons or so of Channel Number Five. He said he'd get back to me on the black lung claim.

I then called a Center of Influence in Clarksburg and explained Janet Bailey's college qualifications and financial situation. I told him I'd be most appreciative if she received a fair crack at a full college scholarship, preferably within driving distance of Merriville. He promised to look into it, saying if she carried the qualifications I stated he would make a sincere effort to ensure she didn't get pushed aside by a high school senior with influence. He asked if she was a relative. I told him she was not, which probably caused him to believe I had found a bright, seventeen-year-old mistress to provide comfort for my old age.

Those calls made, I decided I'd amble to the lounge, grab a cup of coffee and maybe bum a cigarette from the below standard FBI agent who smoked. King Angie nabbed me as I past her office, grabbed me by the arm and dragged me into the lounge. The FBI was probably beginning to wonder about us. "Master Chief, Charles is in my office. He wants to take the physical again. He won't listens to me. Will you talks to him?"

"The Coke Bottle Man?"

"Don't call him that!" she said, giving me a weak grin.

Charles was a tall, six-three, or better, man who'd failed a host of enlistment physicals because of flat feet. He'd been standing on Coke bottles one hour per day for months in hopes he'd develop enough arch to get past the doctor. The sun cometh up and the sun goeth down and Charles continued to retake the physical and each time he failed because of flat feet.

I didn't want to talk to Charles. I had told him once before his chances of getting into any military service equaled that of a fat rat's survival of at a kitty cat convention. There was no chance for Charles, but I could see a chance for something else. "Angie, he's your station's applicant, so he's your responsibility. I'll do it though."

"I knew you would, Master Chief." she said, smacking my upper arm with her fist.

"Uh, Angie -- will you do me a favor?"

"Sure, if I can." She sounded a mite leery.

"I just returned from a trip and my desk runneth over. You've asked me to take time to talk to Charles, so will you --"

"No! Ain't no way! You wants me to fills out your travel claim. Ain't no way, Master Chief. That hussy Irene has got you programmed. I fills out your travel claim, even the one time, your mind is going to tells you to spread-eagles me on that big desk of yours. Ain't no way!" She stomped out of the lounge and into her office bellowing for Charles.

It was worth a try.

"Charles, take off your shoes and socks." I ordered, after I gave him a cup of coffee and accepted one of his weeds.

Charles did it, but kept giving me white-eyed looks while unlacing his sneakers.

"Now, Charles, stand on this burn bag. I'm going to trace around your foot, so stand still -- even if it tickles."

Charles slapped feet larger than a bread box on the paper. I commenced tracing around his left foot with a felt tip pen. I then pulled a ruler from my desk and carefully measured the outline of his foot. "Look at this, Charles. Your foot is a tad over seven inches wide. You see?"

Charles indicated he'd seen.

"You notice here, at the sides of your foot where I tried to slide the tip of the pen beneath your arch? Notice there is almost no mark at all toward the instep. That means you have no arch!

"Charles, you can perch twenty-four hours per day on Coke bottles, Mountain Dew bottles, Pepsi bottles, or Iron City beer bottles. Hell, you could even stand on water cooler bottles, but you are never going to have an arch. Never, Charles, never."

Charles just smiled. "One day, Master Chief, a doctor is going to be too busy to notice my feet."

"Charles, can I hide a ten-wheeled coal truck in a fleet of pickup trucks?"

"Why, no. I don't see how."

"And I don't see how you think you're going to hide your feet in a room full of regular-sized feet!"

"You're saying I'm never going to be accepted?"

"I'm sorry, Charles, but that's exactly what I am saying. You have to realize no military service is going to accept you."

"I wanted to be in the service since I can remember." Charles was trying not to show it, but he was crying.

His statement made me mad at the pampered punks who thought they were too good for the military and believed only dummies joined because they couldn't do anything else. Here was Charles: twenty-eight years old, with a good education, higher than average ASVAB scores and a move-up job at Ashland Oil. Charles never enjoyed a pampered day of life, but he believed he should do something for his country, just like his daddy. Charles' daddy never returned from some minor conflict now forgotten by the public, but a Bronze Star with a Combat V, a Purple Heart and a passel of other medals and ribbons did.

159

Then it hit me!

"Charles, how'd you like to go in the Merchant Marine?"

"Ships?"

"Ship's wider than Buckhannon Street. Ships longer than a football field and taller than an umpteen story building."

"Is it military?"

"It acts as an arm of the military. You'd sail ships all over the world carrying beans, bullets and black oil for the military -- civilian cargo too. You'd make a lot of money, so much you'd only have to work six months per year, if you wanted.

"There's a maritime union school in Piney Point, Maryland. I know one of their department heads, if he's still there. I might can get you enrolled. Hell, with your education, you maybe could get into a maritime academy, but let's see if we can pull this off first."

"Man, I'll take it!"

I shooed Charles out of my office, dug my little black book from my attaché case and dialed the number. I connected with my old shipmate via a sweet sounding secretary.

"Berkeley? Used to be a piss ant second class radioman in *Rank Frank*?"

"Sure is, Senior Chief -- or are you called captain now that you've given up being a boatswain's mate and gone for the gold?"

"I've not sailed as captain yet, but I was Chief Mate in Green Wave and a couple of rust buckets. Congratulations on making master chief! You really learned to suck eggs since you was a piss-ant second class, just frocked to first class. Crewmembers were asking about you at our last reunion in New Orleans. We were all surprised when you didn't muster in."

160

"There was a shuffle in zone supervisors. I was switched to the largest zone. It needed a lot of tweaking, so the captain put me in leg irons and turned me to. How'd the reunion go?"

"We had a really nice ceremony for the guys. We went out on a destroyer and floated a wreath on the water with their names on it. We did that at the exact time the destroyer *Mahan* put a wreath over the side in the South China Sea. We tied together education aid programs we'd been doing bits and pieces through the *Evans Association* and the *Long Beach Fleet Reserve Association.* Time really flies by, Clay. Some of the kids of our lost shipmates are in college!"

The destroyer *USS Frank E. Evans* was cut in two by the Australian aircraft carrier *HMAS Melbourne* in the South China Sea. She lost sixty-eight men, including three brothers and the ship's senior chief's son. I'd transferred to *Forrestal* before it happened, but I'd served with most of those killed.

"Say, Chief Mate. I need something really bad. Can you hook me up?"

"You ain't changed none, Berkeley. Same as in *Rank Frank.* You were cumshawing paint, swabs, or consumables, every time you came to the bosun's locker. Lay it on me."

I explained my need and prepared to do a little old fashioned begging.

"If you say he's a good man, I expect we can fit him in. We have some openings -- not many in deck, but several in engineering. You certain those life rafts don't hurt him none?"

"He walks on them all day at Ashland Oil where he supervises running a big control board -- it covers an entire bulkhead in a big room. It's not a sitting down job."

"I'll get the application in the mail today. You get it filled out with three good references and get it back to me ASAP. Give my secretary your mailing address. Make sure one of the references is

161

from Ashland and says something about him not missing work for physical reasons. I want a copy of his last physical examination, if it's less than six months old."

I signed off with an invitation for him to deer hunt on my property. He said he didn't hunt, but would come to fish the trout stream at first opportunity.

.

"Angie, Light of my Life! Water of my Camel! Sauce of my Pasta!" I cried out, as I approached her and Charles sitting on the small couch in her station. "You'll have papers to fill out and --"

"No you don't, Master Chief!" She jumped up and sidled away. "I don't does no travel claims!"

"Not for me, Angie -- for Charles. He's likely going into the United States Merchant Marine." I stuck my hand out. "Congratulations, Charles. We've got to get eyes and elbows deep in your paperwork when it comes, so try to remember everything you've ever done. You'll probably go to school in late July, the next class. You have to decide whether you want to go into deck or engineering department. I'll tell you about them."

Angie plopped her stern down on the coffee table, bent over and kissed Charles on the lips. I wouldn't call it a friendly, happy kiss. I'd call it a 'It has been done a lot before kiss!'

Angie and Charles?

I phoned Patty around six, not that I really wanted to see her. I simply thought I should tell her I was back in town before she heard it elsewhere and got her feelings hurt.

"Oh, I am thrilled you returned early from your trip!" She sounded excited. "Where shall I meet you and at what time?"

"I'm the victim of one vicious day and it's not ended yet. See you at Moe's around eight, if I haven't cashed in and gone to the Big Recruiting Command in the Sky. OK?"

"May I come to your office? May I come directly?"

There was no way I could deny her, not when she whipped that little girl voice on me. "Sure, if you want, but I might put you to work."

"I do not fill out travel claims." she said, primly.

I would rather have had a sister in the Air Force . . .

I stood when Patty sailed through the hatch, intending to walk around the desk, but she trick seduced me by running directly to me and hanging a lengthy lip lock on me. It wasn't long before she was sitting on my desk with her yellow skirt way above her knees with me sort of bent over her with my hand on her breast. My intended good guy program was suffering severe hits.

Patty shivered, let out a little hiss, slid my hand off her breast and held it tightly against her upper leg. "That felt wonderful! We had better stop."

"I'll bet you have a good many places that would feel even better." I weaseled. "Let's sit on the couch."

"No, dearest. I would want you to do that so much more. Touch me, I mean. Them we would go too far. You make me think Things, Clay-honey and --"

I wasn't real smart, but I was learning how to stop her when she went into her explaining mode. She moaned and leaned back, pulling me down and almost between her lovely legs. Papers hit the deck in all directions.

"Master Chief, I want to talk . . . well, pardon me!" The door clicked shut.

"Angie, Damn it!" I yelled.

Patty turned red as far down as I could see and I suspected she was red further down than that.

"Thank you, Angie." She murmured against my neck, after she had buttoned up and sidled against me again. The scent of her hair made the small hairs stand up on my neck and arms.

"Why thank her? She's always bursting in here."

"Oh, I needed her just then -- and badly too." She gave me a broad toothed smile. "Our kissing made me want to move to the couch! We must stop this. I have known you only since April and already you have touched far too much. But I really do like . . . being with you."

I'd seen a lot more of her than she realized. Her bra and panties were so sheer they couldn't have been seen on a clothesline in a stiff breeze. I tried to hook onto her again but she fended me off. That left nothing to do, except go to Moe's.

Moe broadsided us when we walked in. "You ought to wash your hands before you fool around, Boot Camp. You got inky hand prints all over Patty's as -- uh, hips. Mercy Lord, you young folks! Patty, you like to bit Clay's ear plumb off!"

Patty like to tied herself into knots by fumbling to inspect the sides and rear of her skirt with one hand and inspecting my ears with the other before she realized the ear part was a Moeism.

Talk about red!

She got even redder after she tried to defend herself by saying, "I did not bite Clay's ear. I just nipped a little . . . Oh, damn in hell! MOE!"

Moe laughed so hard he got wobbly and had to sit on a beer keg, but I think he felt sorry for Patty too. He gave her a free beer, something that was becoming a habit.

"I ran across your Ex late this afternoon. "Patty said, when we were finally alone at the corner of the bar.

"I don't have an Ex."

"Irene, your ex-girlfriend. I said 'Ex,' dearest, because you have a current one." She explained, blushing. "I am your steady girlfriend, am I not?"

Her little girl voice was about to drive me out of my rabbit-assed mind! Every time she laid it on me, I wanted to fall down and bite sticks, then just plain jump her bones until her teeth rattled and her ears ached.

"Am I not?" She asked, a bit louder.

For once I was not the object of everyone's curiosity, so I leaned over and brushed her cheek with my lips. "I can't deny your claim to that billet." Not that I seemed to have much control over whether she was or not.

"Oh, good! Curtis will be surprised when he learns we are going steady. Goodness!"

I was relatively certain Curtis would not be overjoyed about our new status, contrary to what he had told Patty about us deserving each other. Furious would be the operative word, once he learned about his first cousin taking up with me on a more than casual basis.

"Irene surprised me, Clay. She spoke with me this afternoon. She was so friendly."

165

"I told you Irene can be really nice. But that's over. Maybe you caused it, or maybe it had already run its course. I don't know, but it's over."

"I surmised it was." Patty said, looking very satisfied. "Irene and a man were looking at rings in Zales Jewelry. Is she serious about him?"

I had a moment of panic before telling myself there was no doubt in my military mind that Patty was in Zales looking for her graduation ring.

"I don't know, Patty. Gunny told me, right after you came on the scene, he'd seen Irene with a good-looking man with iron gray hair. She hinted pretty strongly this afternoon she'd has a guy on the line, but didn't exactly say she was marriage-type serious about anybody."

"Not even you?"

If Patty ever took up sales as an occupation, she'd be a member of the Million Dollar Round Table in her first month. Once she got her foot in the door there was no getting rid of her until she achieved her goal. Whatever it was. I was always apprehensive when she went into her: "Why can't I . . . ?" "I intend to . . ." mode. 'Stubborn' was not a strong enough word to describe Patty's demeanor when she went that route.

"I wish you'd stop poking at me about Irene, Patty. We were better buddies than anything else. I think we're still friends too." I felt that was a true statement. I'd lost the election for whatever Irene thought I should stump for.

"Well, the man accompanying Irene had iron gray hair and he is quite handsome."

About then, Gunny steamed through the door with Charles under tow. "This one of yours, Master Chief? I found him in Chicken Corner telling a dude about big ships."

"Is he drunk?"

"He could sell the act, if he ain't!"

The ability to hold his liquor was not, apparently, one of Charles' attributes. I finally got him to sit on a bar stood and bought him a sissy beer. I then asked why he had sucked down so much booze in the short time since I'd seen him.

"I'm celebrating."

"I gathered that."

"Angie told me to celebrate 'til she got off work. I'm going to be a sailor!"

"Where, might I ask, were you supposed to meet Angie?" If he missed meeting Angie and she found him drunk in Moe's, we were all going to be in the hurt locker

"Right here! I 'splained to Gunny. Angie is going to dress up and we're going to celebrate."

"Right."

Angie came zipping through the door about eight-forty at roughly the speed of a sailor evading shore patrol. It was a totally different Angie than I'd seen previously. I couldn't recall having seen her out of uniform, except in a pair of old slacks and a sweatshirt. She was now decked out in a white-trimmed, black dress that made her appear almost slender She'd done something with her hair too. It didn't look at all like she had moonlighted as a lightening rod -- her usual hairstyle. Angie was quite attractive in civilian clothing!

I figured she'd dismantle me, and stick Gunny's swagger stick where the sun doesn't shine when she realized Charles was plastered, so I caught her by the arm as she passed and whispered, "We had nothing to do with Charles getting gassed. He fueled at Chicken Corner."

Angie gave me a big, happy smile. "He's celebrating."

"He is that."

I guess Angie didn't want Charles hanging with us low lifers because after talking quietly with Patty for about fifteen minutes, she dragged the big lug off. Angie was fair sized, but she looked like a house cat escorting a full-grown wild kitty down the street. Regardless of size, there was no doubt in my military mind who was in charge of that organization.

"Do I detect a little liaison type thing there?"

"I do believe so, Gunny. Charles has been in her office quite a bit since I reported, but I never noticed even one hint of mutual body exchange until today. I thought they were discussing Coke bottle techniques."

"They are getting married." Patty piped up.

Gunny blew a mouthful of Budweiser all over a barfly who was so deep in sauce he didn't even notice. "Angie? *Our* Angie?"

"Yes, Gunny. When Charles completes his schooling." Patty hugged me around the shoulders. "Clay-dearest, it was sweet that you helped them."

"That explains why Angie wouldn't have anything to do with that lawyer striker who's been trying to get into her pan . . . er, date her." Gunny said. "How'd you help, Master Chief? Put Angie in irons and let him crawl around on her 'till it tickled?"

Patty reddened, then giggled.

"I believe I've got him a seat in a maritime school. It was self-defense. I feared he's step on an applicant and we'd get sued."

"You should not tease about his big feet."

"Patty, as a potential school marm, you really should use proper terminology. Cadillac's are big. Peterbuilt trucks and Charles' feet are gargantuan."

Moe leaned over the bar and whispered, "You folks want something to worry about, think of what their kids will be like if they get his size and her mouth."

That comment put Gunny and me right down on the deck laughing, but drew only a gasp from Patty.

"I know you all think you are being cute, but it is not funny. Angie is so happy." Patty said, when we three men stopped laughing. "Clay-honey, Angie is going to ask that you give her away when they marry. She has no near male relatives."

"Oh, Master Chief, you'll look just peachy in your monkey jacket and bow tie!" Gunny chortled and limp-wristed his glass. "And you'll get to wear your cute little medals."

CHAPTER EIGHTEEN

DIRECT ENCOUNTER

We made goal that Friday, exactly goal. I figured there'd be a few more folks who would enlist during the last days of the month. I hoped my recruiters were shrewd enough to keep a couple in their ditty bags I didn't know about and therefore wouldn't have to ship, so we could begin July hot and running with accessions in our sock.

I knew I'd be in the deep, dark kimchee if the commodore found out, but I called my stations, congratulated them, then gave them the weekend off beginning Friday noon. Marcie did well place the conference call. I had all my sixteen stations, plus Deanville stockyard.

After completing the call, I called Patty and invited her to meet me for White Castles, followed by cold beer at Moe's. She accepted and we had a great time laughing and joking with the temporarily free recruiters. Gunny never mustered. That indicated Elizabeth had a child-free weekend. Sometimes during the evening we -- read Patty -- decided we should take advantage of the warm, dry weather by going on a picnic.

So, Saturday morning, I loaded Jarhead into Dad's old Dodge Power Wagon, waved goodbye to Blue Suit who was watching us depart from the picture window and lay course toward Patty's house. Blue Suit didn't want to go on a picnic. There were too many bugs loose in the woods and there was danger of rotten timber falling.

"Jarhead, I seem to recall you managed to fall from grace and got into a fight with, or rather among, several dogs when I took you to Holly River State Park last summer. That was a big vet bill, Bowlegs."

Jarhead pulled his wide paws from the dashboard and stood on my leg, then slobbered up and down my arm. That was his way of saying he had reformed and would not again hang with ruffians. I told him I believed him, but he shouldn't use me for a reference, seeing as I was the fellow who believed the Russians wanted to open a borscht plant in Peel Tree, West Virginia.

Patty cleared her door just as we rolled to a stop. She walked down the gravel path with a heel lifting, bobbing walk that caused her tanned legs to flash in the early morning sun. There was a whole lot of tiny woman inside her plaid shirt and white shorts.

"Hi, Jarhead." Patty greeted brightly, as she placed her basket and cooler into the truck's bed. "I brought you a big bone from last Sunday's ham."

"Hi, Jarhead? Don't I get something too?"

She swung her legs into the truck. Lovely legs. "You would receive a kiss, but Mommy is watching."

"Mothers, Patty, are the curse of the lecher class."

"Mothers are nice. Do you think I would be a nice mother?"

Heaven forbid! Who'd want to do that to such a nice little body?

"Well, do you?"

"I wouldn't be surprised."

"Oh, good!"

That, shipmates, was a scary statement.

The sun barely pierced the thick forest of hardwoods, spruce and hemlock as we worked higher and higher into the mountains. The rough hollows, folded into slopes far below, looked like ground blackened by a recent forest fire. They were not burned over ground. The hills were so steep and the hollows so narrow that one hill cast a heavy shadow against the other as the sun rose toward its peak. The only time a hollow and lower slopes of bordering hills received sun at the same time was around high noon.

Patty must have been reading my mind again because she hugged herself and exclaimed, "Wild, Wonderful West Virginia! Our mountains are so pretty."

They were pretty, but they were not the only pretty thing in West Virginia.

We didn't get to go swimming. The rushing water, probably snow runoff from streams deep inside the mountains, was so cold merely wading in the riffles took our breath away. After wading for only a couple of minutes, we walked hand in hand through the forest bordering the river until we found secluded rocks well screened by brush and trees. Patty set up housekeeping on our selected rock while I cleared away stones by skipping them across the water. Jarhead thought I was doing it for his benefit and damn near jerked me into the river.

"Patty, I'm going to let Jarhead loose."

"Do you think you should, what with his record?"

"I don't believe he's into eating rhododendrons and I haven't seen any other dogs." I said, unsnapping the leash. "He's entitled to a run ashore."

"Here is your bone, Jarhead. Be a good bulldog and gobble it all down." Patty ordered.

"He won't eat bones. He doesn't even like plain meat. He likes Mighty Dog, corn dogs, hot dogs, hamburgers, plain tuna -- and beer, preferably Rolling Rock."

Jarhead slobbered all over her bare feet before taking the bone from her hand. He carried it to the far end of the rock, clamped it between his paws and commenced ripping off hunks of meat. He sounded like a gargling contest.

"Well, I never seen the like -- he made me out a liar! I've bought him bones, but he only pushed them around the yard with his nose."

"Maybe it is the cook."

It might have been. Like Jarhead, Patty didn't have to sound chow call more than once before I was teeth, hair and eyeballs into a fine summer picnic. Either she had accidentally stumbled onto either my weaknesses or she'd done some clandestine research: both deviled ham and egg salad sandwiches, baked beans, potato salad, crunchy celery with honeyed peanut butter and a gallon cooler of strong, sweet tea.

"Did you like the repast, Clay-honey?"

"You know what Tony the Tiger says. Jarhead likes it too. Look at him on top of his bone!"

Jarhead had locked one end of his ham bone into a crack in a rock and was working hard. A pack of hyenas couldn't have made more noise or spread more slobbers around the landscape.

Patty laughed. "He would be totally disgusting if he was not so darn cute."

Jarhead stopped growling and slobbering and looked over his shoulder at Patty with love in his bloodshot eyes. He responded well to compliments. He didn't earn many!

"Patty, that kiss you mentioned . . . "

Nature being what it is, we were soon wrapped together like snakes in spring. She let me stroke her braless nipples through her shirt, but stopped me when I tried to slip inside, probably afraid bears would see. After a time, she sat up, pulled me up beside her and leaned against my shoulder. "Whew!" She exclaimed, fanning her face with a hemlock branch.

"Whew" was right. That girl got more suction out of her soft lips than a lamprey eel. My lips tingled in resonance with the roaring inside my ears.

"Do you think I would be good, dearest?"

"If you're not good, it doesn't leave hope for the rest of us, Patty."

"No, I mean, do you think I would be good . . . in bed -- with you?" she whispered, softly. A pink rose stained her cheeks and worked toward Chinese red.

My good intentions went the way of a reformed thief finding a deserted bank with the vault door open. Bastard children flashed across my mind. I cast them astern. "Cat got climbing gear?" I choked and reached for her, but she averted her lips.

"Have you really thought of how I would be? Tell me, Please."

I had to think that one through. Say the wrong thing and I was a dead kitty cat.

"I'm not certain how to answer your question. I've often thought how pretty you are and I suppose I've thought how lovely you'd be without clothing. How it would feel to run my fingers down your beautiful legs. I like to watch you walk. I like touching you. I know you're passionate. I can't believe the power you put into a kiss! You would be a wonderful lover!"

"You really enjoy kissing me, dearest?"

"More than I can explain. I didn't know kissing was addictive until I met you." I reached, but she again exercised her repel borders bill.

"Are you certain? I did not know I could competently kiss. Clay, I have kissed only . . . a few times all together." she said, as if ashamed.

Talk about a checkered past!

"Would you like to practice some more, Patty?"

"Dearest, all the time I wonder how. It would be with you. I think of how your stern face would look after we had . . . when you are asleep. I also think of how your lean body would look without clothing. What you would do to me. How you would do It. How we would do It together. You Know!"

Patty was about the shade of a Christmas holly berry. I don't believe I'd ever blushed before, but I think she might have me doing it then. She gave me a long, wistful look and turned even redder. She then lowered her face, fumbled at the snap on her shorts, unbuttoned her shirt and came into my arms.

We were getting darned close to the Ultimate Act when all hell broke loose up the river. Men were cussing, kids bawling, women screaming and a dog making short, high-pitched yelps. There was no doubt in my military mind Jarhead was involved.

175

"Stay there!" I ordered over my shoulder to Patty who was making like an octopus trying to button her shirt and snap her shorts simultaneously.

I broke through a clump of brush just in time to see a yelping, whining collie drag Jarhead across some person's picnic dinner. Pots, plates, silverware and food flew north, south, east and west as people rolled out of the way. Jarhead had obviously obtained his goal. The dogs were fused together as tightly as breeding frogs as she pulled him across the grass. The poor little guy's back feet hit the ground only once every four feet or so, but he wasn't about to let her go -- probably couldn't. I grabbed them as they sidled past and pushed them into the cold river where they broke apart, paddled around as if in a daze, then crawled up on the bank and shook water all over the gathering crowd.

"Is that monster yours?" a hard looking woman screamed, digging her nails into my shoulder. "I'll sue if that ugly beast made Crissy pregnant! Crissy is so beautiful and that . . . that . . . Oh, Herbie!" She threw herself into the arms of a short, meek looking man and commenced bellowing like a cow in heat.

"Your dog's not pregnant, Ma'am. I threw them into the water before Jarhead got his roc . . . , uh consummated the act."

"I know he hurt her!" she wailed, sounding like a steam locomotive approaching Big Otter crossing.

The little man collected the wet, disappointed looking collie, then led both his dogs away while talking to them in soothing tones. Frankly, I couldn't why she was so upset. Jarhead had managed to effect liaison with a dog once again larger than himself and Herbie obviously had done pretty much the same thing at some point. The bawling woman must have liked it. Otherwise, Herbie wouldn't enjoy the power position he appeared to hold.

"Jarhead," I told the emotionally unfilled bulldog as we rattled our way through the brush. "You really did it up brown this time.

It's piss and punk time, kid. I'm putting you on Gravy Train and water for a week!"

Jarhead wouldn't even look at me. *"Throwed me in the river, just when I was getting a good grip!"*

Little did that bulldog know . . .

Patty was sitting with her feet dangling in the cold water. She didn't raise her head when we approached. "Patty, you were right. I should have left him on the leash. You won't believe what he did this time."

"I would too. I climbed a tree just in time to see you throw them into the river and I . . . Oh, Clay!" She sprang up and buried her head in my chest. "I am so embarrassed I feel like throwing myself into the river."

"Jarhead does things like that all the time. I'd shoot him, but he does make life interesting."

"Not Jarhead. Me! I am so embarrassed at the things I said and let you do -- and I did. Oh, Lord!"

I held her at half-arm length and looked directly into her eyes. She tried to burrow into my chest again, but I held her tight and maintained lock with her big, gray eyes. "You didn't do anything, Patty, except what is natural. You told me how you felt and I told you how I felt.

"Relationships usually start with flirting, which is nothing more than light sexual innuendos. You and I, we missed most of that stage somehow, but there's nothing wrong with being honest and direct like we were today. The petting? Why not? We're grown folks."

"But, darling, we almost . . . you Know! And being excited, I forgot Jarhead was watching. Do you think he seen?"

"No, he was up the river trying to do the same thi . . . uh, he didn't see anything." I tried to pet her, just to make her feel better, but she didn't want petted. Her eagerness had disappeared and I was glad. I was going to buy Jarhead a six-pack of Rolling Rock because his actions had prevented me from having her. The last thing I needed, other than another Purple Heart, was a little Patterson-Berkeley wood's colt hanging on my pant's leg. Also, I was very much afraid I would hurt Patty. She was so tiny I just didn't see how she could possibly accept a normal man without a lot of pain. I strongly suspected Gunny's lecture on virgin female anatomy was way off-center.

The sun was making its last stand against the coolness of the coming twilight as I crunched across the gravel in front of Patty's sprawling, white, two-story farmhouse.

"Clay, I'm going to be direct again. May we go out tonight? Just the two of us? To a fancy place such as Green Hills?"

My intentions had been to return Jarhead home, then steam about to see if I couldn't alleviate my own emotionally unfilled state. But, doom to me, it was no longer theory that I had the will power of Doctor Leary in a chemical lab when Patty shifted into that little girl voice. It was now scientific law.

"Sure, Patty. Want me to pick you up?"

"I will meet you at Moe's at eight-thirty." She opened the door, hesitated, then threw herself back into the truck and did her lamprey imitation again. Jarhead yelped when we smothered him between us and the upright gear shift. Probably so did her mama -- if she was watching.

I fed the boys, dressed in civilian attire I considered suitable for Green Hills Supper Club, then hit the bricks for Moe's. I was finishing my first beer when a tremor went through the building.

"**EARTHQUAKE**!" a barfly shrieked as he and three other 'flies fell from their bar stools and tried to crowd under a table. I was about to join them, then realized Gunnery Sergeant Thorton and his Lady had failed in their effort to walk abreast through the wide door. They disengaged, maneuvered smartly through the door single-file and lumbered to the bar.

"Elizabeth, this is Master Chief Clay Berkeley, who I told you about. Clay is one of the few anchor clankers I admit to knowing." Gunny said, pulling her tightly against him. "Watch him now, he's a sneaky, little fellow." They trumpeted and danced around while taking friendly little slaps at one another that would have pole axed a raging bull.

"Save the **BEER**!" screamed a 'fly.

I, at six feet and about one hundred and eighty pounds, was near midget size compared to Gunny and Elizabeth. I'd never seen Elizabeth up close, so I examined her critically. She in no way looked old enough to have retired from the Army as a major, as Gunny had said. She had black, shoulder length hair and smooth, tanned skin. She was wearing a well-fitting, yellow dress and a strand of pearls she didn't get in any five and dime store. She was quite pretty and shapely. She was not fat -- just big!

"Elizabeth, do you realize associating with a Marine is detrimental to your reputation?"

She squeezed Gunny around the waist with an arm the size of a mine prop. "I like my little koala bear, Clay -- even if he is one of those horrible Marines. My old Army drill instructor would be quite unhappy to know I am dating a Marine. He, and others, repeatedly warned female OCS candidates about Marines and sailors!"

They muzzled each other a few times, about like two hippos contemplating mating. They broke apart in what seemed four or five minutes, then straddled two bar stools on my port side. Their sterns touched in the space between the two stools. They occupied the same sitting space as three normal sized people. It was a good thing Moe purchased strong stools. Otherwise, the country on the opposite side of the world would have declared war.

Elizabeth leaned over and like to buried my upper shoulder beneath her starboard breast. "I hope you will come and take supper with us soon."

Gunny commenced twitching around like he had a bad case of crabs. I feared the worst.

"Uh, Master Chief -- Steven, Elizabeth's boy, is staying with his dad at Fort Campbell for the rest of the summer and I'm going to be, that is . . . me and Elizabeth are going to --"

"Delbert! Honey, shame on you! It is not as though we are shacking up." She batted porthole size hazel eyes at me. "After all, we are in love."

Delbert? I never knew the "D" in Randall D. Thorton stood for Delbert. The poor man. I loved it!

We had an interesting conversation as to what constituted "shacking up" and what did not. But, I was never able to work "Delbert" into the conversation without making Elizabeth aware I was pinging on Gunny's sissy name.

"There's Patty!" Gunny leaped off the bar stood with the force of a Sherman tank falling boom head to pier.

"There it goes **AGAIN**! It's the New Madrid Fault!" screamed a barfly at the far end of the bar.

"Gracious, what was Mister Burke yelling about?" Patty asked, after she'd kissed me on the cheek (thus marking her territory) and had been introduced to Elizabeth. I didn't know the last names of the barflies after almost two years of association while Patty already knew their full names, where they had worked, where they lived, what sort of family they had, everything. Patty was just too damned smart for words!

"He thinks we're having earthquakes. Something in the beer, I suspect."

Elizabeth took immediate charge. She hammer-locked little Patty under about twenty pounds of solid flesh and bellowed, "You boys are dying to scuttlebutt together. You can spare your fiancée so we can get acquainted." Elizabeth then dragged Patty to a distant booth.

I really did feel the earth quake, when I heard that "F" word.

"Delbert, what did Elizabeth mean, 'fiancée?'"

"Don't call me Delbert!" Gunny snarled, real mean. "I hate Delbert! I agree with what you once said about how, deep down, females have a hard-on for males. I now know that one way they get even is to give us foolish names, or addressing us by the sissy names our mothers gave us. Randall or Randy is okay, but will Elizabeth call me by those? She will not. She insists 'Delbert' has class."

"Gunny," I was afraid to call him 'Delbert' again, "If you don't get off this 'Clay loves Patty' kick, I'm going to borrow an antitank gun off the Army and waste you!"

Gunny looked down the bar to see if anybody was listening. They didn't appear to be, most were so far gone in their cups they couldn't have heard a cow bell next to their ear. "Aw, hell, Clay. Irene hinted to Elizabeth she'd threw you over for Kenneth and now you are getting ready to marry Patty on the rebound. I never said anything . . . not really."

"I'm going to get a recruiter who's married to a Sicilian to put a contract out on Irene. Gunny, who is this Kenneth, exactly?"

"I met him, finally. We ran into Irene and him in Hawk's Nest Bar. Well-turned man. He's a master chief boatswain's mate at the reserve center. He said he was here three-four years ago and liked West Virginia so much he sniveled his way back. He wasn't at the reserve center last time. He was in recruiting. I suspect he was Irene's first travel claims client."

"That blows the bosun's pipe!"

"I'd bet money on it."

Gunny could be quite crude!

Patty and I finally made our escape, but only because Gunny and Elizabeth had an early morning bowling game.

"They are an overpowering couple!" Patty said, emphatically, when we were seated in the elegant quietness of the Green Hills Supper Club. She giggled. "I now understand what you meant by hotels not letting them in more than once."

"Can you imagine them bowling together? I wouldn't want to be driving in that part of town. It'd be hell on the truck's shocks and springs!"

"Dearest," Patty said in her little girl voice, "Elizabeth thinks we are more than we are."

I didn't tell her Elizabeth subscribed to Gunny's rat housed ideas and had probably already helped him polish his dress sword for the wedding ceremony. I did tell her what Irene had scuttlebutted all over town. I finished by telling her it was a pity that such a ridiculous story was making the rounds.

"You think it is ridiculous? Am I that bad?" Her lower lip quivered.

That I didn't need, particularly when I didn't say anything about her being bad. Bad was not a word in my vocabulary when it came to Patricia Lane Patterson. Strange that the word

182

'ridiculous' upset her so, particularly when the word seemed to fit the scuttlebutt quite well.

"I didn't mean 'ridiculous.' I meant funny, sort of."

"I do not think it either ridiculous -- or funny." Patty said, giving me that look again.

I stood up and caught the back of her chair. "Care to dance, Fiancée?"

"I said it was not funny, Clay!"

It didn't seem a gut buster to me either.

That night I dreamed of Gunny and Elizabeth polishing a dress sword and laughing. I didn't see Patty in the dream, but had the feeling she was cheering them on.

The old gal mustered into the dream too. She stared at me for a tick, then smiled. I decided I was never going to understand what I was trying to dream about, not with my animals going totally off-center and waking me up every time I dreamed about the old woman.

CHAPTER NINETEEN

TAKE SEPARATE STATIONS

Patty snapped me up when I crawled out of my truck the next morning in the church parking lot. She gave my cheek a little pat, caress, stroke, thump, whatever, with her gloved hand before catching me under the arm, leading me into the church and down the long aisle to the fourth pew back. She walked with her little sun-streaked head reared back like she was extremely proud of something. I was reminded of Samson.

The preacher reverted from Deuteronomy he'd been hammering on for a couple of Sundays all the way back to Genesis. He must have forgotten to mention a mighty important point in an earlier sermon because, from what I'd seen, he was a real stick to it kind of fellow. He didn't spend a whole lot of time on the ' . . . and saw it was good' parts.

He whipped right into beating The Snake. He peppered Adam, Eve, The Snake and all who came afterwards with a barrage of fire and brimstone with a few bolts of chain lightening thrown in for good measure. I could almost feel sulfur fumes curling up around my feet. It wouldn't have surprised me greatly to have felt the prick of a pitchfork between my fifth and sixth ribs.

The preacher didn't subscribe to that story I'd heard about Adam and Eve getting into so much trouble over a handful of apples. He backed and filled a lot, but there was no doubt in my military mind what those two did to each other. It had nothing at all to do with apples.

There were scads of "Ohing" and "Ahing" going on with a few moans thrown in. Women twitched around in their seats, fanned themselves with funeral home fans and wiped their cheeks and necks with hankies. Men kept crossing and uncrossing their legs and slipping their hands into their pockets. I could almost hear the sizzling. I figured considerable fruitful and multiplying drills would be conducted shortly after that congregation got home.

Patty didn't get all worked up like most of the rest of the folks -- those below the ages of ninety-five, or thereabouts. Either she didn't understand the process and really thought apple theft was involved, or she'd forgotten our little Garden of Eden the previous day and what she'd almost done -- to say nothing of what she had done with her busy little fingers.

The Snake was proud of her!

Mister Patterson mustered me up after we'd filed out of church. He dragged me under the shade of the gnarled cherry tree where the men congregated after services and introduced me around. To hear him tell it, I was practically running the entire United States Canoe Club with no help, except a peg-legged captain and one admiral who wasn't very bright.

The Snake was going to get him too.

There weren't nearly so many people socializing around, the women with the women and the men with the men, like on previous Sundays. I chalked that up to the fact that most of the couples had hauled out of there like the church exploded. They probably wanted to get a session of creating drills out of the way before Sunday dinner. A lot of kids were going play outside, whether they wanted to or not

I'd thought the food in the Patterson house was outstanding in previous weeks, but that Sunday's meal was even better. It was the best food I'd had the pleasure of tasting, and that included meals in some of Spain's better restaurants. We chowed down on country ham, fried spring chicken with giblet gravy, mashed potatoes, creamed peas and carrots, the Patterson's usual fifteen or twenty side dishes and a sliced tomato, leaf lettuce and cucumber salad straight from their garden. The angel food cake was light and moist and big enough to feed those the preacher had cussed out, including The Snake.

Mister and Missus Patterson were a whole lot friendlier toward me than in previous weeks when I'd felt like the duty leper. While I hadn't felt they exactly hated me, I suspected they would have rejoiced mightily had the earth risen up and smote me.

Missus Patterson bragged on how good Patty had prepared dinner and how clever and helpful she was, how she sewed her own dresses, kept a vegetable garden and milked eighteen head of cows before school, and such along similar lines.

Mister Patterson kept addressing me as "Son" and even forced a huge, greenish cigar on me when we went out on the porch after dinner. That puzzled me. He was stingy with his stogies. It was puzzling the way he kept talking about how valuable Patty was to him and how she helped him in buying and selling cattle, timber and coal.

Patty acted different too. She didn't hover around to protect me from her folks like on previous Sundays. She appeared ever so often, gave us a beaming smile, then bounced off with a serene look on her face -- something like you'd expect to see on the face of a fanatical nun watching the burning of a heretic.

Why, the way they treated me, you'd have thought I was a member of the family!

Mister Patterson was really getting whipped up as to how Patty took care of the account books, prepared his complicated tax

186

returns and how she operated heavy farm machinery when Patty came out all dressed up for the movies. She snapped me off the swing, led me off the porch and down the walk. I shifted into my hang-back mode, so I could engineer a cornering look at Patty moving under her flowered dress. I could see considerable under that dress even with what was a light slip or a lining. Whatever it was, it didn't help a lot. That silk dress was thin! What she had beneath it was skimpy too. I wondered if she realized she exhibited almost as much as other young women -- or would have had the neck of her dress been cut Deep South.

I wrapped my arm around her shoulders after we seated our-selves in the movie house, just as the mouse plugged the cat into an electrical socket. Patty reached across, caught my other hand and plopped it down on her upper lap -- right where the heat is. She stroked and played with my hand and unconsciously run her fingers under my sleeve and sort of tweaked at the hairs on my arms. Every time I moved my arm, she'd make a happy little sound, smile at me, then clamp my hand even more tightly against the place where her thighs met the rest of her. I was sweating like a liberal in a redneck bar. It was dark in the movie house, but I could see she was radiating red. I had suspicions she was thinking the same I was, only different. When the lights came on, I was nervous as the cat after the mouse finished with him.

We started at Moe's, but there must have been a mail tie-up. The barflies were short of ready funds, thirsty and mean. They latched hold of me before I hardly got a foot in the door.

"Hey, thar, Boot Camp! Didn't we'uns buy yu uh beer on Washington's Birthday, or whatever th' hell they call hit now?"

After we'd listened to how it was in The Big One, WW Two, and I'd bought enough beer to float Elizabeth, we hauled tail out of there and shifted our flag to Turtle Inn at Patty's request.

187

That place, much touted among the crowd of which Patty was a card-carrying member, was one of those modern, well-lighted dives with pale paneling and odd shaped tables and chairs that looked and functioned like they were the fabrication of drunken Seabees, or sober Air Force Base Engineers. I could hardly move without a tropical fern or some other damned strange looking plant, attacking me. I didn't like the place.

I particularly didn't like the huge, tanned civilian who zipped over to our table almost as soon as we got situated. King Kong stood there flipping Tarzan hair off his babyish face while he prated to Patty about how much fun they'd had in college and how much he was going to miss her now that they'd graduated. He didn't say beans to me. He didn't introduce himself or give Patty room to do so either.

Patty had graduated a few days before. She'd wanted me to attend her graduation, but had been unable to obtain a late-date seat, which didn't make me mad. I could imagine some big, older fellow with a fourteen-inch cigar and a stretch Cadillac complete with paid for platinum blonde wife about one-third his age, grabbing me by the arm and saying, "Hello there! I'm Ralph and I'm smart. I graduated in nineteen-oh-whatever I have a Doctorate in Quadrant Physics and a Master's in Brain Surgery. What is your degree?"

"Oh," I would have to had said, "If my credits mesh correctly, I expect to complete a major in Italian Traffic Management with a minor in Antarctic Freezer Maintenance in the next fifteen or twenty years."

I'd have impressed the hell out of them.

I recalled how Patty acted at her graduation party when she unwrapped my present, a deep burgundy, leather attaché case with her name inscribed on a small, gold plate. She'd gotten tears in her eyes and kissed me right in front of God and everybody.

THE LAUNCHING

My Popeye meter peaked when Old Whoever-the-hell started petting Patty on the shoulder and tittering about some party they'd attended. I couldn't stands no more! "Why don't you drag up a chair and stay a while, Brucie? Two or three minutes, even"

"My name is not Brucie." he said, haughtily.

I stared meaningfully at the skin-tight crotch of his purplish pants. "Really?"

He reddened, mumbled about having to scrub chickens, or some such, then evacuated the area.

"What was that all about, Clay?"

"Just a little male bonding, Patty." I said, smugly.

"Oh," Patty hugged herself. "I cannot believe I am a graduate!"

"Come September, you can pin your hair in a bun, get yourself some granny glasses and a pointing stick to club them with and venture bravely into the Halls of Elementary Education."

"Oh, Clay. I am going to teach second grade. We do not beat them!"

"Missus Wasmer did."

"Did she really abuse you in the second grade?"

"Third grade, actually. But I'm not certain who was doing the abusing. Her nerves were shot. We'd cut a rumpus, The Gates would open and the Wrath of God would descend about our heads and shoulders. She missed her calling. She ought to have played baseball. With her back to the room, she could spot a miscreant, whirl around, then lay a piece of chalk right along the side of his skull. I tell you, she could bean a woodchuck's as . . . er, hit a kid at fifty Daniel Boone paces. She paddled me so many times I started looking forward to them."

189

Patty let go with one of her rich, whooping laughs then leaned back in her chair and had a healthy stretch. Her small breasts perked out nicely. Fine superstructure for its size. "Oh, Clay-honey, I am having so much fun since I met you. I will miss you terribly while I am in Bluefield."

Pestilence! I'd forgotten she was leaving in the morning to get her teaching certification. I felt a bad pang of loneliness. I reached across the table and caught her warm hand. "I'll miss you too, Patty. I'm accustomed to having you around. It'll be lonely with you not here to keep me hope . . . er, company."

"I am glad." she said, quietly. "I will miss you just bunches! I hope the month passes quickly. It should. I have been told I will not enjoy a minute to myself. What are you going to do while I am away?"

"Same as before, I reckon."

"WHAAAT?" she cried, jerked straight up, and knocked her tall beer glass over.

An alert Brucie Clone rushed to mop it up.

I gathered she did not like my answer, but I waited until Mister Show-it-all-off finished wiping the table and departed to get her a refill.

"What I meant, Patty, was I'll just work and hang around. Got nobody to steam with now that Gunny is shac . . . uh, spending his time with Elizabeth."

"Poor dearest. I will be terribly lonely too." she said, patting me on the hand.

I didn't think she needed to know I didn't intend to remain lonely long.

I initially thought it was the Brucie Clone, but it was Brucie himself who brought Patty's beer and set it on the table. "I thought

I'd buy you a drink, Patty, just for old times' sake." He said, cutely, like they had a secret.

We had obviously attended different schools. He'd have gotten his chow grabbing devices ripped off at the wrists had he tried that trick in a CPO or officer's club. Regardless, I believe I would have remained my civilized self if he had not dropped about ten pounds of hand on my arm and said, "Let's discuss that 'Brucie' remark!"

I edged his hand off and stood up.

He didn't love that move and backed up a bit. "I must inform you that I am an accomplished boxer. I received a Letter in college. I played football too."

I gave him one of my best CPO-type glares. "I was on the fleet dogging wrench squad myself." I slid my hand toward my hip pocket. "I carry one with me. It's kind of like wearing your sporting expertise on your sweater, I suppose."

He made a couple of conciliatory remarks, said goodbye to Patty and hauled to starboard. I don't believe he knew that a dogging wrench is a short pipe used to dog down hatches (adjust sailors' attitudes too in olden days) but he apparently had no interest in seeing one.

"I cannot believe how he acted!" Patty said, in a shocked voice. "He intended to strike you!"

"He reconsidered. I'm glad he did. I hate violence, particularly when I'm the one violenced."

She gave a nervous little giggle. "Why do you suppose he acted that way? He acted peculiar when we arrived too."

"I'd say he is mighty jealous. He's not exactly fond of us being together."

"Oh."

"That, Patty, is my considered opinion."

"Oh."

I ordered another beer, seeing as how Pretty Boy bought a fresh beer for Patty and none for me -- a *Senso unico* sort of fellow.

"May I tell you something, dearest?"

That little girl voice again!

"Can't you always?"

"You might not like this, Clay-honey.

I didn't think I'd like raw fish either -- and I didn't.

"I dated him for a while last fall."

"I can see no reason why you shouldn't have. He seems almost half-bright and he's nearly as pretty as Curtis." My voice sounded stiffer than I would have liked.

"I kissed him too."

"The 'few times' you told me about?" Really stiff voice that time.

"Not exactly . . . I kissed him good night a few times, but they were tiny, little pecks, really. I kissed him big twice -- only twice, and those were absolutely nothing in the way of how I kiss you! Clay-honey, I never even considered letting him do *any* of the *things* you have been allowed!

"I last kissed him at Joan's Halloween party. I might have kissed him again, except he became grabby and tried to entice me upstairs. I knew people were doing a lot more than kissing in those bedrooms! When I told him what I thought of that idea, he became quite agitated, so I collected my wraps and left. He was not the man with whom I wanted to . . . er, evidently he thought I would

192

participate in . . . Things. Not with him!" Patty explained, now a flat out red.

I wished I'd doggin' wrenched him. If I had had a dogging wrench.

The old lady in the long, gray dress mustered in again that night, but the dream never progressed past her just smiling at me because I woke up with my animals growling and hissing and trying to crawl beneath the blankets. I was beginning to study on how the animals waking me up related to the old lady type dreams. I couldn't understand why my animals would care what I dreamed, or how they would know. It was all very confusing.

CHAPTER TWENTY

INDEPENDENT STEAMING

Exactly seventy-two hours after I returned from my trip, not counting the weekend, the chief recruiter took me to task for failing to submit my travel claim within the specified time. That told me Irene was serious about no longer filling out my claims.

Shortly after I reported on recruiting duty, Irene had so kindly explained that she would be most happy to fill out the claims and would require only a rough itinerary. The word somehow circulated (probably via Angie, who detested Irene) that I steamed with Irene only because I needed her to complete my travel claims. My friends, of course, deliberately refused to recognize my day-to-day administration burden was far heavier than a simple travel claim. Far be it for them to let loose of a bone they could needle me about!

My complaint was with the system, not with submitting the claim. What with the low rate of per diem, I usually spent all the government gave me plus money out of my own pocket because the per diem granted wasn't enough to cover more than modest room and board. Then, to add to the sorry situation, the bean counters required a lengthy, detailed itinerary and accounting of

194

funds expended in hopes they could recoup a portion of the pittance.

I was not fond of wasting my time filling out the damned form, but now that Irene had stopped doing them, the only person in the entire zone I could have tricked into filling them out was Book. Unfortunately, he needed help filling out his pay chit. I armed myself with a cup of coffee and a weed I bummed from the nonstandard FBI agent and turned to mightily on the very first travel claim I'd personally submitted since reporting to recruiting.

TRAVEL CLAIM; INPUT FOR

NAME: H. Clay Berkeley

RANK: Master Chief Radioman

ORGANIZATION: NRD Big Otter, WV

TRAVEL AUTHORIZATION NUMBER: Unknown

REASON FOR TRAVEL: Supervise and Deputize

PLACE OF DEPARTURE: Berkeley's Knob

DAY/TIME TRAVEL COMMENCED: Tuesday - 0500

PLACE/TIME OF ARRIVAL: Merriville via Pickens - 1100

REASON FOR STOP: Supervise and Deputize

COST OF LODGING: $54.00

COST OF BREAKFAST: $10.00

COST OF LUNCH: $8.00

COST OF SUPPER: $52.00 (*Supper: Six Budweiser sandwiches, plus the two Andy Jackson's I put in the till for the troops.*)

NIGHT MEAL: $00.00

GASOLINE: $00.00 (*Who the hell knows? I pumped the gas out of my farm tank. It'd even out at tax time.*)

OIL/LUBRICANTS: $00.00

MISC. FLUIDS: $00.00

BREAKDOWN REPAIRS: $00.00

I filled the other dozen or so blocks and the applicable portions for the second day of travel, clipped the receipt from the motel to the form, polished a few administrative details, signed it with a flourish and flipped it in the guard mail box.

I realized the Mark One - Mod Zero bilge I'd submitted would be rejected and I'd eventually have to fill out the form correctly, but I didn't intend to do so until I absolutely had to. I saw no reason to cease making life as confusing and as difficult for bureaucrats as my brain could devise. Playing dumb sometimes produces far better results than exhibiting smarts -- particularly when working with bureaucrats. It provides more enjoyment too!

That done, I shifted my Flag to Moe's

Checks had arrived or the 'flies had taken up pimping off women from the Old Folk's Home. They were flush with cash and making like suction dredges on the Mississippi. I went over and tried to get a war story, but they wanted to cuss politicians among themselves and lie about the hot little numbers they'd known in the 'Thirties and 'Forties.

None of my running mates were present, so I held mental muster on everybody I would have liked present.

Patty was learning the teacher trade in Bluefield. Gunny was probably playing in flour. Angie's was probably giving seapersonship lessons to Charles. Book was on leave tending a sick aunt, probably a lie. Keys probably couldn't get his liberty card. Sergeant Major McCormick was probably with his dens of thieves, copying Navy press gang tactics.

It was damned lonely. I couldn't remember when I'd been so totally alone, except when I was driving alone and sometimes when sleeping. I wasn't qualified in TV watching. It looked like a night of reading, for which I was qualified, except there was nothing in the house I wanted to read just then. There wasn't anything available downtown so late in the evening, except skin books. I damned sure didn't need reminders of my womanless state.

After a second beer, my few remaining brain cells cleared their electrical short and started computing again. Underway! Shift Colors!

Pearl's Place smelled good. I'd almost forgotten how pleasant half-naked women smelled after they'd danced and flopped their tools at paying customers during stage appearances.

I ordered a beer while I admired my frosted blonde friend as she jerked and twisted on the small stage. Her daddy might not have left her any money, but her mommy surely gave her some fine tools. After she'd cleaned everyone slack-jawing at the stage bar of ready dollars bills, she bounded off the platform, evaded several hands and fended off half a dozen firm offers while she pranced toward me through the crowed club.

"Hi, Clay! I haven't seen you in weeks, not since you abandoned me in the hotel."

"I didn't abandon you, Claire. I had an appointment that morning. I wouldn't have gotten there had I woke you up."

"You have that right! I'd have taken the remainder of the weekend off." she said, moving a tool to where it really bothered me. "Clay, I don't have to dance for a while. Would you like to sit and talk?"

Do owls hoot?

We found a dark, deserted corner with a two-person sofa and ordered her a drink that didn't cost much more than a ride on the Concorde. After a while, I laid a hint on her concerning the night ahead.

"We've been friends for a long while now, Clay, even before you pulled that maniac off me at Pink Place. Honey, I don't want to see you waste your money."

I understood the game. B-girls didn't like their lovers to spend money in their club, not with so many other cattle to noose, lasso, hitch, hog-tie, whatever. Claire was no different.

"Where do you want me to pick you up after work, Claire?"

She caught my face in her hands and looked me directly in the eyes. "I think bunches of you. Not just for the rescue at Pink Place. I liked you way before that nut grabbed me. You never acted like you had the right to feel me up just because you bought me drinks. You didn't try to buy me. You were always a gentleman and I liked you, so I decided to sleep with you. It just happened that I decided to do it the night that idiot attacked me when I was on my way to meet you. God, I'm glad you were there on time!

"I'm glad I slept with you too. We had some very fine romps. I really appreciate the way you treated me. I really do. But, I don't sleep with married men. Not ever."

"I agree, Claire. Married folks shouldn't sleep around."

198

"Don't tease, Clay. You're married."

"I'm **WHAAAT**?"

"Married. I just hate it too."

"Where'd you get such an atrocious idea? You know I'm not married. You stayed at my house one Saturday night after we went to the Street Fair. Remember"

"Yes, I remember. I had a wonderful time! You weren't married then."

"I'm not married now!"

"Clay, it's not nice to lie to a woman who likes you as much as I do."

"If this is some sort of joke, it's sick. If it's not a joke, then one of us has lost their lashings, and it's not me!"

"It's not a joke. Not to me. I liked you taking me places and treating me like I was your sweetheart, not like I was a girl you picked up in a titty club. Everybody says you're married."

"Then everybody is screwed up like a three-decker soup sandwich! I'm not married. I have not ever been married. I'm not ever going to be married -- not on Halloween, Christmas, or Leap Year. Do you understand, Claire?"

"Small men lie. You are not a small man. Several people, both men and women, have talked about you marrying a young girl. They hinted you had to get married. Is that why you are out catting around so soon? Because she got pregnant and you didn't want to marry her?"

"I didn't have to . . . Damn it, woman! I'm not married!"

"Clay, what your doing isn't right. This is no way to start a marriage. And it is no way to keep one even if you did have to marry -- it being so quick and all."

199

There were going to be some new big winners at liar's dice in The Great Over Yonder, several of them, male and female, once I figured out who had spread such trash.

I threw myself on the mercy of the court and begged.

"Clay, if you need anything, anything at all, I'll help, but I'm not going to sleep with you. I don't sleep around and I'm certainly not going to sleep with a married man. Go home, honey. I'm going to start crying if you stay here."

I hit every bar I knew, but there wasn't one single female on the loose. I called some women from my past, but they either weren't home, or were going with someone. Two of them actually hung up on me! Finally, in desperation, I went to the only other girlie bar within many miles, Pink Place. That was a sure thing, A Pink Place dancer had made sly runs on me when Claire had worked there.

I barely made it through the door before Paige, the small redhead I'd come to see, ask why I had treated Claire so mean. I told her it was all a misunderstanding. I asked her to sit and have a drink, so I could explain, but she refused. She said she wasn't about to mess with a no-count, dirty-minded man so low down he'd knock up a girl half his age, then run off and get married without even telling his girlfriend before he did it.

I returned to Moe's to drink myself silly while I contemplated my enemies and my sins. Murder was on my mind -- or at least a lengthy series of doggin' wrenching once I learned who was trying to drive me totally ape.

CHAPTER TWENTY-ONE

FAIR WINDS AND FOLLOWING SEAS

The chief recruiter informed me mid-afternoon Friday that my travel claim was less than perfect, only the Name, Rank and Organization were pusser. It was en route via guard mail for resubmission. I was pondering my next move on the game board of government administration when Book called to inform me of a very special applicant he was putting on the bus Sunday night ready, willing and able to join the Navy.

The applicant was a seventeen-year-old, high school graduate who qualified for everything the Navy offered. He had absolutely no interest in college, but dreamed great dreams of sailing to distant ports in his bell-bottoms. Probably girls crossed his mind too, particularly after Book had gotten his hands on him. Book had been carrying the lad in his Tracking System for months and frequently offered him as one of his projected accessions. The young man was, in fact, ready and willing, but not able. He never arrived at the examining center because his mother would not sign consent, no matter how Book pleaded.

"Book I told you to forget that kid until he is eighteen. Do I have to come to Fallen Ash and lay a course correction on your skull? Damn it, stop giving me his name!".

"I got th' signed consent form right here in front uh me."

"Book, you can go to the brig for forgery!"

"Master Chief, thet boy's mama's so ugly ain't no way she could even get her uh job in uh bar on East Main Street in Norfolk. She's flat-out, mule ugly!"

I'd seen a few of Book's female friends. I simply could not fathom what she must look like if he thought she was ugly, or what her looks had to do with her giving consent.

"What I decided t' do, after yu done chewed on me like some kinda boot seaman, wuz thet I wuz a-goin' t' have t' decide t' do something. What I done did wuz taken her out last night. I wined an' I dined her 'till her false teeth done fell out. Thet wine wuz near four dollars uh bottle! I writ hit up on my expense sheet. When I got her actin' right good, I done taken her home and put th' Navy in her . . . an' now, I'm a-goin' t' put her boy in th' Navy."

"Master Chief, ain't nobody got more degradation than thet! Why, I bet John Paul Jones didn't have degradation thet good. If yu wuz t' do right, yu'd put how much degradation I got t' the Navy in my evaluation."

Book waited until I stopped laughing before asking is he'd won Station of the Quarter, for the preceding quarter. I told him his Letter of Commendation would be presented by the captain when Irene's people got it typed

"Master Chief, ain't hit yur rule thet th' Station of the Quarter RINC or one uh his recruiters what he wants t' send, gits to go on 'em Educator Orientation Visits down t' Orlando?"

We filled a Navy 727 with civilian educators each quarter and flew them all expense paid to Naval Training Center, Orlando, Florida. There they observed their previous students undergoing recruit training and attending Navy schools. They were given a first class tour of the facilities during which they were invited to inspect the curriculum and offer suggestions. They were usually quite impressed and almost invariably became centers of influence. Money well spent

Their change in attitude, assuming they didn't care much for the Navy before the trip, wasn't difficult to understand. Their previous tobacco chewing, marijuana smoking, girl crazy male students were now bright, clean, well-groomed, girl crazy young men. Their previous gum popping, cigarette puffing, marijuana smoking, boy crazy female students were now bright, clean, well-groomed, boy crazy young women. Their ex-students were studying subjects such as Administration, Electricity and Electronics, Computers and other subjects that required a fair degree of brain power when only months before they couldn't count the number of pencils in their locker. Their ex-students addressing them as "Sir" and "Ma'am" didn't hurt either.

There was no way I was going to expose a plane load of educators to Engineman First Class Eugene "Book" Rodney Arnet, for three whole days! I thought I'd reason with him before I took the only other possible route -- lie. "Book, I never sent you because you said hanging with teachers is no fun. I didn't want to send you where you'd be unhappy."

"They ain't no fun, Master Chief, but Ellen Ann is a-gettin' right damned mean 'bout me a-goin' out and a-stayin' out all night with the boys. That ugly mama didn't help much, even if I did tell my old woman I wuz out a-runnin' with you. I need me some regulation liberty bad! I'm near hard up as one uh 'em you-nicks thet them A-rab fellows use t' keep women straight."

"Book, I don't send recruiters to Orlando to pull liberty. I send them to escort the educators and keep them happy."

"I heerd 'bout 'em EOV's," Book said, darkly.

"Book, are you asking to go on the next EOV?" I thought that ought to confuse him.

'I done said thet. Didn't I say thet? Yeah, I did say thet."

I sighed. It was getting harder and harder to derail Book's mind, probably something in the beer. "Yes, Book, you did. But I have to clear it with the chief recruiter (big fib) because he likes to brief EOV escorts (bigger fib) and . . . aw, hell, Book, he thinks escorts should be young, second hitch sailors (biggest fib.)"

"Angie went. Barbara went. Ferguson went. Lewis went. Hit ain't fair an' hit ain't square I win uh bunch uh times an' yu never did ask nothin' 'bout did I want t' go. Makes me think yu' kinda 'spect somethin' ain't right with me."

There was no doubt Book had his one duck in a row.

"Book, I can't promise anything. I'll get back with you."

"OK. Say, yu'd better not hold any kinda visit down here fer maybe uh dozen weeks. Ellen Ann is right pissed at yu a-keeping me out all last night. She done said she is a-goin' to cut yu. Hit'll take me uh coon's age t' get her off'n her high horse. Hit were her birthday yesterday."

I called the skipper direct because the chief recruiter was at Area. It was just as well he was out of town. He was getting up in years and probably wouldn't have weathered this one.

The skipper let loose with a string of "No's" coupled with gasping noises closely resembling a Hong Kong water taxis' one-lunger engine. When he did start using real words again, his usual clear speech was noticeably absent. I told him I agreed with whatever he'd said, but I still didn't have a viable excuse not to send Book on the EOV.

We kicked it around for about thirty-five minutes while discussing various possibilities: send Book and his recruiters on leave during the EOV; bribe a doctor to quarantine the entire Fallen Ash station until it was over; put Book on restriction for any one of his many past falls from grace. Our worst idea was to send him and his recruiters on a 'training' trip to CRUITCOM in Washington. We rejected that idea. We didn't need the admiral and the president mad at us. Finally, the skipper gave a long sigh. Being a navy-trained salesman, I recognized the sign as a decision made.

"Master Chief, I am going to give an entire airplane load of educators a significant emotional event. I'm going to let Petty Officer Arnet go on the EOV. Let this be recorded as my last feeble minded act in this command."

"Captain, you know I don't blow smoke, but I never before seen you make anything approaching a feeble-minded decision. The decision you just made will be your first."

"I'm being transferred, Master Chief. I'm to report as Commanding Officer of Elk City Reserve Center at the end of the month. The XO will take over until they find an officer who subscribes to the party line."

"Captain, did my pissing off the commodore cause this?"

"It may have contributed, but it did not cause it. I believe someone in CRUITCOM read my research document and became erratic because it is not complimentary to naval recruiting. Frequent discussions with the commodore concerning who commands this district did not help

"I actually believed our situation was improving after the commodore realized none of his districts had a chance of completing the display cases as scheduled and extended their full compilation until the end of the year. He even expressed his opinion that Big Otter had made more progress on the cases than other districts. He did not overly complain about the Hinkle situation either.

"Well, I must get back to training the XO for my job. Notify Book and standby for a ram! Even the Lord might have difficulty foreseeing what Book will do in Orlando."

I returned to my office, notified Book he would go on the upcoming EOV, then locked my safe. I didn't care that it was not yet seventeen hundred and I didn't care if anyone ranking lower than John Paul Jones tried to find me.

I arrived at Moe's and ordered a beer, which came with a few insults from Moe. Things were just not pusser, not by half. My professional life had now reached the same level as my love life, that of whale manure in the bottom of the Marianas Trench.

I contemplated my love life -- something I no longer possessed. I had been totally unable to scrounge up even one female since Patty left, even after I lowered my standards to near Book's level. It seemed every available female in the entire county had been abducted by UFOs, pirates, or maybe vampires. The women on whom I managed to put a full power run acted nothing like I expected. They simply were not interested. My plan to spend a weekend in Marriville crashed and burned too. Gloria had left on an extended cruise in the Caribbean.

My Clarksburg COI let me down too. He obtained Janet Bailey only a partial scholarship. He promised to keep trying, but didn't hold much hope for obtaining a full scholarship.

Pens had the gull hard on the black lung claim, but it was taking longer than I thought it would when I initiated the hook up.

The Hinkle situation had not worked to my satisfaction either. I really wanted to see him punished, but the Bailey's wouldn't give NCIS a statement. So, with our hands tied, I wrote an evaluation that should keep Hinkle from advancing to CPO in the foreseeable future and we transferred him to Guam.

My relationship with the chief recruiter had reached a new low. After a couple of yelling and screaming matches, we stopped speaking, except when duty made it imperative.

Even Moe's beer tasted lousy.

I went home when no one showed up to keep me company and had a few beers with Jarhead. Blue Suit looked really worried. No doubt he was wondering who would provide room, board and TV while the other two members of his family attended Drinker's Hack It School at Naval Hospital, Portsmouth, Virginia

I didn't even get a decent night's sleep. My animals started carrying on when I dreamed of the old lady. This time she was patting my forehead like she was concerned about my well being. When I couldn't go back to sleep, I got a brandy, went to the office, sat in Dad's old chair and sulked. I fell asleep in the chair sometime during the wee hours and again dreamed of the old lady. This time she walked from the double window to my chair, leaned down, hugged me and kissed my cheek. There was no doubt in my military mind that I was teetering on the edge of the pier!

CHAPTER TWENTY-TWO

INTERRACIAL RELATIONS

Book sortied as an escort for the Educator Orientation Visit on a Friday morning. In company were recruiters from Slaty Fork and Fallen Timber and a chief-in-charge to whom I'd given firm instructions as to The Care and Feeding of Eugene "Book" Arnet. I feared the worst. Even a teacher with a degree in Slag Pit Operation had nothing in common with Book, not unless the teacher was into booze, lies and sex -- not necessarily in that order.

Disaster of the First Water struck soon after they arrived at the hotel in Orlando. Chief Harrington, the chief-in-charge, called to inform me Book was missing along with all but three of the male educators. He called back in about four hours to alleviate my fears. The educators had returned from a topless, lap dancing joint. They were, for the most part, drunker than hillbillies on a foxhunt. He called me at home, late in the evening, to inform me Book was again missing -- and so was the female counselor from Big Otter's Silver Run High School.

He called every few hours to report total lack of success in finding either of them. Finally, Sunday afternoon, he called to inform that Book and the counselor had appeared just in time to muster for the return trip. The chief's rambling, partly coherent evaluation of the situation was that they'd been conducting bone jumping drills since Friday evening. He sounded as if he'd been eating baked banana skins, or smoking regulation dope.

I directed Chief Harrington to order Book to proceed directly to my office following arrival at Big Otter Airport and, if she agreed, to send the counselor too. After considering Book could deliberately misunderstand the simplest of instructions, I dispatched the biggest recruiter I could locate on a Sunday afternoon. I told him under no conditions was Book to be taken anywhere except to my office. I had no need to see the recruiters from Slaty Fork and Fallen Timber as they were not from my Zone and not involve in so far as I was aware. Chief Harrington I kept in reserve in the event I decided to put Book up for a court's martial.

I bought a package of cigarettes. Then I waited.

I eyed Book and his new friend for a while before deciding the wine drinking, grape eating Romans couldn't have looked that beat to hell after a Mark One - Mod Zero orgy. I had no idea what I was going to do to Book. There was absolutely nothing I could do with the counselor, her being a civilian. I knew Book far too well to ask him anything. Book had told the exact truth only once in his entire Navy career, then lied his way out of it when he realized what he had done.

The counselor I didn't know, so her credibility was intact. Her virtue was suspect; her having spent almost three days steaming in company with Book. Regardless, I asked the counselor if she was willing to advise me as to their whereabouts during the weekend.

About three and a half feet of lovely legs crossing almost made me lose determination to get to the bottom of the situation I thought of sending Book home and discussing the matter with her in a quiet, cozy bar. Her pouting lips smiling around white, even teeth didn't help much either. I nervously fumbled a cigarette into my mouth and reached for my Zippo, then leaned back to light the thing.

"It began because the depth of Eugene's understanding of black-white problems is simply amazing!"

After I extinguished the cigarette I'd burned to cinders along with two of my fingers, I managed to light another one. "That's where you were? Discussing race relations?"

She gave Book a really loaded smile.

Book smirked.

"Not entirely . . . we did discuss his sincere honesty for a while -- after he called me a 'Coon."

My second cigarette got spit half way across my office.

"He called you a **WHAAAT**?"

"A 'Coon"

"Ma'am, I hope you understand what you've said. Racial slurs are seriously browned . . . er, frowned upon in the Navy. They are chargeable offenses. What Book balled . . . er, called you is an offense. It's serious. It's illegal. Are you certain that is what he called you?"

I was garbling. It would have been nice if Gunny were present so he could see Patty had nothing to do with my sometimes getting tongue tied

"I am certain." She gave Book another of her four-forty volt smiles. "He told me I was the most beautiful 'Coon he had ever seen. I don't consider that a racial slur. I consider it honest."

I carefully lit another cigarette, took a deep drag, then laid in my ash tray. I wished I had bought non-filters. "Ma'am, George Washington was honest. Abe Lincoln was honest. Harry Truman was honest. But I don't see how Book . . . er, Eugene calling you a beautiful 'Coon can be considered honest. Would you please explain it?"

"Don't you think I am beautiful?"

"Damn-in-hell! A blind man would think you're beautiful, but what in the name of John Paul Jones has that got to do with it?"

"You do that so well."

"Do what?"

"Vent your frustrations. It is extremely important to physical and mental well-being."

Some members of this group did not have a full sea bag. Their gear wasn't even all stenciled. I tried again. "Unlike Eugene, I am not an expert in race relations. But, if I called a black person a 'Coon, I do believe they would think it a racial slur. What I need to know is why you don't?"

Book was way over due for well-earned punishment, like keelhauling, but there were problems. I didn't have a ship, let alone one with a keel covered with sharp barnacles. It would also be difficult to get a conviction when the Object of His Affections thought 'Coon was a term of endearment.

"My encounter group believes such words, directed toward a person of any race, are usually taken out of context. The true reason for such expressions --"

"Encounter group?" I broke in, warily.

"Oh, I did not explain! My encounter group at University had so many enlightening ideas as to what polarize the races I formed a similar thing after I moved to Silver Run last year. I feel our little group is progressing toward total understanding . . ."

211

She babbled on for another five minutes with Book interjecting statements almost as brilliant as the Foolish Virgin's Lamps. She certainly enlightened me. She enlightened me that sheer air headiness is not confined to any particular race.

I truly hoped she wasn't very recently pregnant. If she were, their child would have a drift factor exceeding that of the Flying Dutchman. Their child would die young. On Book's side, the kid would be about as bright as a walking pet rock. On her side, it would inherit the desire to merge the KKK, the Black Panthers, the JDL and the PLO, into an encounter group.

"Ma'am, did you, by any chance, go to college in Ann Arbor?"

"I did! How did you know?"

"I guessed."

"Her husband went thar too." Book interjected. "He's some kinda slope head."

I informed her that Book was going to be unavailable for a while, but Angie (who had zipped into her office when she heard of Book's arrival back in town) would entertain her.

I considered sending Book to the next twenty-five racial awareness courses, but I rejected that idea when I realized it would generate a race war. She had anointed Book an expert in race relations and he would believe he was there as a consultant to the graduate course.

Angie slipped into my office through the interconnecting, but rarely used door, after I called her on the telephone. "Where she be? You didn't beat them like a bastard stepchild, murder them, or anything, did you?"

"Book is showing her to the head. I suspect they're laying enlightenment on each other by now."

"Book jump her bones?" Angie asked, wickedly.

"It is, Petty Officer Wallace, my profound opinion they held a fifty plus hour encounter session concerning race relations."

"**SAAAY WHAAAT**?"

"Angie, what would you do if I called you a beautiful 'Coon?"

"I'd smash your face!"

"Then, can I take it, that you, speaking for your race, don't consider 'beautiful 'Coon' to be a non-polarizing term?"

Angie like to tore off the door knob getting out of my office. She whirled around in the passageway and yelled, "Master Chief, have you dropped your load?"

I wondered what the FBI next door thought of that question.

When I had Book standing tall in front of my desk with no long legs to detract him and no opportunity for Enlightenment through Higher Thought, I very carefully began. "Book, I'm sure you know Chief Harrington is a member of the aviation community. At first report, he was landing fighter jets on the bar in the Rooting Creek VFW. The barkeep said he was experiencing a four in five wave off ratio. I understand he has since crawled under the shuffleboard and now believes he is either a woolly worm, or a caterpillar. You caused that, Book. You, in less than seventy-two hours, managed to turn a quiet, stable chief air controlman into a babbling idiot who thinks he's a worm!"

"Yu pissed, Master Chief?"

"No, Book." I said quietly, then yelled at the top of my lungs, **"I'M SITTING HERE WITH SMOKE COMING OUT OF MY EARS BECAUSE I THINK I'M MOUNT VESUVIUS!"**

"Yu pissed, or ain't yu?"

I checked my sea bag for proper stenciling and tried again. "Now, Book, I won't interrupt you, lash myself to the chandelier,

213

or do anything radical while you tell me, in minute detail everything that happened from the time you disappeared with the male teacher. I want you to be explicit."

"OK, but yu got t' swear that explicit stuff if legal-like."

After a complete inventory of my sea bag and a major effort on my part, we got the ship out of dry dock.

"Harry, he's principal uh Blake's Ford, done told me they wanted t' do some kinda paper on lap dancin'. I didn't rightly understand. I know'd 'bout lap dancin' but I don't know what th' paper's good for. I hunted me down uh cop an' axed him where we'uns could find us uh lap dancing joint what done paperin' and I done took 'em t' thar. It wuz somewheres near t' uh town near t' Orlando. I disremember th' name. You done told me t' please 'em, Master Chief. I wuz a-carryin' our yur orders. I done taken 'em because yu told me t'"

I knew I should have jumped overboard years ago when I received the radiogram from the English girl saying she might be pregnant.

"They liked hit real good, but didn't use no paper thet I seed. Maybe hit's somethin' they done t' 'em girls in th' rooms upstairs. Didn't use no paper a-tall when 'em girls wuz a-sitting on their lap makin' like they wuz dancin'. Th' girls seemed t' like paperin' 'cause they kept a-runnin' upstairs with 'em teachers an' . . . I got t' find out 'bout thet paper!"

"To damn-in-hell with the paper!"

"OK, OK, but I need t' know! Hit's got t' be right good. Them teachers really liked thet paperin'. They liked me findin' hit, so they bought me uh lap dance. Boy! She set herself flat down on my lap and danced up uh storm. I liked t' smothered th' way her big titties kept a-bouncin in my face. When she wuz done, I said I liked her lap dance some kinda uh good. She said she'd do hit 'gain

214

fer 'nother seven dollars, but I done told her hit'd cost more'n thet t' get my skivvies cleaned.

"She said, 'Did you get off?'

"I said, Lord, yes! Yu ought t' be 'bout half knocked up!

"So, Helen, thet wuz her name, she done taken me upstairs. Time I got back t' downstairs, 'em fellows must uh got thar paperin' done 'cause they wuz all ready t' go. We'uns done went back t' th' motel an' got hooked back up with 'em women teachers. They wuz by th' swimmin' pool whar thar's uh right good bar. Ain't no t'other kinda bar goin' t' let no one inside after they been a-swimmin' in their skivvies an' --"

"Skivvies? Like in *underwear*?"

'Uh, yeah. Some uh 'em young gal teachers done gone a-swimmin' in their skivvies an' wuz a-playin' kissy face with them other two recruiters and some sailors from Orlando.

"I think 'em old beat-t'-hell women teachers might uh been a-suckin' down the booze while we'uns wuz gone. Two uh 'em old gals done got in uh cat fight over uh bar boy.

"Th' chief done got me an' started a-wavin' his arms around an' talkin' real loud. I couldn't understand near any uh th' words he wuz a-usin'. Jes' a-wavin' his arms around an' talkin' right funny. Yu reckon he wuz a- talkin' in tongues?"

"It's possible. That trip could have caused religious conversion. Now stop asking questions, Book, and go on!"

"Well . . . some uh 'em old gals axed did I know if'n they wuz uh male strip joint fer women, but I couldn't find ary cop. Th' security feller I axed said th' motel jes' hired him thet night 'cause they wuz 'pectin' big trouble from uh bunch uh nuts. Said he didn't know nothin' 'bout no sech place, but he did think hit'd be right good if'n I taken 'em all somewheres else.

215

"They wuz all fine ladies an' I tried to help 'em, Master Chief. I did! I always carry out yur orders if'n yu talk right so as I can understand 'em. Yu don't talk right for uh hillbilly."

We had us another conversation.

"I'm a-tryin' t' tell hit straight, Master Chief. Yu don't need t' yell at me no more. Yu got one terrible bad temper!

"I done had me uh little beer, two-three pitchers, maybe, an' I got t' talkin with Linda. She axed me what did I think 'bout her. I didn't lie, Master Chief. She is th' most beautiful 'Coon I seen. Why, Linda's th' bes' lookin' broad I ever did see!"

I broke my promise. I did interject. I told Book if he ever used the word 'Coon again when he wasn't talking about the furry animal that wears a black mask, I was going to get a helo from Fort Knox and drop him feet first from way, way up. I further explained I didn't want to damage Kentucky by dropping him on his head. Then, with slightly less effort than it takes to walk a pig backwards, I got him underway again.

"Linda done tol' me I wuz honest and unlighted. Said she never had met no man with no schoolin' thet wuz so unlighted. Said she had some whiskey an' she'd like t' give me uh drink if'n we'uns could find us uh room by our ownself somewheres. We'uns couldn't go t' either one uh our rooms 'cause we'uns wuz both doubled up with someone else so as they wuz two uh us in uh room. She said neither uh 'em different people might like us a-drinkin' whiskey in the rooms. We'uns talked 'bout hit fer uh while an' decided we'uns both did need uh shot uh her whiskey. I done got us uh double room, so as th' two uh us wuz allowed in hit, yu see. She said not t' use our names, so I used yur'n. Hit's right bad t' spell."

"I heerd this leetle noise when I wuz a-shuttin' th' door. Master Chief, thet leetle noise wuz her skivvies an' stuff a-hittin th' deck! Hit turned out thet she didn't have no whiskey! I had t' order us some.

216

'This ole boy what brung th' whiskey started axin' me all kinda questions 'bout us all. Where'd everyone come from? What kinda work did they really do? Wuz anybody I knowed mad at his motel? I done told him I wuz Clay Berkeley, when he axed my name 'cause thet's how I writ th' room card.

"Wait uh minute! I know what yu're a-thinkin' 'bout! I didn't do thet. I didn't misappropriate myself as no master chief! I never told nobody I wuz Master Chief Berkeley. I said I was Clay Berkeley. Thet's yur civilian name and yu can't misappropriate no civilian! Anyhows, he wuz uh fine feller. He even said they'd be a-watchin' out if'n any uh us tried t' stay in uh Manor House Hotel ever again. Hit wuz some kinda good fer him t' done thet."

I slowly and carefully conducted another mental sea bag loading drill before I explained he could go on another EOV just as soon as the Master Chief Petty Officer of the Navy accepted a job as towel boy in the Vatican's hot skivvy house. I knew I'd screwed up as soon as I said it. Book had never heard of the Vatican and probably thought the master chief was holding out for a little more money. I further explained that the next time he told his wife he was with me when he was not, I was going to tell her exactly where he had been, what he'd been doing and who he'd been doing it with.

"When does thet thar start a-workin' Master Chief?" he questioned, concern spreading across his freckled face.

"Yesterday."

"What 'bout Thanksgiving? Maybe this year?"

"I told you, Book, it started **YESTERDAY**!"

"Then two women thet ain't th' same, neither one uh 'em, is a-goin' t' be some kinda awful bad pissed off at yu, Master Chief."

When I finally figured out what, he had said, and who he was talking about, I questioned his last garble.

217

"I phoned my Old Woman a' said yu wuz a-keepin' me here 'til Monday. She decided right then on uh trip t' sees her mama in Seattle. Said she'd come back maybe on Thanksgiving, but she waren't sure jes' what year. She ain't a-goin' t' like yu messin' up her trip. She thinks loads uh her mama!"

I wondered how much GSA would make me pay for the desk when I destroyed it by banging my head against it.

"Linda is a-countin' on me t' help her out some. She don't like t' stay by herself an' nobody else. Th' slope head is gone on some kinda business in Pittsburgh pert nigh ever weekend. Master Chief, yu think he might be a-stayin' thar to cheat on Linda?"

It was a great pity The Pill had not been available at the time when Book's mother was in heat.

CHAPTER TWENTY-THREE

SEARCH AND RESCUE

The next morning, sexually unfilled, hungry, but too hung over to eat, and feeling as secure as Dolly Parton wearing an age-weakened tank-top on an Italian autobus, I took another look at the rejected travel claim and gave it another shot to confuse and dismay the Counters of Beans. I copied the authorization number from my travel orders to block two on the travel claim input, made a few adjustments to the times and scratched out 'Supervise and Deputize' and wrote 'I&I' in the code block. Irene would think I meant 'Intercourse and Intoxication,' but I meant 'Inspection and Instruction,' which was also an unauthorized code. I then wrote a note on a government form for memo's and stapled it to the travel claim.

MEMORANDUM

FROM: Northern Zone Supervisor

TO: Administrative Officer

SUBJ: Travel Claim, Resubmission of

1. I trust this resubmission of my Travel Claim will prove satisfactory to the Naval Finance Center.

2. If it requires additional work, will you kindly provide one of my past travel claims you gundecked -- sailor talk for forgery, fraud, cheated on, lied about, etc., so I can copy your work.

Respectfully,

H. Clay Berkeley

After that evolution, I went across the street to the only Mexican joint in the entire county to talk Pedro the Pepper Puller into fixing me one of his great hangover meals. They would burn the lung warts off a Las Vegas showgirl, but they surely sweat out the booze. While I was eating, Pedro sold me a chance on the Spanish lottery El Gordo scheduled for drawing around Christmas. I also loaned him twenty-five dollars so he could balance his till before his wife came in and discovered his last horse didn't win. No one ever said Pedro's was cheap.

I had just returned to my office and settled into my chair when one of Angie's recruiters came tearing through the passageway door like a flasher leaving a NOW convention.

"Thank God you're back!" she screamed, flitting around the office like a drunken goony bird. "Angie went to Barfield County to run police checks!"

The Grand Dragon of the Ku Klux Klan owned Barfield County in every way but deeded property. There was a total of six black families in the entire county. When asked by a national TV program why he allowed those and no other blacks to live there, he replied: 'Cause we'uns always owned them.'

The male citizens of the county were almost entirely moonshine drinking, dope smoking, minority hating Neanderthals who thought females were created solely for their personal enjoyment, however they chose to define it. Barfield County led the entire state in rape, sexual assault and domestic violence and those figures reflected only known cases.

We recruited about one male per year out of that county, but there were always more women trying to join the military services than there are females working in the Kiev Street Sweeping Brigade. It was the rare Barfield woman who passed the entrance examination with high enough score to enlist. The citizens of Barfield County didn't spend much money on education, nor did teachers generally remain employed there for long.

We didn't maintain even a part-time station in the county seat of Creed's Bluff because we couldn't keep equipment in the office, engines in the cars, or recruiters out of the hospital. Another reason was so few males qualified for enlistment -- even marginally. The very few recruited from Barfield County were walk-ins at Angie's station, which was about thirty miles from Creed's Bluff. Barfield County was unsafe for visiting male white folks and terribly dangerous for all minorities, so I ran the police checks Angie needed when she had an applicant with Barfield County affiliation. I would no more let one of my black or female recruiters to go to Barfield County than I'd have taken up practicing aircraft landings after reading the procedure out of a book.

Angie -- black, female and alone, was now somewhere in Barfield County! She had about the same chance of escaping rape as a pretty Albanian woman in a World War Two concentration camp.

I headed for the state line and hit the southbound interstate at full bore Pinto acceleration just in time to cut off a North American Van Lines truck. The blast of his horn almost blew me off the freeway. After a ball-busting run down the interstate and a few miles on a two-lane highway, I screeched to a halt in front of a funeral parlor across the street from the courthouse.

The usual group of dirty haired psychopaths were mustered in front of the court house, picking their teeth with Buck knives while swapping hound dogs, guns, pick-up trucks, girlfriends and wives. Four or five of them gave me the finger as I crossed the street and climbed the courthouse steps, but I didn't object. I wasn't a complete idiot.

I knew the county sheriff only to speak to. He was a half way normal fellow who somehow managed to win elections in an area with few normal voters. He was a long way from having all the links in his anchor chain, but I'd never heard him of shooting anybody just to get a kickback from the undertaker. I figured I was half-safe with him, so I knocked on the entrance to his office and entered.

"Well, howdy do, Mister Berkeley. I tell you this Navy gal of your'n is the cat's meow!" the sheriff boomed. "She's right funny."

Angie whipped a sly smile on the sheriff and winked at me.

I explained in a rambling manner that I'd been driving past and noticed the Navy car, so I stopped to see which of my recruiters decided to goof off in Creed's Bluff. We discussed the crime rate (high), the tax base (low) and the salary of the sheriff (followed the tax base) and had a cup of his good coffee. After my blood pressure dropped to something less than that of a jug per day stump juice drinker with a four pack a day habit, I told Angie we had to go.

My pressure peaked again when we passed the local carriage trade in front of the courthouse. I received a few fingers and some cat calls. Angie received whistles and racial slurs mixed with sexual acts they wanted her to perform. I kept my mouth shut and prayed Angie would maintain. I kept one hand on Angie's arm until I had her locked in her car.

When I had Angie safely back in our building, I led her into my office, stood her at attention in front of my desk and lifted safeties. After I said harsh things to her, I calmed down a mite and continued. "Petty Officer Wallace, what you done today ranks right up there with the intelligence of a mentally retarded, three-toed sloth! I tell you -- if brains were horse manure, you couldn't fertilize a bonsai pine. Who in the hell do you think you are, the Wonder Woman of Navy Recruiting?"

"I ain't putting up with nothing from that Old Dragon!" Angie said, sullenly, as she poked at her eyes with her knuckles.

"And them people down there ain't putting up with you! Interbreeding is a way of life down there. They're all near degenerates. In plain English, they're flat crazy. The best of them make Charles Manson look like a guru who eats watermelon seeds and blesses tumble bugs.

"Barfield County goons kill people -- and each other too, with pickaxes, chain saws, crowbars, dried kitty cats and anything else they got to hand. Don't you ever read the papers?"

"It's not right, the way they treats black folks down there." She cleared her throat and sniffed. "I wanted to show that Old Dragon --"

"Angie, if you can get your FBI buddies down the hall to arrange for the Second Marine Division to provide security, you can organize fourteen protest marches, set fire to the KKK headquarters, castrate the Grand Dragon, and ride your unicycle stark naked down Creed's Bluff main street waving a flag proclaiming 'Rednecks suck bull dongs' so far as I'm concerned, but --"

Angie started laughing.

"Damn it, Angie, this is serious! I fully expected to find you dead in a ditch with your uniform hiked up around your neck after

223

twenty-five snuff dipping hicks had played jackhammer between your legs! Can you understand that, Angie?"

She stopped laughing and gave me a long stare. "You cares about me, don't you, Master Chief? Not just because I works for you. You cares what happen to me. You really likes me!"

"Of course, I like you, Dummy! Why wouldn't I like you" You're a great person. Oh, I get tired of your smart mouth and your H. Rap Brown, Gloria Whatever-her-name-is routine and your Jane Paula Jones 'I'm mean and I'm bad' attitude, but I like you. Hell, Angie, everybody likes you and you scared the living shi . . . er, hell out of us! Then there's always the fact that if something had happened to you there'd been the piper to pay. And I'd have had to hold an investigation and fill out all that damned paperwork!"

I never thought Miz. Righteous Navy would commit an Act of Fraternization, but she did. She kissed me right on the lips!

"You one sweet man, Master Chief. You ain't none too choosy who you sleeps with, but you one sweet man."

I committed a Navy Sin too. I patted her cheek that was now a little damp, then slapped her on her solid butt and ordered, "Get the hell out of here, Petty Office Wallace. Go put some folks in the Navy before I really get mad at you!"

If anyone learned of our Mutual Admiration Exchange, also known as fraternization, we'd both be filling out employment applications at McDonald's

I was extremely happy to see twenty hundred roll around. My nerves had taken about all they could hack for one day. Moe's slop chute was in my immediate future.

CHAPTER TWENTY-FOUR

ESCAPE AND EVASION PLANNING

"Gunny was here, Said he'd be back. He looked awful low. You two get caught playing in someone's patch?"

"Moe, I've not seen Gunny for days. I haven't been in any kind of patch in so long I'd have to reread *Sex in Three Easy Lesson*s before I'd know what to do with one."

"Sure does clamp down on variety when a man's contemplatin' formation steaming. How is Patty, anyway?"

The ACLU wouldn't support printing what I said to Moe.

"That's another sign, Clay -- touchy as a boar hog with warts on his belly. Anyway, this beer's for you, Courtesy of them."

"Thanks for the beer, fellows." I waved the bottle at the 'flies, wondering why they had bought me a beer. Either they'd changed President's Day, or they were buttering me up because they expected imminent breakdown in mail service.

"No need fer thanks, Boot Camp. We'uns 'll get plenty off'n yu when we'uns win our bet."

Bet? What bet? I had the uncomfortable feeling I was being set up by the barflies, but I didn't pursue the matter, for fear asking would activate their snare, trap, deadfall, whatever.

After about forty minutes, Gunny dragged into the bar and grunted at me before he ordered a double, straight Jim Beam.

"Something wrong, Gunny?"

Nothing.

"Now that you mention it, Gunny, if I discount an EOV that destroyed the morals of educators in three states, a near run-in with the Bums of Barfield County and the sex life of a steer, things are going quite well in my world."

"Yeah, mine's great too." Gunny said, glumly.

I asked. I weaseled. I connived. Finally, I begged, but Gunny wouldn't let me in on his troubles. He did get more talkative after I told him about the Angie-Barfield County episode.

"That girl's got more cojones than three-quarters of the men in this country." Gunny said, solemnly. "If I were governor of that state, I'd declare martial law in that county and put the National Guard in there until God could get around to sorting them out."

"That'd cost too much. I'm inclined to round them up, fit them out in high altitude parachute gear and heave them out of a transport plane over France. Think about it, Gunny. Within a year, they'd have most of the women in France barefooted and knocked up. Hey! A new species -- a Frog with culture and cojones!"

That got Gunny laughing.

"Say, where's Elizabeth, Gunny?"

"She's manning a booth at the mall. Election's coming up. She'll be along."

"Think her boss'll get reelected?"

"Sure will. He's served for twenty-odd years and every citizen in the country owes him. He intends to retire after his next term. I think Elizabeth is going to run for sheriff then."

"She'd be a good one, Gunny. Anyone who served as an Army MP major sure could pack the load as sheriff."

"Yeah. I'll get a lot of flack about running with a doggie if my old Corps shipmates ever learns about that!"

Running with her wasn't all he was doing!

Elizabeth arrived about a beer and a half later looking as bright as a new minivan and about the same size. She grabbed Gunny, put a fathom and a half of tongue down his throat and squeezed him until he grunted. She then said something I couldn't hear.

Gunny leaped straight up in the air, clicked his cordovan's together, lit flat footed on the floor, grabbed Elizabeth around her waist and swung her until her feet were at least one-quarter of an inch off the deck.

"The Russians done **DROPPED IT**!" screamed a 'fly.

"That's great!" Gunny yelled. "Now we don't have to formation steam!"

Elizabeth batted her hazel port holes at him and shook a cigar-sized finger teasingly, "Not until we decide we're ready, Delbert."

I knew there was a story in there.

Elizabeth clutched Gunny's spade size hands and jammed them beneath her breasts until his hands were out of sight past his wrists. "Clay, I don't know what Delbert has told you, you two being so close, but the crisis is past. We are not going to have a baby."

Gunny grinned like a raccoon in a pollywog pond. I could understand that. Paul Bunyan's father would have felt the same way under similar circumstances.

They weren't trying to charge their batteries, probably in consideration for Elizabeth's temporarily delicate condition. It was quite subdued, really: a couple of hugs, one or two suctions that would have cleaned paint off a fleet tug, a little thunder level giggling, gooses that would have made Superman jump, and some grunts and wheezes that didn't hurt the ears more than a heavy metal band at ten paces Even the mouse caught in the sweat pool beneath their stools survived nicely.

When they got tired of doing whatever it was to each other, they bid a gracious good night to all within yelling distance. They locked like collided battleships when they tried to pass abreast through the door, but they made a graceful maneuver that didn't hurt the door jamb much, then lumbered down Sycamore Street at about ten miles per hour.

"Talk about Mister and Missus Godzilla! They meet in a sideshow?" Moe asked.

"In the rare possibility you don't know, they met at the court house. Elizabeth seems like a really fine person, but I figure Gunny's going to have to moonlight as a hit man just to keep them in food and beds."

"And I'm going to have to hire a full-time carpenter to keep my stools and door casing together if they keep prematin' in here."

Moe gimped down the bar to conduct beer replenishment for the 'flies while I contemplated a newborn version of Gunny and/or Elizabeth. It boggled the mind.

The wall phone on the far wall rang and rang until my favorite 'fly staggered over to see what was causing the noise.

"Hey, Boot Camp!" He pointed at the phone. "Hit's fer yu and hit'll cost yu beer fer me answering 'stead uh yu. Hot damn! Our bet is lookin' better all th' time!"

Bet? What damned bet?

"Clay-honey, Blue Suit answered the telephone at your house. He said you were at Moe's."

"Patty, you have no idea how glad I am to hear your voice."

"Me too, considering you did not call this weekend."

"I couldn't track you down! And the warden up there was less helpful than a Quaker in a bar room brawl."

"They do not like to give out information. It has been difficult here, but it is almost over."

"I'm sure looking forward to having you back here. Patty, I expect you to meet me in Moe's after you arrive in town Friday night. If you want, I'll come to Bluefield to pick you up."

"Could you meet me halfway, or rather a bit further?"

"Meeting you halfway will be a change. You usually come lunging at me."

"I do not, Henry Clay Berkeley! You have more hands than that Indian statue thing!"

I could almost see her coloring. I also could imagine how Gunny would tease if he knew the 'H' in my name stood for 'Henry.'

"Dearest, could we have the entire weekend together in Elkins? Please?"

The barfly was right. The Russians really did drop IT.

"Why Elkins?"

229

"Elkins is such a pretty town. Listen, I will ride the afternoon bus to Weston and meet you at the bus depot about six o'clock Friday evening."

"Uh, Patty -- what about your folks? Aren't they expecting you home Friday night?"

"I can spend the weekend with my steady if I want! Anyway, I will tell them a great big fib . . . provided I can think of a suitable one."

Devious little minx!

"I must run, I have a big day tomorrow, dearest." she shifted into her little girl voice that made the hair stand up on the back of my neck. "You know we cannot -- I won't. Oh, damn-in-hell! Clay-honey, we must have two rooms. I hear the Palace Valley Inn is very nice and not too expensive. Please try to get adjoining rooms I have never stayed in a hotel and I would be nervous in a room off by myself."

"OK, Patty. Whatever you want."

"Good night, darling." Patty said, then shifted into that little voice again. "I love you."

Two rooms? The Russians had not dropped IT, but then, they didn't have to. Patty's 'I love you' rocked my earth in its pivots.

I really didn't want more beer, but I needed to give serious thought to what I was going to do. I bought the rare package of cigarettes, non-filters, and curled against the corner of the bar.

Angie had done some fine undercover work and discovered Patty did understand the basics of birth control. I no longer feared getting Patty pregnant, but Pill or no Pill, Patty was too vulnerable. Gunny was right. Patty was not the sort of woman you shacked up with for a while because it was mutually beneficial, then sailed away. I enjoyed Patty's company, more than any woman I'd known, but there flat wasn't going to be any launching of a life together. Formation steaming was out!

Patty had, on a limited basis, permitted me to touch her important areas, but I was greatly afraid I'd touched her most important one as she had touched mine. I was now aware she was in love with me. I knew damned well I was in love with her. I'd known for weeks -- maybe since I first dated her, but had never admitted it to myself. I didn't want to be in love with Patty or anybody else. Marriage scared me more than war. I had to get rid of Patty and I had to do it without hurting her feelings. I didn't know much about love, but I knew enough to understand hurting the feelings of one you love was not an appendix in any operation order.

I mentally cut and paste ideas through three beers before I devised a means by which Patty would terminate our relationship and believe it her idea. I then went home and got drunk with Jarhead. Blue Suit got a bit tight on catnip and even lapped at Jarhead's bowl of beer. I guess he decided if he had to live with a family of hell-raising, female-chasing, no-good drunks, he'd just as well join the group.

CHAPTER TWENTY-FIVE

JOINING OF FORCES

I'd barely gotten the truck door open when Patty came legging it out of the Weston Greyhound station, her overnight case swinging beside her. I intended to give her only a friendly peck on the cheek, but she wasn't having that. I almost dropped her when she leaped against me, threw her arms around my neck and kicked her heels high into the air behind her. She immediately began doing some very good work with her lips, which she also used to transmit happy little sounds. You couldn't have gotten a feeler gauge between her most prominent forward protrusion and my chest.

"Uh, folks, I don't think you better oughta had go any further out here in front of God and everybody. We got us a strong bunch of church goers in this here town." advised the elderly man who came puffing up with Patty's two big bags.

After I cooled her face down with a handy fire hose, I loaded her gear and we drove away in the cool, mountain air.

"I do not know why I act as I do." Patty said, still crimson. "I'm not totally inexperienced. I've kissed, but never on a public street in front of 'God and everybody.'"

232

"Young girls get crushes on older men." (Seed One)

She gave me a quizzical look

I learned that a couple checking into individual, adjoining rooms was not the norm in Elkins, West Virginia. The desk clerk studied us carefully, checked my credit card and our registration cards, then asked our relationship.

"We have no relationship. Does she look old enough to be my girlfriend?" (Seed Two)

And another quizzical look from Patty.

Patty exited her room wearing what was, for her, a shockingly tight, white sheath dress. It was the shortest dress I'd seen her wear, about one-half inch above her knees. She'd done something different with her hair too. It was no longer the wavy-curly mass I was accustomed to. It now hung around her neck in soft waves. I couldn't understand how she accomplished that in the few minutes she had been inside her room, but I knew it wasn't a wig. There wasn't a wig maker in the universe who could have matched her streaky taffy hair color.

For once I did not execute my hang back mode. I didn't think I could stand it, so I caught her hand and marched her smartly to the elevator.

"Clay, are you that hungry?" she queried, after she twice snagged her heel in the carpet.

"Pretty hungry. One gets hungrier earlier -- when they get old." (Seed Three)

Patty looked as if she was doing some heavy brain burning.

"Was your steak okay Patty?" I suspected they kept the dining room lights dim so folks couldn't see the wilted lettuce and the freezer burn on the beef.

"It seemed a little tough. How was your ham?"

"It seemed tough, but I believe it was my teeth. They're not what they once were. I'll probably need false choppers before long. (Seed Four)

I had been positively dazzling throughout supper. I discussed, knowledgeably and at length, the high divorce rate in the Navy (Not true, but Seed Five.) How lonely long deployments were for married people (Seed Six) I even whipped in an amusing tale about a commander friend who had married a woman ten years his junior and divorced within six months. The punch line was that the commander told shipmates he had not enjoyed his marriage, not even his honeymoon. He claimed it was very confusing because he never knew if he should tear off her clothing and throw her on the bed -- or burp her. (Seed Seven)

A loud gasp by Patty indicated the anecdote had gotten the desired results.

Patty reached across the table and caught my hand just as I was setting the now empty bottle of not very good red wine back on the table. "Clay-honey, may we go into the lounge? They have a wonderful group playing tonight. I heard them in Charleston."

"Are they loud?"

"Sometimes, but they play all types of music."

"Loud music hurts my ears. I don't understand why you young folks listen to such stuff. Much of it is dirty too." (Seed Eight)

Silence. No strange look.

The band was outstanding, just as Patty said. They played to every age group, eighteen to eighty. After a couple of slow dances, I was beginning to enjoy the drink with the umbrella when the band lit into what I figured was The Chimpanzee Mating Dance. Patty snapped me out of my seat and heaved me right in the middle of the entire troop before I regained my balance. Her movements inside that tight dress in her stocking feet looked impossible!

"Aren't they just great?" Patty bubbled, fanning her face with her little purse.

"I suppose chimpanzees think so, but it caused a bad stitch in my side. I'm way too old to do dances like that. (Idea Nine)

Patty slowly collected her things and stood up.

Then she sat back down.

"Clay, I thought you were the most wonderful man, almost from the first hour we met. As I learned more about you, I realized you were a highly intelligent man who hid his sensitivity behind a gruff, give-a-damn exterior. You related to your recruiters in a kindly manner I would not have thought possible in the military. Angie, Gunny, Keys, and all of the recruiters I met, believe you to be God's Gift to the Navy I certainly thought you were God's Gift to me!" she said, in a badly quivering voice. "I no longer believe that. Irene is correct. You are a calculating man who cares for nothing. You are not selfish. You do not even care for yourself!

"Clay, I have never made love, but that does not mean I am totally ignorant. I do not understand why you treat me as you do. I am talking about you fondling me until I almost cry from pleasure, then suddenly acting as though you can hardly stand to touch me. I wanted to make love with you . . . Oh, so badly. How many times did I go with you thinking we would make love? Several. Many. It was, admittedly, partly my fault. I was fearful, but I never, never treated you as though I did not want you! I now realize you do not want me as a mate."

"Patty, listen! You don't understand --"

"I will not listen! I will tell you something you do not understand. You will always regret you did not accept what I wanted so badly to give. By damn-in-hell, you will always love me too!" She burst into sobs, whirled out of her chair and ran from the room in her stocking feet

People looked at me like I'd skinned a live kitten.

I collected her shoes and bird-dogged her track. I knocked on her door, but received no answer. I entered my room and made a few passes around the place before I tried knocking on our connecting door. That evolution didn't make it either. I tried to phone her room via the switchboard, but the desk clerk threatened me with bodily injury. Word had gotten around.

I wanted a drink in the worst way. I wanted a gallon of booze, but I wasn't about to go to the bar. I feared lynching after having heard comments from lounge patrons when I left to catch up with Patty, so I had to settle for what was in the room reefer.

I drank a brand of beer I'd never heard of, smoked a cigarette, popped another beer, undressed down to the buff and crawled on the turned-down bed. I lay there in deep thought for a long while, but always reached the same conclusion. I had done what I thought fitting and proper, but I was, to use a British term, "A Right Bastard," for keeping after Patty the way I had. I was an even bigger bastard for keeping after her once I realized kissing and petting was more than simple playing around to her. Gunny was right. Some things do hurt worse than getting shot.

The beer tasted like Hudson River water and the tobacco tasted worse, so I did my nightly wash up, returned to bed and snapped out the light. My emotions were such I couldn't sleep, so I tossed around thinking of the one thing I was trying to forget. I sincerely hoped Patty would soon meet a man who would accept what she wanted to give in the manner she wanted to give it. I didn't see how she could miss. Loving Patty was easy. Trying not to love her was not only difficult, it was impossible.

Sadly, the situation was not totally new to me, although the English girl had not said the things Patty had. When I'd met Mary in Palma and learned she wasn't pregnant, I told her we no longer had reason to marry. Mary never said one word. She simply walked out of the Antrim Bar, returned to her hotel, packed and flew back to England. I never saw her again.

There was, however, an immense difference between Mary and Patty. I never loved Mary. Patty was going to cause me a multitude more self-hate than Mary ever had. I knew I couldn't replace Patty with any other woman. I was a dead kitty cat!

"May I come in, Clay? Please?" Patty asked, slipping partly through the connecting door.

I snatched the sheet over me. "Wait a couple of minutes 'til I get dressed."

"NO!" She walked to the side of the bed and snapped on the light. "Look at me, Clay . . . I purchased this gown for my hope chest. I intended it for my wedding night. Look at me!"

Patty was wearing a white, floor length gown that had not the hint of a doubled fold of cloth anywhere. Even the tiny mole above her left breast was visible through the sheer cloth.

"I will buy another -- if I ever need it. It will not be white though."

"Patty, honey. Please return to your room. I'll dress and we will go some place. Any where you want." I begged.

"I will not! You are going to make love to me." She raised the long gown slowly upward, pulled it over her head and dropped it behind her. "I told myself you are going to be the first man to have me. By damn-in-hell, you are going to be! Turn loose of that sheet and let me in the bed!"

I was too stunned to respond, so Patty, gloriously naked, put a knee on the side of the bed, braced herself and gave the sheet a big tug that didn't accomplish her mission. She instantly shifted from prissy schoolteacher type to Mark One - Mod Zero hillbilly gal. "Henry Clay Berkeley, if you do not crawl from under that fool thing and grab onto me, I am going to clobber you!"

After she had made her point and crawled into my arms, she whispered in a soft, scared voice. "Clay-honey, I understand what to do, but please try not to hurt me."

Much later, after periods of foggy, near sleep and sessions of the closest love making I'd known, she woke me with soft touches of her hand. "Look!" she giggled. "It likes me. Look at what it is doing!" she giggled again and moved my hand to her body.

"No, please. Do not move your hand. I want it right where I put it! Oh, I tingle! My breasts feel as though they might jump out of my skin!"

Patty slithered from beneath, scrambled on top of me, then spread-eagled across my body. She raised herself on her hands, positioned her perky, little breasts just about even with my collar bones and looked down at me -- big, gray eyes straight on. "Clay-honey, I intend to see that you will never want another woman, not ever. You have one. You are never going to rid yourself of me, Henry Clay Berkeley. I do not give one damn-in-hell how old you become!"

"Patty, honey," I said, when I could pry her lips loose. "You will not have to buy another gown. Use the one you have for our wedding night."

Patty did not act at all surprised. The little devil knew I was going to propose, or whatever it was I had done. Sandbagged! Again!

"This is our wedding night, dearest, but I will wear it again the night of the ceremony." She blushed, peculiar considering her current state of dress and what she had been so enthusiastically doing. "Until you remove it from me."

We received some very disappointed and hateful looks when we edged into the Patterson house carrying Patty's luggage -- disappointed toward Patty and hateful toward me.

Her mother appeared ready to attack me with whatever she could lay to hand. Her father probably spent the weekend cleaning his double-barreled shotgun and oiling his blacksnake whip. He was likely still trying to decide if he wanted to use the gun so I'd marry Patty and make her an honest woman, or run me out of West Virginia with the whip.

It got right peculiar when Patty told them.

Missus Patterson let out a cry and swayed a bit, then hugged and kissed on us like she had gone plumb off-center. I thought she was going to do hand springs right there in the living room. I don't know if she rejoiced acquiring me for a son-in-law, or if she was simply overjoyed her daughter was going to relinquish her status of Fallen Woman and redeem her good name.

Mister Patterson shook my hand twenty or thirty times, gave me a cigar, gave me a second one, then gave me the whole damned box.

It took us a while to get away from them; we made our break while they were arguing about who first knew we were going to marry.

"If I were a suspicious man, Patty, I'd be inclined to believe your folks want to get rid of you." I told her after we'd arrived in Moe's and I was playing catch up on the beer free weekend.

239

"They do . . . in a way. Mommy believes I am already an old maid, but she has thought that since I turned eighteen. We have had many, many mother-daughter talks. She once hinted I might be frigid." Patty blushed, mightily. "Oh, if she only knew!" Patty touched her lips lightly against mine and breathed, "I was, you see, dearest, waiting for you."

I'm not real sharp, but her location gave me a good idea and I took advantage of the situation.

"Hey! Stop it! This ain't no quickie motel. You two are goin' to have to get married if you keep that stuff up!"

"We are, Moe. Soon too." I told him after I let Patty up for air and gave her an opportunity to hose down her red face. I had actually jabbed back at one of Moe's comments and won!

The barflies executed a nice rendition of Here Comes the Bride by clicking their beer bottles together.

"Well, Boot Camp -- hit looks like yu done got reeecruited your ownself!" yelled my favorite 'fly. "We'uns knowed yu wuz a-goin' t' do hit. Knowed hit fer months, even unto t' first time yu brung Patty in here. We'uns made us a bet. Not uh one of us bet fer yu t' jump slick outta gettin' spliced to her. Yu owe us lots uh beer!"

"First Angie, then Irene, now you. Gunny's probably next." Moe muttered. "It must be something in the damned beer." And then brightly: "Maybe I can get kickbacks from the preachers! And the beer companies!"

CHAPTER TWENTY-SIX

PLANNING SESSION

I campaigned mightily for keeping it simple and we had our first tiff when Patty insisted she would never feel married unless we married in a church. In that I had no church in particular, none at all in fact, it made perfectly good sense to her that we marry in her church. She wanted a military wedding in her church and by her pastor. I don't believe her preacher would have liked what we'd just been doing when we (she) resolved he was the one to marry us. The Snake loved it!

"Clay-honey," she said, rolling beneath my arm and laying her perky, little breasts against my rib cage. "Men simply do not understand the importance of the wedding ceremony."

Bet me! I could think of only one other church ceremony that scared me more, but I hoped that one wouldn't occur until far beyond the allocated three score and ten.

"I want people to see us married, Clay. I want every female to know you are no longer available. I want the girls who teased and snickered at my lifestyle to know I found exactly that for which I hoped. Dearest, it might be mean, but I want to brag!"

I leaned and kissed her almost pug nose. "I understand, Kitten. You can hire sixteen elephants, a rock and roll band and talk Angie into riding her unicycle naked if you want, but I have to tell you something."

"What, dearest?"

"If you don't turn loose of me and stop that, you're going to be in a heap of trouble!"

Patty rolled on her back and slowly extended herself in invitation. "Bother trouble!"

Patty totally committed herself to keeping me away from other women. I thought she'd slack off a bit when she started teaching school in late August, but it didn't work out that way.

She'd go home from school, grade her papers and carry out other tasks as necessary -- cut a few switches, maybe, then arrive in my office at least a half an hour before I quit. We usually went to Moe's for a beer before going to my place for two or three hours. What with Patty living at home, we could never spend an entire weekday night together, not without me getting blacksnaked by her daddy. Her daddy struck me as an unsuspecting sort of fellow, but her mama surely wondered at Patty's sudden interest in folk lore, particularly when the festivals lasted from Friday evening until around midnight Sunday every single weekend. Patty certainly wasn't a saint anymore, not since The Snake came upon her bearing apples that night in Elkins.

I could have organized the crewing and commissioning of a guided missile destroyer-leader with less effort than the planning of our wedding.

First the invitations. Patty invited ten thousand, or so, a goodly part of West Virginia, dozens from adjoining Kentucky counties, but none from Barfield County. Then she got to me.

"Clay, you must invite more people!" she poked at me, after I'd come up far short of the hundred names I think she expected.

"That's the entire muster list, including embarked personnel." I didn't have anybody to invite, save for Missus Post and other neighbors, a few distant relatives, some old shipmates, recruiting associates, Cletus and his clan, eight-ten COI's, some folks I grew up with, Moe, the barflies and Captain Markham.

"What about your present captain, the commodore and the admiral? It is customary to invite your superiors."

Patty charged full bore at transiting to Navy Wife when she noticed an advertisement for books in a Navy Institute Proceedings magazine. She quickly became the proud owner of a small library of Navy related books she thought useful: *The Navy Wife; Naval Orientation; Naval Customs, Usage and Tradition; The Bluejacket's Manual; The History of the Navy*, six volumes, deluxe edition -- and of all things, *Naval Operations at Sea*. After speed reading them, and other manuals she found in my office, she considered herself the resident authority on the Navy.

"I don't know the admiral; I've only seen him once. He wouldn't come, but you're right. It is proper to invite him. You can invite the XO who is acting CO. He's harmless. The commodore isn't coming. If he does, I don't!"

"But, dearest, he is your superior. It says in the --"

"He is not my superior! He is my senior, but he damned sure is not my superior!"

"But the book --"

I caught Patty by the shoulders, sat her down in a chair and knelt in front of her.

"Patty, look at me and listen. I'm proud of you taking an interest in the Navy. I'm overwhelmed at the knowledge you've squirreled away in such a short time. But, honey, what we write

243

down in the Navy, and what we actually do, are different things. Listen to me.

"A long time ago, Day One plus however many years, Moses hobbled his way down from Mount Sinai lugging two flat river rocks with words burned on them by the finger of God. Those stones were the equivalent of books in those days because the Children of Israel didn't have printing presses, and the Egyptians had a monopoly on papyrus reeds. Of course, God could have used whatever He wanted, but I guess he wanted to use the local product.

"When Moses got down to the camp where he had left the Twelve Tribes, and maybe a few Gentile stowaways, he found the people making golden calves and holding maximum liberty call. Moses got so mad he cast the stones to the ground, then stomped them into such small pieces the Lord had to go on overtime for forty days and forty nights to burn a new set.

"After Moses received a new issue -- and probably a good chewing out for breaking the initial issue, he returned to camp, sounded General Quarters, Man Overboard, or something similar. He then held a complete muster of All Hands. After he got their report chits straight and reviewed their service records, he held captain's mast and slew every other ten thousand with the jawbone of an ass. He then read The Plan of Forever from the new set of stones.

"About one week later, after they had gotten the guilty parties buried, they went right back to making golden calves, stealing apples and holding liberty call.

"Patty, folks back then didn't pay attention to that book, which was *Commander in Chief Universe, Operation Order Number Zero Zero One hyphen Earth*, and they pay little attention to it now. Those Navy books you have were not written by the Finger of God. So, we're definitely not going to be slain by the jawbone of an ass if we don't adhere to them."

"Why, Clay-honey -- you read the Bible!"

I wondered if Adam had a similar problem with Eve when he tried to explain why he didn't want The Snake hanging around the orchard.

Then the wedding attire. Mine wasn't a problem. I had a dinner dress uniform hanging in my closet, ready for service.

Not so Patty! She wore out her mother, her aunts, and every close friend searching for a wedding gown. She was thinking of hiring a search party from Kelly Girl when I questioned her intentions during a lengthy Saturday afternoon search at a Charleston mall.

"Patty, there can't be many different wedding dresses in this small city and --"

"Perhaps I should go to Richmond . . . or even Washington."

"Patty, I do think you want to be married before you have to do it in a wheelchair, but it's not going to happen unless you decide on a dress. You've got everybody climbing bulkheads!"

"But, Clay-honey, it has to be right!"

"Is it so complicated? They're all white."

"It cannot be white!"

My gyroscope tumbled again.

"Dearest," She caught my hand and pulled me down on a mall bench and whispered, "It is not like we just petted. We did *It,* Clay -- a bunch of times. I am no longer . . . pure."

"By damn, you taste pure to me!"

"**Clay!**"

I think, seriously, she wanted all ten thousand, or so invitees to believe we'd conducted bone jumping exercises throughout the county, except maybe on the courthouse lawn on top of the statue of Stonewall Jackson and his horse. That, of course, would have been extremely difficult.

Finally, after The Great Search, she settled on an ivory gown and was satisfied.

And the reception. That time, I believe Patty did employ Kelly Girl to search the entire county. She wanted an establishment that would hold ten thousand, or so, had facilities to serve food, and wouldn't charge more than five bucks for a seven-course meal, booze extra. She hinted she might go as high as six-fifty if they would throw in the booze. She had her daddy so upset he made joking comments about selling his farms, moving to Miami and taking up domino playing with Cuban immigrants who had access to a better class of cigars.

Both of her folks were out to get The Snake.

She finally selected the Moose Lodge, but wouldn't disclose the price per plate, with or without booze. Her daddy winced when the subject came up and spoke of giving up cigars. I later learned that Patty was not spending her folk's money, but using money she'd earned over the years buying and selling livestock on her own behalf.

"Clay," she asked, one evening while perched on the corner of my desk, "Do you realize you are out of uniform?"

That question killed a whole sheet of number crunching and word weaving she'd only recently let me resume. It is extremely difficult to crunch numbers and weave words when legs as pretty as Patty's keep crossing and uncrossing on the corner of your desk. I didn't say anything. I knew she'd tell me.

"I read in Uniform Regulations that jewelry is not to be worn on the naval uniform, except items of personal nature, such as a belt buckle with the name of a ship in which one has served. That is proper terminology. One does not serve *on* a ship. One serves *in* a ship."

"I served in the good ship *Frank E. Evans*."

"It is not your belt buckle. It is your tie bar. The tiny letters read 'Mam's.' That could not have a personal meaning."

It did, but I surely wasn't going to tell her why. It was time that my favorite 'fly had a new tie clasp.

I put the computer feed in a drawer and locked my safe. "Patty, I don't believe in burning books. I love books, but I'm about to give torching certain ones serious consideration. Now, what I propose is take you to Moe's, ply you with liquor, then take you to our future home where I will take advantage of your drunken, defenseless, young body."

"Oh, I like that idea!" she squealed, clapping her hands together. "May we forgo the liquor?"

The Snake must have laid a whole bushel of apples on her!

"Patty shredded your liberty card yet, Master Chief?" Keys teased, when we were seated in Moe's.

She didn't need to. I didn't have enough strength left to have used it. "Not yet. Patty is very understanding and --"

"Sure she is! Next, you'll be telling she's going to let you steam around topless places --"

"Elnathan! You're getting nasty again!" Missus Armstrong screeched.

"I am understanding, Dottie. Topless clubs are no longer on his itinerary. He can go to such bars as he wishes, but we will have a little disagreement about a certain beer parlor in Merriville!"

I didn't need to listen to more, so I excused myself and went to the head. It didn't really surprise me she knew about Gloria. I was beginning to believe she could read minds. I was giving the mind reading possibility deep thought on my way back from the head when I picked up on Patty's conversation.

". . . so, when Angie and I overheard Moe telling an Army recruiter that women who work in topless clubs often refuse to . . . er, associate with married men, it provided the idea to expand the fib my friends were already spreading in areas of temptation about Clay having gotten a young girl pregnant. Since pregnancy is known as the actual reason for some marriages, we expanded the fib a tiny bit and reported Clay had married. My friends did a wonderful job spreading that fib, but you would not believe the amount I had to reimburse them for expenses. Pearl's Place was the worst! Drinks in Pearl's are terribly expensive and -- Clay! Oh, my God!"

"Oh, my God' was correct, or it would be when I got her in private. I'd suspected half of the people I knew of lying to Claire, but not Patty. It never crossed my mind. I also had not known people were telling every female in a two-state area that Patty was pregnant -- by me!

Patty's story of destroying my sex life stoked conversation for several minutes. Patty acted proud of what she had done and even giggled about it. That generated a question or two in my mind. How in the hell had she known I would shoot over to see Claire as soon as she left town? Had she done something to influence Gloria to take a cruise? How in the hell did she know I was going to marry her way back then when I had not a glimmer I would do such a thing? Patty was not only a stubborn genius -- she was a plotter and flat sneaky!

We had a lengthy conversation later that night about her having sent people to Pearl's, and throughout God-World, to accuse me, falsely, of having 'married some young girl' as Claire had put it. I mentioned other falsehoods too -- such as a pregnancy that could not have occurred, except via Immaculate Conception.

Patty said it was done in self-defense and that 'I have the perfect right to protect what belongs to me.' She also stoutly maintained her friends simply used the wrong tense about my being married. About to be married was, in her mind, only slightly different from actually being married.

When I told her she should never attempt to teach grammar if she had no more concept of tense usage than that, she explained in five hundred words, or more, that tense usage didn't apply -- it was the form of the thing that counted. She maintained there was no legal difference between 'betrothed' and 'married' under old English Law that, according to her, had not been repealed in Virginia after the Revolutionary War. It followed, of course, that West Virginia, a part of Virginia until 1863, never repealed it either.

I could see the life ring floating away, but made one more desperate grab for it by pointing out a major flaw in her reasoning. I told her we had not then been betrothed, married or anything else. Therefore, her passing The Word to God-World that I was married had been a lie. I explained it could not be called anything but a lie -- and a whopper too, because I then had no intention whatever of marrying her, or anybody else.

"Henry Clay Berkeley, you must have known we were going to marry. Goodness, dearest, I did everything, except tell you outright -- many, many times.".

CHAPTER TWENTY-SEVEN

THE LAUNCHING

We married on a cool, September morning.

I had no concept of cool. I was scared. I was wondering if there was a precedent for conducting abandon ship drills at weddings when the organist hit the first notes of The Wedding March, something I'd referred to, only weeks before, as The Death March. I looked to my best man for moral support, but Gunny, who had proven his bravery untold times, was deathly pale. He later said he'd twice nicked himself that morning while attempting to sheathe his sword.

As Patty walked proudly up the aisle on her father's arm, I realized, once again, I'd been terribly wrong in initial evaluations. She wasn't just cute, borderline pretty. She was the most beautiful of women. I was so proud of her I got tears in my eyes.

I did and she did and it was done. The launching of our marriage was completed.

I lifted her veil. Her eyes were wet too, but her bright, broad toothed smile told me a lot. It told me I now possessed everything a man could possibly desire, something I was too stupid to understand before our night in Elkins.

I kissed her tenderly, but at length.

I froze with stage fright at the reception when I lifted her gown to remove the garter. Patty leaned down like she was going to help me, blushed brightly, then whispered, "Silly, you've been a *lot* higher than that."

Angie was in good position to catch the bouquet, but Elizabeth did a combination Packers/Celtics act and grabbed it just below the chandelier. Gunny turned pale and swayed like a destroyer broadside to a long swell.

The acting CO caught the garter. He handled it like he's never seen one before, let alone fondled what one packaged.

All was shipshape and Bristol fashion until I made a head call and Curtis-baby slithered in, looking like he'd sucked down his share of the booze Leprosy! I realized in that moment the possibility his nasty genes could have derived from the Patterson clan. Hopefully, they originated from the Longly bloodline in which case none of them were lurking about in Patty's body. Regardless, it was far too late to worry, so I stuck out my hand and made a couple of nice comments.

"Patty is ecstatic, Clay, but she won't be in that condition tonight after you force her to engage in sex. You'll have to, you know. She's an ice box. Hey! That's a pun -- ice box, get it?"

I didn't have either a dogging wrench, or a dried kitty cat, but I made do. I then stuck a towel in the head and flushed it until water streamed across the tiled deck. I didn't want Curtis to lay there unconscious. He was, after all, family.

I prayed The Lord would forgive me for thumping on Curtis just after I had left His House. I thought it likely that He would. He probably disliked Curtis too. I hoped Patty wouldn't notice my knuckles that Curtis insisted on skinning with his teeth. I didn't

251

want to tell her what he'd said -- and lying to her was flat out of the picture. I had already discovered trying to lie to her worked about as well as a rubber ax on an oak tree.

Gunny did, of course, notice and queried what had caused my skinned knuckles.

"Well, *Henry*, I'll go and shift your new cousin-in-law out of here before something really bad happens to him. Which it will . . . if he gets smart toward me. OK, *Henry*?"

I hoped something would happen to Patty's preacher, for using my full given name when he asked the 'Do you' question. Something out of the ordinary, like The Snake supplying a mean, ugly woman with an apron full of apples. I wondered how one put in an order.

We ate the dinner, danced a couple times, then got the hell out of there.

I had offered Patty the world for our honeymoon. I had pay saved, a goodly amount of cash I'd inherited with the farms and the proceeds from my folk's life insurance. The annual profit I realized from the farms and related sources had also piled up until it equaled a tidy sum too. I wasn't rich, but I didn't have to worry about weekly blood bank visits.

Patty chose Elkins. She wanted the exact room in which we first made love.

The hotel clerk, the same one as before, wasn't inquisitive like when we had last registered. He checked us in and congratulated us on our marriage, a happening blabbermouth Patty blurted about at the reception desk. I made note to later remind her I'd told the clerk we had no relationship when we last stayed in the hotel. Her telling him we just married must have told him we developed one during that night. That would, of course, generate a huge blush.

We toasted each other with champagne the hotel graciously provided. Rather than waste it, we drank the entire bottle; otherwise, it might have aged too much.

We accomplished a few other things too.

"Clay-dearest," Patty panted, nervously buttoning and unbuttoning her blouse. "Would you please run out . . . er, down to the bar and have a drink -- just a tiny one?"

"Not *now*, Patty!"

"Yes. Now! For no more than fifteen minutes. Please."

I hoped no one in the lounge would recognize me from the last time. It is extremely difficult to honeymoon while dangling from a sugar maple at the end of a noose.

Patty was wearing her white gown when I returned to the room, the one she had worn so briefly only once before. She welcomed me back by initiating her greatest kiss thus far in our odyssey. Finally, she pulled away. "Clay-honey, do you remember what I told you I expected you to do with this gown?"

I nodded that I remembered. She was so beautiful my throat was dry!

"Do you not think I have had it on long enough, dearest?"

CHAPTER TWENTY-EIGHT

FORMATION STEAMING

We returned from our honeymoon and set up housekeeping in our slate roofed, fourteen room farm house. I hoped Patty would be comfortable in the house, which had slowly evolved around a two-room, log cabin built as a follow-on to a crude hut built in 1710 by the original Henry Clay Berkeley. The house had been expanded one or two rooms at a time until it was now an odd, sprawling, two-story structure. Different size and shape doors and windows, manufactured in different eras, made the house strange to the eye. It was even odder inside because ancestors had matched uneven floors with steps and had cut doorways through walls where one would not normally expect to find a door.

Mister Pollard, the farm manager, maintained the unoccupied house during the years I was steaming around the world. Consequently, the house was spit shined and Bristol fashion when I returned to West Virginia on recruiting duty. The house was in the same condition as the day Mom and Dad passed out the door for the last time, then died together when the bridge they were crossing in Mom's new Mercury collapsed into the Hemlock River. The house would undoubtedly outlive the Berkeley Line, of which I was the last

Patty loved the house and all that was in it. She seemed unable to refrain from touching the old furniture dating from various eras, including some hand crafted by the early residents. She positively loved the four-poster bed with the high, hand-carved headboard with which she was well familiar before our marriage. She quickly decided there was no reason to spend our money to redecorate our house that didn't need one single thing. She did buy and hang a set of pull drapes across the master bedroom picture window, which faced the orchard and Berkeley's Knob. Squirrels, rabbits, raccoons, bears and deer *Know* things -- according to Patty.

Jarhead went into his ass mode and remained there. Patty could barely stop walking, let alone sit, without him wanting to flop his big, ugly head across her feet and slobber on her. Blue Suit was so happy at having a soft lap to curl on that he took up running his sawmill full time.

There was one change in their lifestyle our pets probably didn't like, They were barred from our bedroom. They were sometimes evicted from other rooms too, for varying periods of time. Patty wouldn't allow them to watch any lovemaking, except for random pats and kisses. Pets *Know* things.

Missus. Jenkins was quite happy when Patty decided she needed her housekeeping services only two days per week. Missus. Jenkins had wanted to cut her days of work for months, but stayed aboard because I badly needed her.

If such a thing exists, we settled into the routine of married life.

Patty's school was a couple of miles distant from my downtown office. We, therefore, usually left the house about seven-fifteen, executed a goodbye kiss that probably gave Missus Post conversational tidbits for the entire day, entered our respective vehicles and separated to earn our beans and bacon. Some morning departures were positively frantic, depending on the Snake's influence on our get-out-of-bed time.

255

I didn't know if it was The Snake's influence, or Patty's crusade to keep me safely in her bed and well away from random women who might cross my bow. I favored whatever it was, even if it did keep me in a weakened state. I was sleeping more at my desk than I was in my bed. I don't know how Patty got anything approaching adequate sleep.

Workday evenings, when Patty had only a little paperwork to do, she would come directly from school to my office. Usually, on those nights, we would stop in Moe's to catch up on the latest scandal. Moe always had something to say that would ensure the lighting off of her color generator. Moe dearly loved to see Patty blush. He maintained he had not seen a woman blush for forty-five years.

Evenings when she had lessons to prepare, I stopped at Moe's before heading home. I missed her being with me. I usually left after one beer, but a good conversation with my ex-running mates turned me into a party animal after which I had as many as two beers. I had crashed and burned Big Time!

Our married life settled into a warm, comfortable routine. I had found a snug harbor.

I gave Angie to Charles in marriage in October when he returned from his first cruise in the container ship *Sealand Voyager*. Angie proved the old adage that all brides are lovely. Gunny refused to compete for the garter. He put his huge hands behind his back and hung around the fringes of the single males so Elizabeth would believe he was trying. Gunny caught it anyway. Charles ringed the hilt of Gunny's sword with the garter. The following day, Gunny and Elizabeth announced they would marry during the Christmas season.

I figured I'd be a pro at weddings before long. I'd already filled two of the three main male billets and would soon fill the third as Gunny's best man.

We continued going to church with Patty's folks and taking Sunday dinner with them. Mister Patterson always gave me a cigar after dinner, but not before he had taken Patty aside and questioned how I was treating her. I guess he didn't want to waste a perfectly good cigar on a man he might have to blacksnake and mutilate.

Wednesday nights were their return visit to our house. Patty reported her father had, on their first visit, walked around our home farm before I arrived home from work. She said he was scheming to see if he could join forces with us in some manner. I told Patty he'd have to talk to Mister Pollard because I didn't know beans about farming, trading cattle or selling coal and timber. Patty informed me she had already given thought to our situation and I need not concern myself with matters outside the Navy. She explained in several hundred words how she intended to study the day books to learn our financial situation. Since she had already beaten me to parade rest with words, I didn't correct her mistaken idea that we were barely financially secure.

Jarhead had, with exception of minor falls from grace, been in good behavior mode since Lady Lou gave birth to regulation blue tick hound puppies. He was probably fulfilling a vow.

Blue Suit got a little too much catnip and went off-center in early October. He raped Missus Post's tabby cat. He then whipped up on Braxton's half-wild tomcat until the cat looked like he'd been run through a wood chipper! Blue Suit then took off into the meadow for the remainder of the day. The outside world proved too much for him. He reverted to type when he returned to home and custody at dusk.

Patty held captain's mast and awarded punishment of stopping his treats and restricting his TV watching for one week.

Blue Suit's wild liberty must have told Jarhead something was missing in his life. He went AWOL a few days after Blue Suit's escapade, grazed through Missus Post's flower bed, pissed on her yellow rose bush, then hit the beach on liberty. He stopped down the road and collected Carlos the Crazy. Patty found them sampling the merchandise at Hancock Kennels. Missus Hancock told her they had gang banged Lady Lou, after which Mister Hancock kicked the barn door flat off its hinges, then steamed off to the local slop chute to lay plans for moving to Canada.

Patty decided to 'scold' Jarhead as she had Blue Suit, but she wouldn't let me observe. She said it would interfere with her authority. She claimed animals were similar to children and she knew how to control children. She inferred I believed Jarhead's conduct to be fitting and proper and in keeping with that enjoyed by sailors and Marines.

Patty chose the far corner of the backyard to conduct captain's mast. Jarhead, having been a material witness at Blue Suit's mast, knew what was coming and refused to go. She clapped him in irons and dragged him along smartly. When she got him in position, she cupped his head between her hands and laid it on him. I couldn't hear what she said, but it must have been good because she blushed a lot.

Patty might have known about child control, but she didn't know much about regulation English bulldogs. Consequently, her reasoning with Jarhead didn't quite make it.

Jarhead went AWOL eight days later, chased Missus Post's chickens until they stopped laying, worried the yellow rose bush clean out of the ground, chewed on what flowers he'd missed the last time, then took extended shore leave. Patty found him at Nutter's farm, locked tight with their Irish setter with Carlos the Crazy in support position.

Patty asked Mister Pollard to build the backyard fence even higher, move everything more than one foot high distant from the fence and put complex latches on the gates. She now accepted that Blue Suit was an accomplished manipulator of latches. She suspected everybody of being an accomplice. She called the electric and gas companies and told them she would do the monthly meter readings and mail the figures to them. She cautioned the milk tanker driver, the feed truck driver, and everybody else who might visit the farm on business. I knew her efforts were a waste of time because it was only a matter of time before Jarhead got itchy and dug his way out. I didn't tell Patty that. I wasn't a Californian and didn't want a concrete yard.

Patty and I were ambling through our orchard one frosty Friday evening, picking up the random apple and pear that animals had not captured, when she hit me right between the running lights with one hell of a question. "Clay-dearest, do you believe in ghosts?"

That question caused rapid inventory of my gear locker and entire sea bag.

"I have my doubts, but creditable folks claim to have seen them. Why?"

"I have seen ghosts." she said, in a quiet, little voice.

"When?"

"Oh -- since we arrived home from our honeymoon."

"Ghosts? You've seen ghosts. In our house?"

"Not all were in the house. Jarhead and Blue Suit have seen them too."

"Patty, I know our animals communicate well, but they can't talk. How do you know they saw ghosts?"

"Because they act odd when I see one! Jarhead whimpers and hides beneath something and Blue Suit crouches between my ankles. He arches his back and hisses. Both are frightened silly!"

"You were not frightened?"

"Nooo, not really. Apparitions are more interesting than frightening."

"You were awake when you saw them?"

"Yes -- although I have experienced dreams that might not have been dreams."

"You haven't been hitting that really old stuff in the liquor cabinet, have you? Dad left that, or maybe his dad."

"I do not drink alone! I barely drink at all!"

"Honey, I'm not doubting your word, but what makes you believe you've seen ghosts?"

"Because I have! You failed to inform me there are ghosts on this property. You let me learn of them by myself!"

"Uh, Patty -- how could I have told you about ghosts if I have never seen any? If there are ghosts hanging around, I don't know about them."

"Yes, you do!"

"I do?"

"You told me some of the interesting things written by your ancestors in those old journals in the library, but nothing about them seeing ghosts. I have now read those journals and found lots concerning apparitions in those journals. You thought I would be afraid!"

"The old timers believed in all sorts of superstitions most people don't believe in today.   Yes, they're people who believe firmly in ghosts, witches and such.   Some even believe in vampires! My Father claimed to have seen a band of Indians climbing the exact hill we are standing on, but I suspect he'd been hitting the stump juice he kept in the blacksmith shop."

"Your mother was not an old timer and I find no indication she was a drinker."

"Mom didn't believe in ghosts!"

"She did too believe in ghosts! She recounts, four times, or more, of seeing apparitions walking through this very orchard and crossing the ridge toward Big Otter. She also observed strange beings when she was pregnant with you."

"Are you telling me Mom kept a record of things like that?"

"She most certainly did! I found her diaries in her dresser drawer, dating from when she was a teen. Did you not know that?"

"Honey, you will find lots of things in the house that I don't know about. Remember, I joined the Navy and left here when I was seventeen. Except for short leave periods, this is the first I've been home since. There are drawers, closets, chests and such that I've never opened -- at least not since I was a kid, maybe not even then. Lord knows what is in them.

"Let's go to the house. I want to see Mom's dairies."

"No!"

"No? Why not?"

"Because there are items personal to her that you should not read, you being her son. We will keep them for our descendants, who will not have known her personally. Come. I will prepare hot chocolate and read a little of her diaries to you."

"I don't understand why you don't want me to read them, Patty."

"Would you like your son to read details of what we did in Elkins?" Patty queried, turning red.

"Uh, no."

"Then you do not want to read the actions of your mother and father! Her diaries should not be destroyed though. What she set down is family history. They will be of great interest to future generations as the old journals are to us. Please understand I am not keeping anything from you. They did nothing wrong. Their activities were human. Very human!"

I understood my birth was not a result of Immaculate Conception. The Snake had come upon my folks at least once, thereby generating a Be Fruitful and Multiply evolution. But, like most people, I never gave thought to the union of my mother and father.

Patty squirmed beside me into a huge, old-fashioned chair, turned the cloth-covered book to where I couldn't see the inside pages and started to read:

"'Dear Diary, I have much I want to write, but my time is limited. I started teaching again today and I have lessons to prepare. Oh, but I hated to return to teaching after our magnificent honeymoon at White Sulfur Springs! So many remarkable and revealing things have occurred since Bertram Lee Berkeley and I began our life together. (Has it really been only twenty-four days?) I write not of our wedding night -- that was breathtakingly glorious! What he and I did throughout the entire night encompassed all that I ever dreamed --'

"I am not going to read the remainder of that paragraph, Clay-honey.

"'I write of the aged woman I noticed crossing the orchard last evening just before B.L. returned from the stock sale. I know what I saw, even though B.L. laughed when I told him. I believe he is hiding something from me.

"'The woman crossed the orchard just past the row of pear trees and hobbled her way up the slope. I could see her plainly. I decided I was seeing a ghost, for I did not know her and I know every person within miles and miles. She could not be of this era because of her clothing. Her gray dress, which dragged the ground, appeared to be of a rough material -- not a material I've ever seen. She was carrying a small bag in her left hand and a shiny, worn branch in her right hand -- a walking cane, I suppose.

I did not actually see her cross the ridge, for she disappeared beside the walnut trees near the crest of the hill. She did not disappear behind anything! She just disappeared! Have all those wonderful acts between B.L. and me affected my mind? It certainly affected my --'

"*Sooo*, Henry Clay Berkeley, your mother never seen ghosts, huh?" Patty asked, in a sly, little voice.

"She probably fell asleep and dreamed it. I know I did."

"You dreamed what, dearest?"

"I dreamed about an old woman in a funny dress a couple of times." I didn't think I should tell her about Jarhead howling and trying to crawl beneath the pillow and Blue Suit hissing, not when their actions tracked what Patty said about them being frightened when she thought she'd seen ghosts. Strange, odd, bizarre, whatever.

"Then you have seen her too! What did she do?"

"Nothing. I didn't see her. I dreamed her. I dreamed she stood beside the bed and another time I dreamed of her when I fell asleep in a chair in the library. That's all."

Patty twisted around in the chair and locked her big, gray eyes into mind and radiated a very penetrating look "Did this occur after we married and you did not see fit to tell me?"

"I first dreamed about her after I met you. I don't recall exactly when all I dreamed about her, but she once gave me a dirty look. It was the night you got pis . . . er, mad and threw me out of your car when I wouldn't jump your little bones, if that was what you intended. I was upset when I went to sleep. A little drunk too."

"Oh." she said, turning a bright pink. I asked her why the blush, considering that her blushing stage ought to be long, long past, what with The Snake's influence and all. "Shhh, let me read another passage.

"'The Christmas Program is going to be a success -- my first as a teacher of a one-room school! The children are learning their parts well ahead of when I thought they would do so.

"'I had to discipline Clark Elliott this morning. He threw a spitball at Jerry Lane, missed and hit Helen James near her eye. I spanked his little tail and sent him home! I trust he will receive a good thrashing from his mother, this being the second time I've sent him home this week. He is such a mean little devil! Oh, I so dislike the discipline function of my profession.

"'I saw the old woman again this afternoon when she passed through the gate between the barnyard and the orchard. She did not open the gate. She passed through it! She looked much younger today, but I believe she is the same person. She was badly stooped before. She was walking very erect today. She is a tall woman -- extremely tall. Her hair was a rich reddish color, not gray, as before. She was dressed differently too. She was wearing a fawn-colored dress I suspect was doeskin.

"'I later went to the orchard and tried to follow the path that she walked. I discovered an old footpath. It is more a slight ditch than a footpath, but the ditch was probably worn into the soil by the many feet that has tread upon it. I asked B.L. about it this evening. He said his grandfather thought it a long-ago route from the Indian village on top of the hill to the river below. Interestingly, B.L. said his father had rocked the path time and again, as had his grandfather, for they feared water washing down the path would turn it into a deep gully. He said the soil was too soft, like many wet spots in this area and would not retain rock. I did not argue with him, but the soil does not appear wet in that area. I believe Indian ghosts did not want the path filled with rock!

"'I believe I know who this lady is! I believe she is Margaret Louise (Tinny) Berkeley -- the first non-Indian woman ever to set foot on our hill! I believe this because of a description I read in one of the old journals praising the color and abundance of her hair. Is the ghost she? I believe so, but I have not spoken to B.L. about it. I really believe he is hiding information from me! Does he believe I am afraid of spooks? Probably! I am, after all, the weaker vessel – so he believes. (Males never learn, do they?)

'"I spoke with Edna Post's grandmother today. She agrees with me! She said Berkeley women were long known for functioning as midwives and for their ability to treat the ill. She said it would have been common for them to walk to a distant cabin to deliver a baby, or to treat an ill person. She said the woman has been seen by others, but not by her. My protective husband had to have known of her, and he denies there are ghosts among us! I'm going to jump on B.L. when I get him in bed tonight and tear his ears off, then I am going to -- er . . . you do not need to hear the rest of this narrative, dearest."

I sort of turned my head away and wiped my eyes. It was difficult to hear what Mom had written as a young woman -- a woman who died long before she aged. I couldn't think of anything I'd seen that she had written, except her signature on my report cards. Mom was twenty-eight when she married and probably taught school for six or seven years before that. Likely she had enough of fooling around with school kids and chucked the whole thing when I appeared.

Patty touched my cheek beneath my right eye with the soft tip of her finger "It is fitting to cry, dearest. I cry too, when I read what your ancestors wrote. Their lives were terribly arduous, particularly those of the females, but there was much joy in their lives too.

"Your mother was a wonderful, happy woman with few stones in her path. You were one of those stones as a teen, what with your playing tricks on people, fighting, staying out late and raising all sorts of Cain. She knew about your girlfriends too!

"I believe, from what she narrated, that your father was quite different from you, but not entirely so. He was insular in nature, having lived his entire life in West Virginia, except while fighting in the war. Her writings suggest he was a kind, loving husband and father, but he drank more than she wished. I see no indication they argued, but she worried greatly about him drinking."

"I don't remember them arguing, but I recall times when Dad stomped out of the house and went to his hidey-hole in the blacksmith shop where he kept a jug of stump juice. He'd hang there for a while, smoke his pipe, then return to the house in a good mood."

"Her last sighting of the elderly woman is interlaced with personal items, but it is the most interesting. You will not believe it!

"'The woman I believe to be Margaret Louise Berkeley appeared beside my bed last night. I initially thought I was dreaming, then realized I was not. She had aged somewhat since my last sighting and was again wearing a dress made of the rough material I now believe to be a fabric used in colonial times, which the settlers called linsey-woolsey – fabric loomed from linen fibers and the fleece of sheep. She stood there, smiling, cuddling the old family cradle in her arms. An antique dealer would call it primitive, but that cradle is my favorite antique of all the antiques in our home. It is handcrafted from shaved chestnut and appears never to have been sanded. It is worn and stained. It was likely crafted to hold the first child of Henry Clay and Margaret Louise Berkeley. I suspect every Berkeley baby born since occupied that cradle.

""She faded from view when I punched B.L. awake. That man can sleep! B.L. grumbled about my dreaming weird dreams and rolled over. I went to sleep too, but not directly. I didn't let B.L. go to sleep, not that he wanted to do so after a bit of coaxing on my part.'

"I will not read the remainder of this paragraph, Clay-honey, but I will read the next few. They are so sweet!

266

"'Why do I love B.L. so much? He and I do not like many of the same things. He is not a reader and does not enjoy discussing current events. He enjoys loafing with his pals for hours on end, but has little in the way of conversation to offer when he returns home. Oh, he is a Diamond in the Rough just like my father, but he is a fine, brave man. It must be true that opposites attract. I simply could not imagine loving any man other than B.L. I am so happy he chose me when he returned from the war. (Who actually chose whom, I wonder?) He could have had any woman in Big Otter County, him being the bold, handsome hero that he was -- and still is. How many men won so many medals in battle and received field promotions from sergeant to captain in the United States Army? Not many, I'm sure! I am so lucky a woman!'

"Clay-dearest, I simply would have loved to have known your mother. She felt much the same about your father as I feel about you. Wait! There is more that I wish to read.

"'I discovered today I am pregnant! Oh, but I prayed for this! I now realize why the ghost of Margaret Louise was holding the cradle and smiling. The Berkeley Line will continue, if I bare a son! I once tried to speak of the continuation of the Berkeley Line with B.L., his brother not having an interest in ANYTHING, except running hounds and drinking with his cronies. B.L does not seem concerned that his family name might die out. Dear Diary, I sincerely hope I am wrong, but I do not believe B.L. will have a brother long. The man is drinking himself into a grave as have other past Berkeley's. This is a pity. He is a fine man in other ways.

"'Today is the first time I have seen B.L. shocked. I brought him a cup of coffee, splashed a tot of whiskey into it and cuddled on his lap. Then I told him! I thought he would drop me to the floor. He is now wandering about the barnyard with his pipe in his mouth. I'm going to call to him after a bit and ask if he realizes it is unlit! I suspect he is greatly tickled about my pregnancy, but I will never know. B.L. is terribly poor at displaying emotion. Oh, I hope it is a boy!'"

Patty thought I was crying, but I wasn't. I was only sniffing -- caught a cold while walking in the orchard, probably. Master Chiefs do not cry!

"Clay-honey -- just think! We will maintain tradition when we use that cradle for our children!"

That comment caused me to lose my anchor and every foot of chain! "Uh, Patty, I been meaning to speak with you about that. You spoke of descendants when we were in the orchard today, probably because of what Mom wrote. The Berkeley name did survive one more generation when I was born, but that is the end of the line."

Patty threw the back of her hand against her mouth, which had fallen open, then said, "Why I uh . . . may I ask why, Clay-honey. We are both young and healthy."

"Because, my beautiful lady -- I do not want kids!"

"But, we must have children! That is what people do when they marry. They produce children!"

"Patty Lane! You are using birth control, aren't you? You are not pregnant, are you?" If she wasn't using pills, there'd be hell raised in high places. If she was pregnant, I was going to borrow Gunny's sword and fall upon it!

"I am using birth control and I am not pregnant!"

I pulled Patty from beside me and cuddled her on my lap. "Kitten, if I wanted children, there's no one I'd rather have them with than you. But, Puss, I do not want children, not at my age. I am, after all, twelve years older than you. Any child we had would not be of age until I was, at the earliest, in my 'fifties." I didn't think I should tell her she was too small to bear children, not her -- the mental reincarnation of stubborn, hardheaded Sir Winston Churchill!

"I remember what you said one night in Moe's about liking children roasted. You did say that, but you blamed the saying on some old movie star, a Mister Fields. I thought, then, that you were being funny. Now I learn you hate children. Maybe you even hate me!"

Patty leaped from my lap and tore out of the library door. I heard her sobbing as she tore up the stairs toward our bedroom. We had experienced our very first fight. Patty crying was a knife in my heart, but I wasn't going to change my mind about having children. I didn't know any children, but I was certain I wouldn't much like the little imps if I did.

We made up before we went to sleep – twice. Children were not again mentioned.

CHAPTER TWENTY-NINE

RELIEVED FOR CAUSE

I wandered into my office a bit later than usual Saturday morning to find both of my phone lines blinking like a fourteen-year-old boy viewing his first blue movie. Angie came running in while I was trying to decipher the acting CO garbling on one line and the chief recruiter bouncing off bulkheads on the other. The commodore was on her line! When they all had stopped screaming like a cathouse madam fresh out of towels and hot water and slammed down their respective telephones, I went directly to Harry the Bat's news stand in the lobby and bought a copy of the Star-Journal newspaper. There it was, on the top right column of the first page.

LEADER CALLS NAVY RECRUITING "A JOKE."

MINORITIES DENIED ENLISTMENT

I was a news item . . .

Patty must have broken the record for the highest speed ever recorded in Big Otter County; she arrived in my office, streaming tears, in less than fifteen minutes after I called her.

"My Lord, Clay-honey," she wailed through quivering lips while wiping tears from the corners of her mouth. "Those are off-the-record comments from our interview -- the parity thing too. I never published any such material!"

"I know that, Kitten. The question is, how did it get into the Star-Journal? Stop crying. There's nothing to cry about."

"I have no idea how the newspaper obtained it, Clay. Those comments were never typed in the smooth. I transcribed my notes on the word processor, printed it, and then blue-penciled what I did not want included in the published interview. I then gave it to Joan for smooth typing. I destroyed the rough after she finished. Oh, what to do?"

It took an effort to get her calmed down, but when I did we formulated the likely scenario of events that caused the article.

I called a Star-Journal reporter after learning the editor was not available on Saturday to discuss where they had gotten the material. She would not discuss the article, but did say they had gotten it from a reliable source.

Personally, I wouldn't call Curtis reliable.

"Come on, honey. I've been yelled at enough for one day. I suspect Round Two is about to commence and I'm not going to stick around so they can bless me again. Let's go to Moe's and sort this thing out."

"They are going to fire you! Oh, damn-in-hell!" Her cheeks were bright with steadily flowing tears.

"Yes, I expect they will fire me. I've given them a sea bag full of shi . . . er, stuff to throw at me, but it will take them a couple of days to get their duck in a row." I caught Patty beneath her strong, little chin and kissed her. "It's not your fault, so stop crying. I still love you, bunches too, even if you did do a Delilah on me."

The Delilah comment wasn't a particularly bright attempt at humor. It turned Patty's overflow valve full open. I had to hold a patching and shoring evolution to stop the tears from flowing by petting and kissing on her. Of course, I believed the hair cutting story as much as I believed the apple caper. I had recent, first-hand knowledge of how Sampson lost his strength.

We accepted Moe's nasty welcome about showing up before he got the bar set up, got a cup of coffee and settled in the far booth where we hashed it out until we obtained a good picture of how and why this had happened to us. The root cause of our dilemma went back a long way.

Patty had bested Joan at every turn since the fourth grade. Joan wanted to be the class monitor, but Patty was appointed. Joan wanted an office in the 4-H Club. She did not get one, but Patty did. Ditto Future Homemakers of America. Ditto Girl Scouts. When they were older, Joan wanted to be president of the Honor Society, but Patty won hands down. Joan wanted to be the valedictorian when they graduated high school. Patty bested her in that too. In college, Joan stood for the editor of the Campus Crier, but Patty was selected. The only place Joan ever excelled without Patty besting her was the cheerleader squad in high school. Patty didn't try out for that. The skirts were too short and she didn't like the skivvy flashing bit.

It didn't take us long to understand that Joan had recognized our interview, taken as a whole, was not something I would want to tell the media. She had made herself a bootleg copy of the rough, thinking she would keep it until she could use it in some way to embarrass Patty, myself -- or both.

It followed that Curtis was probably already hatching a plot to get even with me after I'd laid a little practical leadership on him at the wedding reception and he had leaped all over the document when Joan told him of its existence. The fact that the publisher of the Star-Journal and I had a short donnybrook in the Holiday Inn some months prior certainly didn't hamper his efforts at getting the information into the print media.

Getting me in trouble with the Navy aside, they hoped I would get so angry with Patty that our marriage would suffer. Curtis, for his part, failed to fully analyze the Background and Assumptions Annex of his Operations Plan. His Intelligence Estimate Appendix was flawed too.

Nearly one year after my parents were laid to rest, the Navy took me in and provided a rudder when I most needed one. It provided a sense of direction and a feeling of being part of an organization that had weathered many a storm. Once I proved my willingness to accept the ways of the Navy, I was welcomed into a brotherhood that demanded everything but my soul. I loved the mystique of the Navy, much of which was inherited from the age-old British Royal Navy. It converted me from an uncertain youth into a confident, successful, satisfied man. The United States Navy, in no small way, functioned as my family.

But now, there were other considerations . . .

Patty had changed me forever. She'd made me an even more confident and satisfied man. I fully realized future increases in my success would be a direct result of Patty's intelligence, concern and support. She provided comfort and happiness I'd never before imagined. There was nothing the world could give me to replace the feelings I had when she hugged me in her sleep. It was terrifying to think of life without Patty. Like the Navy, I owed Patty a debt I could never repay.

I thought of how it must have angered Curtis when I married his cousin. Our marriage probably twisted in his guts, but not nearly so much as when he discovered we were ecstatic with each other. The Navy had moved to Number Two -- Big Time Number Two. Curtis had not counted on that.

A wail from Patty jerked me from my musings.

"Oh, Clay-honey, I destroyed your career. You don't know beans about farming and I cannot earn enough to support us. What will we do?"

I, once again, realized we had yet to discuss our finances since we married. Since she did not know our worth, she obviously had not yet gone through our financial records and farm accounts as she had said she intended to do. But my career was her real concern, not money, so I did not bother explaining we were in excellent financial shape even without my Navy salary.

"Patty, you didn't destroy a thing. You warned me Curtis was mean and sneaky some months back. Remember? I already knew that, but didn't see anything like this coming.

"I'm not as upset as you might think, Kitten. Mad at Curtis -- yes. I'd like to fall upon Curtis and smite him mightily beneath his fifth rib. Maybe I will. But this situation isn't all bad.

"People in the Navy know a lot about each other, Patty. It is a fact that I have an outstanding reputation in the fleet. What I'm telling you is people in powerful positions are going to be asking questions about why I was relieved for cause. I heard only last week that a four-star admiral -- a straight shooting hard nose -- is asking questions about Captain Markham having been removed from his command.

"Patty, this situation might get heat applied to certain parts of people who are long past due. If that admiral really rattles cages in the recruiting command it might result in major policy changes. It could get them doing something constructive, instead of initiating idiot ideas that don't work, then blaming recruiters for not using them correctly."

Patty's lower lip was quivering again and rain clouds were forming in her gray eyes. "But, dearest, everybody will believe you exercised poor judgment by telling me what you did. That cannot enhance your reputation."

"Honey, all they can do is transfer me. Free speech is still legal in the US of A. They can't discipline me, other than sticking a Relieved for Cause letter in my service jacket. They can't write a bad performance evaluation, not with my record of production. None of it will hurt me. I'm as high in rank as I intend to advance. Patty, I'm ready, willing and able to return to sea."

"You will go to a ship?"

"Probably not as ship's company. There are mighty few master chief radioman billets in ships. I'll go on an admiral's staff, probably a carrier or cruiser-destroyer group staff. Staff's shift ashore when they are not at sea. That means I'll be home more."

"I will still be alone many nights!" Patty sobbed. "This is horrible! We just got married!"

The barflies started muttering among themselves. They appeared ready to hold a torch and pitchfork drill on the guy they thought was mistreating Patty, so I kissed her so they'd keep their beer hooks off me. I wanted to kiss her anyway. I wanted her to stop crying. There wasn't much worse than seeing Patty cry. That aside, who wants torched and pitchforked after being informed he is the prime participant in a walk the plank drill?

I stayed away from everyone connected with recruiting until Monday when I mustered in my office at the usual time. No one had tried to find me since Saturday to tell me, officially, to pack my sea bag and hit the bricks. They were probably having trouble getting their duck in a row. Firing a master chief required a trailer truck load of concrete documentation.

I held a conference call and told my recruiters what had happened. It took a while before I was able to quell a mutiny.

Angie was all for holding a protest march in front of the federal building -- after she pulled every hair from Joan's head and knifed Curtis. She made a few pointed remarks as to what she was

275

going to do to the commodore's private parts too. Book thought the Air Force was behind it and wanted to bring a logging truck filled with wood hicks to town to clean them out. Petty Officer Lewis made dark comments regarding the power of the Mafia. Chief Hagland intended to defile the statue of the Merrifield Mayor's Union great-grandfather and get fired too.

I was finally able to calm them by reassuring them that the end of creation would not occur with my transfer. But they knew, and I knew, that they were going to have it very rough if my relief was a Slimy Creature instead of a Mark One - Mod Zero Senior or Master Chief Petty Officer. Their future skipper had not yet been identified either -- a concern of the first order.

CHAPTER THIRTY

PROCEED ON DUTY ASSIGNED

I telephoned my detailer in Washington, Master Chief Radioman Abraham Lincoln "Reb" McGee, once my boss in *USS Forrestal*. I informed him of my impending homeless state and requested orders to a cruiser-destroyer group, preferably in the Pacific.

"I just heard the Slimy Creatures fired your navy blue ass. Acted up, did you?"

"Yeah, you could say that. I shot off my big mouth and it got into print."

"Well, Motor Mouth, now you've got me owing CRUITCOM a replacement and there is none in the pipeline. They're going to suck hind tit 'till I can suck some fool into the job."

I knew how that worked. He had talked me into recruiting duty by buttering me up with promise of assignment in West Virginia.

"Lay it on me, Reb. San Diego or Long Beach -- or Mayport, Charleston or Norfolk?"

"Sorry, none of those ports."

"Yokosuka, Japan or Naples, Italy?"

"I have zero master chief seagoing billets open!"

"Just what in the hell have you got, Reb? Did you get told to broadside me to a do-nothing billet?"

"I'm not going to tell you what cretin tried to order me to do just that this morning. I told him I'd be beating holes in the Chief of Naval Personnel's desk before I detailed a prime man to a rinky-dink job!"

"Reb, what *is* on the deck plates?"

"I have one each shore billet in Puerto Santa Cruz, Spain and Honolulu, Hawaii."

I put Reb on hold and called Patty. She went totally bonkers.

"No sea duty? Oh, wonderful! Forgive me, dearest. I am sorry you did not get a staff. No, I am fibbing. A whopper too. Oh, my prayers worked. I am in love with your detailer!"

We (she) picked Naval Communications Station Santa Cruz, Spain.

"Well, now, Clay . . . you don't sound so disappointed now that you made a decision. Spain is great duty, but you know that, having been stationed there when you were a wet-behind-the-ears chief." Reb said, after I told him to cut orders to Spain.

"I'm happy with it, Reb. A wonderful girl reminded me of what I'd be missing at sea."

"Isn't taking an American girl to Spain sort of like taking a bottle of Sneaky Pete to a wine tasting in France?"

"Not this one!"

"Uh, right. I sort of forgot you're married. I received your wedding invitation, but couldn't get away. She must be gold plated in all the important places to have harpooned you."

"She's in the very top drawer -- all by herself. Call when you do your next European detailing swing. We'll take you tapa hopping around Andalusia and you'll see."

"I will surely do that, Clay. Well, a couple of my lines are blinking, so I better go. I'll cut your orders with a thirty-day delay in reporting. You will need that with a wife."

The chief recruiter telephoned about seventeen hundred to inform me the commodore had directed him to act as my replacement until a relief could be ordered in. Upon receipt of transfer orders, I was to proceed on duty assigned.

I'd never owned much in the way of personal belongings and had not considered transfer a hardship. I normally received transfer orders far in advance. On the day of transfer, I picked up my orders, tickets or travel advances, then left the command. It was as easy as finding a good time in Costa del Sol. The State of Matrimony changed that Transfer was now about as easy as finding a good time on Adak Island, Alaska.

Passport: I didn't need a passport for transfer to Spain, although I had one. All I needed was orders and a Navy ID card. Patty, being a civilian, had to have a passport. She really needed two, a no-fee one that would permit her to remain in Spain without a long-term visa and a regular one in case she wanted to travel to countries that did not recognize the no-fee passport. We finally got Patty's paperwork mustered and shipped to the Bureau of Naval Personnel and the State Department.

Housing: I had never lived in government housing, nor had I ever lived on the economy overseas, except for a two-year period in a *residencia* on the outskirts of Madrid. There I was housed, cared for, and fed great meals by a chubby Spanish Senora and her fat, extremely relaxed husband. I could no longer live in an everything-taken-care-of *residencia*, not with a wife.

I knew the Santa Cruz Family Service Center would send us a 'Welcome Aboard' package that contained information needed to survive in Spain; however, the package would likely not arrive until after we left West Virginia, so a telephone call was in order.

Patty accompanied me to the Reserve Center where, with the blessing of Captain Markham and Irene's hubby to be, I leaped on the Defense Department telephone system. I soon managed to hook up with the master chief I would relieve -- Hector "The Inspector" Seeley, who had supervised me mightily in *USS Frank E. Evans*.

Hec improved my morale. My billet would be Operations Master Chief in a department manned with two hundred and twenty-five radiomen, electronic technicians and a handful of other ratings who operated and maintained eight work centers, including a satellite earth station. The commanding officer was the CO I'd served in *USS King*, my first seagoing CPO billet. He was a great CO and we had gotten on well. Hec said the department head was an excellent administrator, but really shaky when it came to working with the fleet because all she knew about ships was most were gray.

I motioned for Patty to pick up an extension telephone when Hec started talking housing. Hec, himself, lived aboard the Naval Station, but I could choose either to live on-station, or ashore. Patty started waving her free arm in the air, acting crazy, when Heck said he could hook me up with the beach front quarters of a transferring Naval Oceanographic Center officer if I wanted to live ashore and if we were willing to live in a hotel until the officer departed. He explained the ashore quarters was a two-bedroom cottage a few miles from the communications station. He said the place rented partially furnished, which, in Spain, meant some sort of heating and, maybe, a cooking stove. There was no lengthy discussion necessary. We -- read Patty -- opted to live ashore so she could 'experience' Spain.

Patty simply bubbled all the way from the Reserve Center to Moe's She babbled at length how wonderful it would be to play in the sand and waves. Patty had never seen a beach.

Patty told Moe all about Iberia, a subject in which she was quite knowledgeable. She'd stayed up in recent nights reading every Spain-related book she could locate in the Big Otter library, in the public school system and at the college.

Moe said he was going to miss her. He hemmed and hawed, then reached across the bar and made a couple of clumsy passes over her wavy-curly hair. Patty stretched on the bar railing and kissed him. She told him, in two hundred words, or more, she was going to miss him too.

The result was an offer for Moe to vacation in Spain. He said he would likely come if he could bring a friend. Patty told him he and Missus Moore were welcome at any time. Moe then hauled down the bar, probably to start drumming up the price of airline tickets via barfly consumption.

"Patty, do I understand Moe might come to Spain with Missus Moore -- *our* Missus Moore?"

"You do not mind, do you?"

"Of course not, but I'm a bit off course now. I've heard rumors about them shacking up, but I never believed it."

"Clay! They are not 'shacking up.'"

"Moe's not bringing her to Spain because he likes her silver hair and trim stern. What do you think they're doing together -- playing mumble peg, maybe?"

"I call it loving each other."

"I suppose that's a consideration, but my God, they both probably voted for President Roosevelt."

"Does that prove something, Clay?"

"It proves they differ from most of their generation by shac . . . er, living together without benefit of wedlock."

"My Aunt Joyce and Missus Moore are best friends. I have known her . . . forever. I did not really know Moe before we started coming here. They have lived quietly together for years and years. Her husband left a peculiar will. I do not know the details, but she loses her property if she remarries." A dangerous glint flashed in her eyes. "Do you call what we did before we actually said our vows 'shacking up'?"

I knew the answer to that question.

That got me a warm smile and a pat on the cheek. "Of course, you do not think that, dearest. I consider our first trip to Elkins our wedding night. You do too, do you not?"

I knew the answer to that question too, which got me another smile and pat I wondered if Margaret Louise Tinny had bugged Henry Clay Berkeley along similar lines for eighty-one years. There was no record of their ever having married, other than jumping over a stick.

"Missus. Moore is so sweet and wonderful! She explained various things during our first visit to Foxfire that helped so much.

"I expect you remember when I left you alone at the table for so long on our first date. I was so terribly ashamed I had acted out a lie. Oh, I was terrified you would storm out of Foxfire and I would never see you again once I told you about that stupid bet!

"Missus Moore caught me crying in the bathroom. She immediately asked what you had done to me. I replied it was what

I had done to you. I told her about the bet, and about the feelings I was having for you. I told her it sounded silly, but I believed I had fallen in love with you shortly after we met. I told her I wanted you for my own, but what with your reputation and what I had done, I did not see how that was possible.

"While bathing my face with a damp cloth, she said she could not understand how such a sweet and pretty girl could experience problems finding the man she wanted. She was surprised I did not know males rarely initiate marriage, rather it is the female who moves the process from courtship to marriage. She said if I really and truly wanted you I should go after you with every asset I had -- or could make you believe I had. Dearest, I did exactly as she said and it worked beautifully!"

"I must get that woman a little present, for helping you catch me. A Cadillac, maybe."

That statement got me a lot more than a smile and a pat, causing Moe to yell at us to knock it off.

"Clay-honey, I am going to have to have bathing suits. I fear they are quite expensive. I spent all my cattle money on our wedding. I have been depositing my salary in a savings account in event we experience a financial problem. So, dearest, I really have no available funds."

"Patty, tonight, you keep your nightgown on. We are going to talk finances."

"If we cannot afford them, we cannot."

"Patty, I'm not going to discuss our worth in a slop chute in front of God and everybody, but we are far from poor."

"Oh, then may I purchase two or three bathing suits? We can afford them, really?"

Some days . . .

"Patty, get the swimsuits. You'd better buy them here. You could buy them in Spain, but you wouldn't like them."

"Why not, dearest?"

"Because, most have four strings and a tiny piece of cloth for the bottom -- and no top."

"No top? I must have a top! Oh, damn-in-hell! I will never get to play on the beach."

"Wait a minute! I didn't say every woman runs the beach with their as . . . assets hanging out. Most Spanish women wear tops. It's just that European women from the northern countries and England have big tit . . . er, breasts and like to show off what they have, you see."

"Then I can wear a top!" Patty said, brightly. "I have nothing to show. My breasts are no larger than a tea cup -- or was it a shot glass?"

The poor mouse drown beneath my stool in the pool of instant sweat.

Patty giggled. Then she giggled some more. Then, she let loose with her rich, whooping laugh and laughed until her hanky was completely soaked from wiping her eyes.

"Oh, Clay -- I have waited simply weeks to get you on that. I was beginning to think you would never provide an opportunity. You should have seen the look on your face!" she said, then let go with another round of whooping laughter.

I wondered, for the eleventy-eleventh time, what had happened in her childhood to cause her peculiar sense of humor.

"Oh, dearest, I thought it so funny when Elizabeth told about you getting tongue tied after our first date. I would have given bunches to have seen that."

"You're not mad -- not even a little?"

"No, of course not. My breasts are small, but larger than a shot glass or a tea cup! And you seem to enjoy them, Henry Clay Berkeley -- small though they are. Mine cannot possibly droop when I age." She remembered where she was and looked around to see if anyone was listening, then lowered her voice. "My breasts work just fine, thank you, kind Sir. I could not bear the pleasure if they tingled any better when you stroke them!

"No, dearest. I am not in the least angry. You were confused and troubled because you could not accept just how attracted to me you really were. I do wish I had known your thoughts regarding me that night in Foxfire. I would have said to damn-in-hell with that stupid lipstick bet! We would not have had to wait almost four whole months before making love!

"Clay-honey, may I do something when we get home?"

"I never yet told you no."

Patty became very red, leaned over and hooked me around the neck with her slender arm and giggled in my ear. "I want to put my little boon-dockers under your bed. You may play with my tea cups, if you wish. In fact, I demand that you do!"

CHAPTER THIRTY-ONE

RELIEF IN SIGHT

Over the next week, we sorted through the house to decide what we wanted to take with us. We finally decided on about four thousand pounds of household gear, although I, as a master chief, was entitled to ship twelve thousand pounds. I was certain we would return to the States with a lot more than four thousand pounds after Patty eyeballed the fine furniture of Spain.

We had a small disagreement about the bed. Patty wanted to ship our huge, old-fashioned, four-poster bed with the tall, hand-carved headboard. I could see no reason for dragging that monstrosity to Spain. She slipped her little boon-dockers beneath the bed and demonstrated its value. She used various training aids -- tea cups included.

Just as the packers arrived to prepare our shipment, Patty lugged the old cradle into the room where we'd staged various small items we wished to have shipped. "Whew, that thing is heavy!"

I took immediate, firm action by picking it up and toting it back into the sewing room from whence it came. At least that is what I started to do. Patty jerked it out of my arms and slapped it back on the floor, almost straining her milk.

"Leave the cradle alone!"

"We're not taking that thing! It has no value to us in Spain. Here either, for that matter."

"It was your mother's favorite antique -- and I am taking it!"

"Patty, look . . . you have a whole damned house filled with antiques -- fourteen rooms full of old stuff. And, Kitten, half a barn loft and three-four outbuildings full of maybe even older stuff. You surely cannot take it all. We've separated everything we need and we don't need the cradle!"

She puffed out her lower lip, set her tiny hands firmly against her neat waist and locked eyes with me. We'd not been long married, but I'd already been the sad recipient of that action. Satan, himself, and a squad of Marines could not alter her decision once she adopted that stance.

Five days before we were to leave, I was at the farm shop, when a Navy car passed the Post place, turned into my gravel lane and stopped in the barnyard. I recognized the master chief who limp boned it out of the car. I figured it was my relief -- a man I'd known in Vietnam.

Bob Mac donough had served as the only CPO on a Vietnam-based LST with a fine CO and XO, two inexperienced reserve officers and a crew of eighty-six. He'd been acting first lieutenant for ten months, the ship's only CPO, and the chief boatswain's mate rolled into one. He'd experienced fire at sea, shelling, casualties, and a running fire fight with a junk off a Southern Philippine Island where he'd helped rescue some folks, including the Filipina he later married. He earned his entire swashbuckler qualifications in one tour, but the ordered tasking of his LST made him suspicious of those high in the chain of command. The commodore was not in for an easy time. My recruiters were, if anything, better off.

I took him into the house and introduced him to Patty who ordered us into the library, then charged off to get chips and nuts to go with the beer in the library's small reefer. Then, wise woman that she was, she left us alone.

"Clay, the acting CO and the commodore will have three coronaries and delayed cases of herpes when they find out, but I ordered all my recruiters to Big Otter. Officially, it will be my initial training session so the Navy will pay for their food and lodging. Unofficially, they're going to throw you a going-away bash starting at Moe's at twenty hundred, Friday night. Book wanted to hold it at some topless joint, but Angie ate him out like a boot seaman. She said it'd been placed Off Limits by your wife. She told me why too!

"You left me a fine bunch of people and an excellent working plant. I appreciate taking over such a fine organization. I hope Angie watches my back as well as people say she watched yours. The way she acts right now is I'm no more valuable than a bull that won't breed. You must tell me about this guy Book. I'm having trouble believing him.

"I got some poop on the new skipper. It's thought he will be selected as an admiral within the next couple of selection boards. He's an ex-POW. He's said to be a regulation sailor who hates Slimy Creatures worse than the North Vietnamese. It doesn't look good for the commodore.

"You received some phone calls.

"A senior chief named Larson said to tell you he'd fixed the black lung claim and 'The check is in the mail'.

"A Mister Jeffers, listed as a COI in the telephone flipper, was sorry to hear you'd been transferred. He asked me to tell you Janet Bailey was awarded full scholarship. She is also eligible for a student loan, if she needs one. He seemed to think you had a personal interest in her."

"I've never met her, Bob, but her parents are high grade folks and they've had a long spell of hard times. The black lung check Pens Larson call about is for them. Look in the Merriville Station folder in the safe if you want to know what happened."

The party started quiet and maudlin, as do all such functions, but it got to jumping after the presentation. The troops gave me a walnut desk set engraved with my rank, name, title and the period I'd served at NRD Big Otter. Patty received a bouquet of roses.

Angie and Book grabbed me along about midnight and pulled me into a dusty room just off the passageway to the head. Inside the room was mustered a host of recruiters and support personnel, Irene, and a woman so fresh and lovely she'd have made a young Sofia Loren envious. A battleship had nothing on her super-structure!

Angie functioned as spokesperson. "Master Chief, you hears 'bout Longly and his little problem?"

"No, but I'm glad he has a problem and --"

"Shut up, Master Chief. Listen. Tells it, Lewis!"

"Master Chief, I didn't have nothing to do with any of this, but a couple of swarthy looking fellows snapped Chief Longly into an alley and laid some groups on him. They explained if he wanted to remain a happy, healthy beaver, he'd better request a transfer. Things like kneecapping were supposedly mentioned. His requested transfer was arranged, probably with the help of his buddy, the commodore.

"A senior chief, who was once running mates with the journalist detailer, put in his fid. Chief Longly received orders to a bird farm in Yokosuka, Japan, which the journalist detailer claimed was the worst billet available."

There was a loud round of applause and drinks waved in the direction of Senior Chief 'Keys' Armstrong and toward the fresh, lovely Missus Lewis with the superb superstructure -- late of Catania, Sicily.

"Shut up!" Angie ordered. That ain't all. Let me tells it.

"The commodore's too cheap to pay to gets his income taxes and personal paperwork done, so he makes his admin officer do it for him -- all sorts of other stuff too. His admin officer told somebody in our NRD that he ain't even happy at making his people do the commodore's private stuff when they barely gots time to do official stuff.

"What happened is that some person reported him to the Navy Department for misuse of his position. What he done did was commit fraud and abuse. He'll likely gets his wrist slapped, maybe fined, and told to retire."

Everyone raised their glasses to Irene. Like I said, she can be one sweet woman!

CHAPTER THIRTY-TWO

STOWAWAY

Patty cried when we said goodbye to her folks. She'd never in her life been separated from them for longer than one month and then only as far away as Bluefield. This time, less leave periods, it would be for three years. Patty sobbed and carried on and refused to get into the car until her mom and dad promised to visit us in Spain starting in early July. I thought the requested period for the visit was odd, considering summer months were her father's busiest time -- and Patty knew that.

"Kitten, why were you so specific about your folks visiting in July?" I asked, after we'd gotten on the road. "Spain is beautiful any month of the year."

"Uh . . . well, I . . . no real reason." she sniffed.

We were about three hours northeast on a crooked, two-lane road en route Baltimore to ship the car when Patty pointed to a sign along the highway. "That little motel looks nice. Let's stop for the night."

"It's not even three o'clock in the afternoon!"

Patty looked at me with accusing eyes. "*You* said we'd leave home two days in advance of our flight date so we could take our time getting to Philadelphia. *You* said we could play tourist!"

"I know I did, but there's nothing around here to see."

"I do not necessarily have to see something, dearest. I want to do something!" she blushed, and moved her hand. I damned near ran off the road.

I had a serious talk with Patty our last night in the United States because she had me shorted to ground. I very thoroughly explained the capability of the normal male. She didn't buy it, not even after I told her my trying to make love again would be like trying to push a log chain through snow.

I damned near crawled up the boarding ramp. Our fellow passengers on the United Airlines Military Charter probably thought I'd been drinking. I'd have been in lots better shape if I had boozed the entire night.

I slept all the way across the Atlantic. I didn't even dream. I slept the sleep of the totally tuckered out until Patty started petting me on the leg and jabbering about the green sea of winter beating foam from the chalky coastline. Either it was something she had read -- or she was writing a poem in her head.

"That's the coast of Southern Spain coming up. We will be landing in a tick."

"Yes, dearest. The pilot said so. I thought I'd wake you so you could see it too.

"Just think, Clay-honey, we will soon be in the beach hotel you told me about -- *Playa de la Sol*-- Beach of the Sun. What a beautiful name!" She twitched around in her seat, sighed softly, and hugged herself. "We can take a nap! Sleeping in a bed after this airplane seat will be wonderful!"

Not necessarily, Buccaneer . . .

"Dearest, I have been reading this naval manual while you slept. I do not understand something."

"What, honey?"

"Travel claims."

I'd have lurched clear across the next seat, but my loosely buckled seat belt grabbed me. I held a complete inventory of my gear locker before I said anything. I wanted to ensure I had not missed something important. I decided I had not.

"I've never said one harsh word to you. Not one." I whispered. "Not even when I discovered you'd destroyed my love life in Pearl's and a couple of other places -- West Virginia and Kentucky. But, now . . . Patty Lane, you shut your face about travel claims! I mean a-number-one-ditty-bag right now too. I do not ever want to hear that word again. Do you understand?"

"But, Clay-honey, you never completed a single one since you met me, that I know of. The Navy Finance Center is very likely in a tizzy. I do travel claims now!"

Every man, who is not a complete moron, should understand when he cannot win, particularly when he has not a glimmer of what is going on.

"You're going to ask, regardless. Lay it on me."

"It is clear we cannot claim travel expenses for Jarhead and Blue Suit, even though we will pay their transportation to Spain."

"So?"

"So, darling," she said, in her little girl voice. "Can we claim a stowaway? And I want you to remember that I love you desperately."

"A stowaway?" I asked, wondering what desperate love had to do with a stowaway.

Patty took my right hand and placed it on her lower mid-section. "This stowaway."

That was when I fainted and made a spectacle of myself in front of God and everybody -- just as the aircraft touched upon the soil of Spain.

The End

Author: F. L. H. Hudkins

(The voyage of Clay and Patty Berkeley continues in Book II – The Cruise and III – Fiddler's Green of Snug Harbor Series.)

ABOUT THE AUTHOR

Author was raised on a hillside farm in West Virginia. He had his first paid job at the age of seven, riding ancient horses engaged in pulling hay shocks from meadow to stacking point He worked on his parents' farm and for neighbors until he enlisted in the Navy at seventeen.

He was double-hatted in his last Navy billet as Command Master Chief of the United States Sixth Fleet and Communications Readiness Officer. He shipped as Radio Electronics Officer in the United States Merchant Marine after retiring from the Navy

He is married to the former Agueda Caceres Perez of Madrid, Spain. They have five children.

THE LAUNCHING

www.ingramcontent.com/pod-product-compliance
Lightning Source LLC
Chambersburg PA
CBHW070919260626
47162CB00007B/2723